Lock Down Publications and Ca$h
Presents

Crime Boss 3

Road to Revenge

Written By

Playa Ray

First Edition 2024

Printed in the United States of America

Lock Down Publications
P.O. Box 944
Stockbridge, GA 30281
www.lockdownpublications.com

Like our page on Facebook: Lock Down Publications
www.facebook.com/lockdownpublications.ldp

Stay Connected with Us!

Text **LOCKDOWN** to 22828 to stay up-to-date with new releases, sneak peaks, contests and more…

Like our page on Facebook:
Lock Down Publications

Join Lock Down Publications/The New Era Reading Group

Visit our website:
www.lockdownpublications.com

Follow us on Instagram:
Lock Down Publications

Email Us: We want to hear from you!

In Memory Of:

Mary Alice Bradley Robinson
~August 16, 1941 - October 14, 2023~

"Pray for me, and I'll pray for you.
Watch how God moves."
Catilina L. Lester – Mason

Chapter 1

"Hello?" Anthony answered his cellular phone angrily, hating the fact he was roused from a pleasant dream which was something he rarely had.

It's been six months since the night Anthony walked out of Fulton County Jail a free man, though he still had visions of the U.S. Marshals coming to claim him at any given time. Since then, he'd been under the thumb of Ebony and the watchful eyes of Rick and Bull; with whom he'd found himself working alongside in distributing drugs to Ebony's "employees", and collecting what was owed to her.

Never in a million years would he have guessed that she was involved in such criminal activities but now that he was cognizant of it, he remained under the impression that there was more to Ebony Davis than she'd let on; especially since he didn't know what kind of ties she has with Rick and Bull. Perhaps she had them doing *special* details.

"Aren't we a bit grumpy this afternoon?" Ebony's voice filtered through the earpiece. "Did I wake you? I mean, I would hate to assume that you're still in bed at this time of the day."

"It's not good to make assumptions," Anthony replied, swinging his legs over the side of the bed as he sat up, planting his feet inside his house shoes. "Is there something I'm supposed to be doing at this time?"

"There's always work to do," she answered. "Right now, I need to know about the bird that flew south. Have you heard anything?"

Anthony was slowly shaking his head because he already figured that this was her reason for calling at such hour. "No, I haven't." He told her. "I watched his house for two hours last night, and he's still not answering his phone."

Ebony was quiet on the other end.

"Are you there?"

"I'm calling a meeting tonight," she responded. "Six-thirty, location three."

As always Ebony disconnected without giving him a chance to respond, but he quickly became accustomed to this within the first week of release. He figured she intentionally did that to get on his nerves, and to of course, remind him that she was the boss. He was her indentured servant.

However, her officious deportment didn't bother him one bit because he didn't feel anything like a subordinate in her presence. He looked at it as if he was working off the debt he owed her for helping him out of a situation that he saw no favorable way out of, which was fine by him because he was able to continue his search for Marvin and Janelle whenever Ebony granted him a leave to visit his mother back in Atlanta.

Now, clad in a pair of sweatpants and a T-shirt, Anthony got off the bed and left his bedroom en route to the bathroom. Placing his phone on the towel shelf, he brushed his teeth, and washed his face. The kitchen was his next stop where he toyed with the coffee maker until he was able to get the brewing process in motion. After placing a skillet on the stove, he retrieved two eggs and a stick of butter. Before he could do anything with the items, his cellular vibrated atop the marble-top island that sat in the center of the kitchen. Placing the eggs and butter on the counter, he grabbed his phone, and regarded the screen that displayed a photo of his mother indicating that she was the one calling.

"Hello?"

"Hi, my son!" Carol beamed. "How are you?"

"I'm okay, Mama. How are you?"

"I'm bless, baby!" She replied. "My ankle is still a bit swollen, but I'm slithering around just fine."

"I don't know how you tricked yourself into thinking that you could still play basketball," Anthony said, pulling a butter knife from the silverware drawer. "You're almost a hundred years old."

"Whatever!" Carol responded with a giggle. "It was for the church. The children needed another player and I volunteered. I couldn't score a basket to save my life, but I had fun. Are you driving up for the weekend?"

"I don't know yet," he said holding the phone between his shoulder and ear while cracking the eggs on the edge of the skillet and pouring them on top of and already sizzling butter.

"Why don't you know?" She inquired. "Aren't you off on the weekends, and why won't you tell me what kind of work you're doing?"

"Because it's not that important."

"If it's illegal," Carol started, "the police won't think it's not important. It's true that you're a grown man, and you can live your life how you want to, but I hope and pray that you're not foolish enough to be doing anything illegal after escaping that last situation. Can't you see that God gave you another chance?"

"I see that, Mama."

"I understand that you wanted to get away from Atlanta," she resumed, "but Macon isn't that much better from what I've been seeing on the news."

"Every city is full of crime, Mama," Anthony acknowledged, raking his scrambled eggs onto a saucer. "Just because there's crime in Macon that doesn't necessarily mean I'm involved in any of it. I know you're worried, but I'm asking you not to worry. Could you do that for me?"

Carol exhaled through the phone. "I'll try and you still haven't answered my question."

"What question?"

"About this weekend," she replied. "I've been telling the people at my church about you, and it would be nice if you would attend this Sunday, being that this is the weekend of our feast."

"As of now," he started, "I still don't know if I'll be able to make that drive, but I should have confirmation around six-thirty tonight. Just be expecting a call from me around seven."

Hanging up with his mother, Anthony poured himself a cup of coffee then carried his breakfast into the living room, where he took a seat in his recliner and powered up his plasma television to catch the rest of the twelve o'clock news. It was on a commercial break, so he delved into his eggs, forking a large amount into his mouth. With room for another load, Anthony dug in again just as the news came back on. The first thing that graced the screen was a photo of a person he was very familiar with, which rendered him frozen; fork poised in mid-air, and mouth agape revealing un-masticated eggs.

"Welcome back to *WXGA* news at noon," the anchorman promulgated.

He was seated beside his co-anchorman as the initial picture filled the wall screen behind them.

"If you just tuned in there's been a development in the case of the charred corpse that was found in a wooden area just outside of Warner Robins last Wednesday. After conducting several tests on the remnant of the skeletal, authorities were able to identify the corpse as twenty-three-year-old Christopher Roundtree of Macon, Georgia, who was reported missing on the twenty-seventh of January. According to the local medical examiners, Roundtree sustained a gunshot wound to the left side of his skull before being doused in a combustible substance known as zodine and set afire. As of now, homicide investigators are looking into…"

Anthony couldn't believe what he was hearing. *"What could Chris have possibly done to deserve such a humiliating death?"* He wondered.

Chris had been working under Rick and Bull before Anthony came into the picture. Though conversation were kept to a minimum while dropping off drugs to him, not once did Anthony get the impression that Chris was the type to do anything that would bring such tragedy upon himself. He wasn't a gang member, nor did he live in a gang-infested neighborhood, so the authorities couldn't sell their gang-related pitch to the media like they always did whenever a minority was found murdered. Maybe he accumulated a slew of enemies while under the sub-employment of Rick and Bull. There was not telling what kind of criminal activities those old men had him carrying out before relieving him of his duties on the day before he was reported missing.

Chapter 2

After concluding her call with Anthony, Ebony checked her watch to see that she had a little over twenty minutes left of the hour recess that Judge Carl Jackson had bid his courtroom. Being that she hadn't eaten breakfast and didn't know when she would be able to sit down to a decent meal, she decided to take the elevator down to the cafeteria where she ordered a turkey sandwich, mixed fruit cup, and a glass of pink lemonade. Once she paid for her order, she turned from the check-out counter and scanned the place for a table to sit at. That's when, to her surprise, she spotted Attorney Ellen Martinez, who was seated all by herself. Ebony didn't know why, but she didn't even entertain the thought of joining the lawyer as her feet were already in motion.

"Do you mind if I join you?" Ebony asked, now looking down at the older Latina attorney who seemed preoccupied with her pasta salad and bagel.

"Not at all," Ellen replied after regarding Ebony for a split second before dropping her eyes back to her meal.

Ebony placed her tray down on the table then took a seat across from Ellen. Her motive was clear, but she didn't want to bombard the lawyer with questions she probably had no business asking. She was always inquisitive about anything she could learn about her father, but she had the feeling that she would have to tread lightly with Ellen Martinez. Therefore, she chose to take a bite of her sandwich, and wash it down with her lemonade before plunging in.

"I've never tried the pasta salad," she started. "How is it?"

Ellen nodded, but never regarded Ebony. "It's pretty good," she offered. "The best I've ever tasted in fact."

"Well, I guess pasta salad will be on my agenda for Monday," Ebony said before taking another bite of her sandwich.

After washing it down, she resumed. "May I ask you a question, Martinez?"

"Mm-hmm." She had bitten into her bagel.

"How close were you and my father?" *To hell with treading lightly!* She thought.

For the first time, Ellen Martinez held Ebony's gaze for what seemed like an eon, though her eyebrows were furrowed with uncertainty. "What do you mean?"

"Did you two have a relationship outside of the courtroom?"

She diverted her gaze but said nothing.

"Look, Ellen," Ebony pressed. "I already know that my father wasn't a good husband to my mother. They divorced because of his infidelity. I can't hold a grudge against you for being the other woman. You're human."

"It wasn't like that," Ellen purported, only holding Ebony's gaze momentarily before taking hold of the briefcase beside her chair and heading for the exit.

As she watched the older woman leave, Ebony mulled over her last statement. *If what she and Tyrone Davis had wasn't "like that", then what was it like?* Ebony wondered. Clearly, Ellen had furtively intimated that they had something going on because that was definitely not the answer that Ebony would give if asked whether or not she'd fraternized with any attorney outside of the courtroom, being that all dealings were conducted inside the court room and on record. So, her answer would be a flat out no.

This will definitely require further investigation, she thought.

The rest of the day seemed to breeze by. It was sad that Samantha was sick, and had been out all week, which left Ebony with no one to philander with during work hours. Now on her way home, Ebony toyed with the idea of driving out to visit her friend, but didn't risk contracting influenza, and having to take a large amount of days off especially when her career was beginning to flourish. Plus, she had a meeting with Rick, Bull, and Anthony in less than two hours. She'd already orchestrated with Rick and Bull the night before.

One of her workers had become MIA, three days ago, making off with a pound of marijuana. The amount was inconsequential to her, but Ebony had a low tolerance for the act he committed and had been anticipating the day when one of her subalterns thought it was okay to cross the seed of Tyrone Davis; so that she could make an example out of them.

Entering her home, she voice-deactivated her alarm, then marched toward her bedroom, where she deposited her briefcase and pocketbook onto the bed trading her pumps for a pair of warm boots considering the forty-degree weather. As she was tying the last boot, the terse honk of a vehicle's horn sounded outside. Already knowing who was blowing for her, she retrieved her keys and pre-paid phone she'd gotten from Rick and exited the house without reactivating the alarm. Securing the locks on the front door, she made for the black SUV, casting a glance at the house close to the end of the street, where the ever present group of men were standing out in the yard. Though there were five present, Ebony had already ascertained that only three resided at the home along with and older woman. She'd also deduced that they were drug dealers, and a part of a street organization known as Solid Nation.

"Do they ever sleep?" Bull asked as soon as Ebony climbed into the backseat of his truck.

Seeing that he was referring to the S.N. members, she said, "It doesn't seem like it, but as of now, they're no factor."

"You still don't think they know who you are by now?" Rick inquired from the front passenger seat as Bull backed out of the driveway.

"It's hard to say." She was regarding her neighborhood through the tinted windows. "It's not like I've had any close encounter with either of them. Hell, they probably don't even watch the news."

"I'm still skeptical about your jogging route," Rick told her. "Too many people have been mugged at that park after hours and a mugger recognizing you as a prosecutor won't cause them to relent. It would only present them with a motive to make you a part of the homicide files."

"Nice euphemism, Rick!" Ebony said to the back of his head. "You sure know how to make a woman feel safe. So, I'm supposed to just stop exercising?" She asked. "Let myself go? Turn into some…"

"Join one of those gyms in Macon," Rick cut her off. "It's what outside joggers do when it gets cold, being that they have indoor tracks. We can't look out for your well-being if you're foolishly putting yourself at risk."

Ebony didn't care to reply because Rick had a valid point. Yes, she was cognizant of muggings that took place at *Hester Park*, but for some reason, she'd been feeling invisible ever since she'd chosen the place as her new jogging site. Maybe it was because she carried her gun in a waist pouch, and a small canister of mace in her hand while making laps around the huge park. The pouch and protective spray were at Rick's insistence when he found out that she was actuating the public place. Now he was insisting that she use a gym's inside track for her safety as if people don't get mugged upon leaving such a place. Yet, and still, she knew that the older man meant well, which meant that she would have to find time out of her busy schedule to acquire a membership.

It had taken over thirty minutes to reach Clubhouse Grocers, or Location Three, which was one of their five meeting locations. As Bull searched for a spot to park, Ebony didn't bother with surveying the lot for the car she'd bought for Anthony, being that he was never punctual, but to her surprise, Bull pulled into a spot, parking alongside the burgundy Lincoln Innovator that Anthony was seated behind the wheel of. Not wasting any time, he dismounted, circled the SUV, and climbed in behind Bull.

"You're on time for once," Ebony acknowledged, studying his face as if to perceive his reasoning.

"I've been sitting her for almost twenty minutes," he responded before shifting his gaze to the view outside his window. "Did anybody catch the news?"

Anthony looked to the backs of Bull's and Rick's heads then regarded Ebony, who seemed to be the only one paying him any attention.

"There was a body found outside of Warner Robins last Wednesday," he explicated. "Today, it was identified as Chris. Did you know he was reported missing."

Ebony shook her head. "I haven't heard anything about that."

"Somebody shot him in the head," Anthony went on, "then set him on fire. Who would do something like that? He wasn't affiliated."

"Which doesn't mean that he couldn't have pissed off the wrong people," Ebony offered, then took in the view outside her own window.

"Chris was a good worker, and I don't feel like he should have gone through such an ordeal. He had his own life outside of what he did for us. Right now, my main concern is Zachary."

She turned to Anthony. "We've been playing nice for three days. Now it's time to turn up the heat. I just hope you're ready to take it the extreme."

***

It was close to nine o'clock when Rhonda was finally able to place Asia inside her crib, thankful that the nine-month-old infant had ultimately fallen asleep after being up since ten in the morning. After giving her baby a peck on the cheek, Rhonda journeyed back to her bedroom where she began undressing for her shower. Now, with a towel wrapped around her she made for the bathroom wondering why Zachary hadn't called to check on her and the baby yet, when he would usually call three and four times a day. They'd been together for twenty-one months, so she could tell when something's wrong with him, which is how she was able to discern that he'd been acting strange for the past few days as if he'd done something he had no business doing. She already knew about the drug dealing. He was doing this when they'd met, but this was something totally different. He was acting like he robbed a bank; only coming home at nighttime after leaving his car parked on the next street; using the back door as his means of entry and exit, and constantly asking if anyone had been by the house looking for him.

Just last night, he called and asked her to peer out the window to see if she could spot an unfamiliar vehicle parked along their street. Just so happened, she was able to spy some dark colored Lincoln sedan that was parked across the street, though two houses up. Plus, she was able to tell that someone was occupying it. Once she'd conveyed this to Zachary, he told her to make sure that all doors and windows were locked, set the alarm, and not to open the door for anyone, which had her scared out of her mind and unable to fall asleep until she'd watched the unfamiliar car drive off. She hadn't heard from Zachary since.

Stepping out of the shower, Rhonda wrapped the towel around her, dried the bottom of her feet on the floor rug, then made for her bedroom where she dried off before donning one of her cotton fabric pajama sets. After applying deodorant under her arms, she stood staring at herself in the vanity mirror attached to the dresser. She had never said anything to Zachary about it, but she had grown insecure about the postnatal weight she'd gain. She came to find that she'd gained twenty-seven pounds after giving birth to Asia which showed in her face, thighs, and stomach. Her not eating healthy, nor conforming to some kind of exercise routine wasn't helping her one bit.

Rhonda pulled the bottom of her pajama shirt up to gander at her now protruding belly, and to study the unchanging patter of the stretch marks that pretty much became a plague to her once beautiful caramel complexion. As always, she couldn't help but grab her stomach and jiggle it in her hands. While caught up in the moment of doing this, she was interrupted by the annoying buzzing sound of the doorbell which startled her. Trepidation kicked in as Rhonda rushed to the living room window to see if that cabalistic Lincoln was parked anywhere out front, but when she peered through the Venetian blinds, her eyes immediately landed on the unmarked squad car parked out at the curb in front of the house. Not being able to see the front porch from there, she made for the front door, where she used the transom to identify her visitors. Just as she expected, there were two uniformed police officers staring back at her which made her wonder if the authorities were included in Zachary's instructions on not opening the door for anybody. Whatever he'd done, she knew that she was surely about to find out as she disarmed the alarm, disengaged the security lock, and pulled the door open.

"Is there a problem officers?"

"Are you Ms. Rhonda Giles?" asked the bulkiest of the two older black male cops.

"Yes, I am," Rhonda answered, now wondering if she was about to be hauled off to jail for whatever her boyfriend had done. "What's the problem?"

"We're looking for a Zachary Taylor," the same officer promulgated. "Is he here?"

"No, he isn't." She shot a glance at the other officer who was studying her as if to perceive any signs of lying.

"Well, we have a warrant to search the residence," the same officer spoke again holding up a sheet of paper that had *WARRANT* in bold-typed letters at the top, and a bunch of extremely small-typed words beneath it.

Rhonda's heart seemed to stop beating. Now, she was sure that she was going to jail because there was a possible chance that there were drugs in the house being that Zachary was known to keep his supply there. Plus, there were a few handguns though they were legal to keep inside the home. Rhonda just hoped no one was harmed by them.

As she was locking the door back, the quiet officer disappeared leaving her and the other officer standing around the living room in silence. The only sound that could be heard was that of the remaining officer folding the warrant in his gloved hands before stuffing it into his pocket on his coat. Other than that, Rhonda waited to hear furniture being turned over, which would incontestably be supervened by Asia's fitful bawling, but the house was quiet until the officer return with another officer whom Rhonda assumed was stationed outside the back door just in case Zachary happened to be there and tried to make a break for the alternate exit. As the third officer stopped in front of her, she noticed that he looked vaguely familiar to her.

"Do we have to tear the place up?" he asked, gesturing with his right hand. "Or are you going to comply?"

"I don't know where he is," Rhonda answered, holding her arms out helplessly. "I haven't seen him in two days."

"He hasn't called you?"

"The last time he called me was last night," she answered, glancing over at the quiet officer, who was still watching her, then back at the one with whom she was speaking to. "What has he done?"

"Where's your cell phone?" he asked, repudiating her question.

"It's in my bedroom."

Without another word, he spun on his heels and marched out of the living room. Again, Rhonda listened for the sound of furniture being turned over, but he shouldn't miss the phone that was visibly atop the dresser. Although she didn't know how things were going to turn out for her and Zachary at the moment, the quietness of the house seemed to put her mind at ease, especially knowing that her little angel was still fast asleep. The quiet also made her wonder why she hadn't heard the occasional chatter from the officer's radios since they'd been in her presence.

Were there no crimes being reported at this time of day? She wondered. *Were these guys even carrying radios.*

Before she could make a furtive attempt to evaluate their bodies to see if they were in possession of the transceivers, the third officer re-entered the living room with her pink cellular in hand. "This is what you're going to do," he said, now standing directly in front of her. "You're going to call Zachary and tell him whatever you need to tell him to make him rush home. I don't give a damn if you have to tell him that you're dying. Get him here!"

"You want me to make up something?"

"You're a woman," he replied, holding the phone out to her. "This should be a piece of cake."

Gingerly accepting the device, Ronda chose Zachary's number form her contacts while trying to come up with something to tell him that would get him to rush home, and not inadvertently send out a warning, or maybe she should say something that would warn him that the cops were here to collect him. If they should catch on to her ploy, she could be hauled off to jail and charged with harboring a fugitive, right? Surely, she couldn't let that happen. If she were to go to prison, what would become of her little Buttercup?" Child Services are so strict now. A mother would pretty much have to join a nunnery and have God as her attorney in court to regain custody of her children. Rhonda was definitely not trying to go through that.

"Hello?" Zachary's voice boomed through the speaker concluding her thoughts.

"Where are you?" Rhonda asked, still unclear of what she was going to tell him and did her best not to make direct eye contact with any of the officers; especially the quiet one.

"Why?" he asked, sounding concerned. "Is something wrong?"

"I'm having those pains again," she answered, going with the first thing that came to her head.

"How bad is it?"

"Real bad," she told him, making effort to sound as if she was really in pain. "My right leg is numb and the pain in my abdomen is severe. I'm doubled over right now. You really need to get me to the hospital right now, Zachary."

"Damn!" he swore through the phone. "Do you have Asia ready?"

"You'll have to do it when you get here." She added more grunt to the response. "Right now, she's still asleep. Are you on your way?"

"I should be there in about twenty minutes," he promised. "Just stay strong, baby. All right?"

"I'll try."

After concluding the call, Rhonda stared at the phone for a brief moment before raising her eyes to meet those of the officer standing in front of her. She couldn't make any sense of the look that he was now giving her, but there was a sinister sneer on his face that seemed to corroborate the look in his eyes, which sent chills down her spine. Something wasn't right about this, she inferred. Not only did three regular police officers arrive in one, official-looking unmarked squad car, but there was still no chatter-not even white noise emitting from their radios. Maybe these guys weren't what they claim to be.

"Women are so good at deception," the man in front of her now asserted, relieving her of the phone. "It was proven back in biblical days when Eve deceived Adam, and that prostitute deceived Samson. I guess it never stops huh?"

"I was doing what you told me to do," Rhonda protested. Now she was convinced that these guys were not of the law, and she quickly pegged the guy she was speaking to as a misogynist. The hatred in his voice was evident.

"No." He was shaking his head. "You were doing what you were put on this Earth to do. That's to bring destruction to mankind."

"Enough!" the quiet one finally spoke, gaining everyone's attention. "He said that he would be here in about twenty minutes. Therefore, everything needs to be set up before he gets here. The car needs to be moved, she needs to be incapacitated, and somebody should take position at the back door just in case he uses that as his entrance. I'll move the car." With that he exited the living room, leaving the three of them alone.

Rhonda had already deduced that these men were not police officials. Therefore, whatever they had planned for her and Zachary, did not include the inside of anybody's jail. It frightened her to realize that she could end up like a lot of women that were found murdered, after being sexually violated, but that couldn't be these guys intentions. They were after Zachary. Surely their minds wouldn't be on something so vile, right? Hopefully, it was just a home invasion, and she, Zachary, and Asia make it out alive; but how would Zachary look at her once he realizes that she was forced to use deception in order to lure him into a trap?

Rhonda's thoughts were interrupted when the misogynist tossed her cellular onto the sofa before storming out the room. At that moment, she was afraid to move, which was why she didn't bother to look back to see what the other man was doing. She would be able to hear him if he were to do anything other than what he was doing the last time she caught a glimpse of him.

Momentarily, the misogynist returned with one of their dining room chairs, and a roll of Scotch tape which was what Rhonda used to seal boxed packages of Dominant perfume that she mailed out to different customers for the company she works for. *So, this is what the quiet one meant when he said, "incapacitated,"* she thought as the chair was placed in front of her.

"Sit your ass down!"

The venom in the man's inflection impelled Rhonda to act immediately. As soon as her bottom made contact with the soft cushion, he dropped to his knees, and began binding her right leg to that of the chair with what seemed like a redundant amount of tape. After severing the tape with a compact knife, he produced from his pocket, he starts on the other leg. This is when Rhonda decided to take a gander at the other man to see what he was doing, but he was nowhere to be found. The very moment she realized this was when the sound of disturbed furniture reached her ears, ensued by Asia's wailing which sent her mother's instincts into overdrive.

"My baby!" Rhonda exclaimed, now looking down at the man who seemed to be having the time of his life with the excessive usage of her costly tape. "Please, don't let him hurt my baby!"

"Shut the fuck up!" he voiced, not bothering to look up at her. "Nobody gonna hurt that piece of shit! You just better hope that thieving ass boyfriend of yours shows up within twenty minutes. If he doesn't, your baby goes into the oven!"

Now Rhonda was as frightened as she had ever been in her entire life. It's just been confirmed that Zachary had stolen from the trine, but what could he have possibly stolen that would have this man threatening to put her baby in the damn oven? One would have to be an extremely sick individual to even think of such a thing, she thought just as the man got off his knees and stood behind her.

"Place your hands behind your back!" he ordered.

Rhonda did as she was told just as the quiet, older man re-entered the living room standing just beyond the threshold. Their eyes seemed to lock instantaneously, and for some reason, Rhonda was beginning to sense that he was the most reasonable one out of the triad. *Perhaps, he's the leader of their gang,* she thought as the misogynist tightly bind her wrists together, and the agonizing cry of her baby strummed on the strings of her emotions. There was never a time when Asia cried, and Rhonda didn't rush to her side, which is why her heart was aching. Her mind was telling her to jerk against her bindings.

Her baby needed her, and there was no way...Then, while still holding the man's gaze, a thought entered her mind. It was irrefutably a desperate thought, but it was all she could think of. She's usually a good judge of character. Now, she decided to test the water with this guy to see if her assessment rang true about him. "My baby's hungry," Rhonda finally spoke, maintaining eye contact. "Could you please let me feed her, so she'll go back to sleep?'

"That's not my call," he answered in a composed tone, then lifted his gaze to the other man. "Once you finish with her take up position at the back door. If he comes in that way, subdue him by all means, but don't kill him."

There was no response from the misogynist as he severed the tape with his knife. Leaving her incapacitated as he was instructed to do. She heard him stretch the tape again and wondered what other part of her body needed binding. It was confirmed when he cut off a piece and slapped it over her mouth. Then, he marched dutifully out of the living room, presumably to take locus at the back door. He was told not to kill Zachary. Did this mean that they were going to survive this ordeal? Maybe they just wanted to rough him up for whatever he'd stolen from them. She thought. Still watching the man that was still watching her, and what did he mean that it wasn't his call? It was evident that he was the one running the show, or maybe he was just a lieutenant in their sect and was only following orders that were handed down by their absent leader.

"Did you find anything?" he asked the heavy-set man that now re-entered the living room.

He shook his head from side to side. "Nothing worth mentioning. If he has a secret compartment, we'll have to make him tell us where it is."

"I doubt that he has one," the quiet one replied. "Besides, we're not here to recover anything. It's already been counted as a loss. Right now, we'll need another chair. Then I'll need you to cover the front door, and please close the door to the baby's room."

Without a word or even a nod of the head, the heavier man made off to do as he was told. Rhonda listened to her child's cry indicating that he'd completed one of his tasks. Moments later, he reappeared, carrying another one of the dining room chairs, in which he sat next to hers. Then he made for the opposite entrance. Once he was gone again, the quiet one extinguished the light, leaving them in total darkness, save for the light of the night's sky that barely breached the living room curtains.

Though Rhonda was still frightful of the outcome of the situation, the darkness seemed to bring her tranquility. At least she wasn't under the watchful eyes of the quiet one being that he was now peering through the blinds as if to monitor Zachary's arrival. Though he'd been using the back door lately. Rhonda felt that he would use the front door, being that he was under the impression that he had to drive her to the hospital.

This still had her wondering how things would be between them after tonight. Surely, he would have conflicting feelings towards her, which would ultimately cause him to leave, or maybe he would be understanding as to what she was forced to do, and they could go on with their plans of getting married and having more children.

The man at the window whipped around at the first sound, which was a few seconds before the larger one dashed through the living room at a speed that Rhonda didn't think he possessed, carrying a handgun. By the time he cleared the living room, Rhonda could hear the sound of her boyfriend scuffing with the misogynist. She was hoping that he'd overthrow the sick bastard but knew that he wouldn't be any match for the big guy and his gun in which she hoped that he didn't have to use, though she braced herself for the sound.

Zachary stared daggers at Rhonda as he approached and was forced down onto the chair beside her. She diverted her gaze as the misogynist began taping Zachary's legs to the chair while the bigger man kept his gun aimed at Zachary's head. At this time, Rhonda had lost all hopes of her and Zachary holding it all together after this. He was already looking at her as a traitor. Ashamed, she looked over to the quiet one, who seemed to be staring through Zachary's soul from across the room. His visage was unreadable, which was the same facial expression he maintained while crossing over to them and standing directly in front of Zachary.

"You are one stupid individual!" he spoke at a length, shaking his head." "Not only did you run off with a measly pound of marijuana, but you didn't have good enough sense to skip town, nor move your family to a safer location. That's like committing murder then turning the gun on yourself."

Chapter 3

After the meeting with Anthony, Bull, and Rick, Ebony managed to make it home a little after seven o'clock. During her Uber ride, she pondered what Rick had said about *Hester Park* being a dangerous place to resume her jogging routine, and how she should join a gym instead. She had just gotten accustomed to the new environment after moving to Wilkins, so this would be another headache she'd have to overcome; or should she buy a treadmill and join the circle of fools who actually believe that they are not too lazy to take up a running course?

"Definitely not!"

Entering her home, Ebony used voice activation to set her alarm then journeyed off to her bedroom where she undressed before setting off to take her shower. As the streamy, hot water lightly pummeled her dark skin, she began thinking about Samantha, which made her realize how much she was in dire need of sexual relief. It's been almost three weeks since they'd been sexually active, and she hadn't been with a man since Jason. Masturbation would usually be her nostrum, but she'd been so caught up in her busy schedule that once she was done with her homework, exercising, and eating dinner, she'd be too tired to do anything else. After drying off Ebony brushed her teeth before making it back to her bedroom, taking her hair out of its bun, and it seemed as if Samantha had sensed her crossing the threshold because that familiar ringtone began playing on her cellular that was lying on the bed beside her pre-paid phone. Ebony re-directed her steps to retrieve her phone.

"Lincoln County Health Clinic!" she answered with a simper on her face. "How may I help your sick ass?"

Samantha sounded like she was laughing, coughing, and choking all together. "You're a real special case. Did you know that?"

"Of course," replied Ebony. "And why does it sound like you're getting sicker and not better?"

"Don't let the sound fool you," Samantha said, coughing a little. "I'm actually feeling better by the day. By Monday morning, I should be good as new."

"I sure hope so." Ebony took a seat on the edge of the bed. "It's been quite lonely without you. I've had no one to flirt with during the day."

"What about Aaron Taylor?"

"He's only your surrogate lunch partner whenever you can't make it," Ebony claimed though she'd been entertaining the thought of giving him what his randy eyes have been begging for ever since they'd met. "And, by the way, Judge Manning rescheduled Tracey Marlow's case. So, you'll have to handle that one on your own sometime in the future."

"That sucks!" Samantha expressed. "What about Edwards? I guess I'll be preparing for this trial also, huh?"

"No."

"Huh!" Samantha underwent another coughing spell. "Was his case also rescheduled?"

"He's on his way to prison."

"What!" Samantha was in disbelief. "You mean to tell me that he'd finally broken down and accepted the twenty years after going on and on about being a sovereign individual who's exempt from obeying the laws of the United States?"

"Of course," Ebony answered looking down at her other phone that was vibrating beside her displaying Rick's number on its screen. "Um. Sam?"

"Yes?"

"I have an incoming call," she asserted. "If it wasn't important—"

"I understand babe," Samantha cut her off. "Just promise that you'll call and check on me tomorrow."

"I promise."

"Great!" Samantha exclaimed. "In the meantime, I'll continue corroding my bowls with chicken noodle soup and ginger ale.

"Sounds good to me," Ebony offered. "I'll talk to you tomorrow."

"Alright Love."

"Love," Ebony switched phones. "I'm listening."

"Get dressed!" Rick commanded through the earpiece before hanging up.

Disconnecting, Ebony took a deep breath before leaving the phone on the bed and making for the dresser to find a fresh pair of underwear to put on. Though she'd given her consent to her men to pose as police officers, in order to catch Zachary, she didn't actually believe that they would apprehend him on their first endeavor. Since it just so happened to play out that way, she knew that it was time to get it over with.

The day she decided to deal with Bull and Rick, Ebony knew that she was going to accumulate a massive body count. As of now, she was only at number three, which consisted of the old man that occupied the house she now lives in, her grandfather, and Christopher, one of her workers. That number was definitely going to change tonight! Black jeans, a sweater, and boots were Ebony's choice of accouterments. Not knowing exactly where Zachary's abode was located, stripped her of the ability to surmise Rick's ETA. Therefore, being that she still hadn't eaten dinner, Ebony decided to help herself to some canned spaghetti and meatballs making sure to keep her phone in her pocket, just in case Rick shows up.

The call didn't come through until she had eaten and was loading the used dishes into the dishwasher. After setting the timer on the washer, Ebony pulled the vibrating phone from her pocket, and opened the text from Rick that read, *"I'm outside."*

She replied, *"Okay"*, as she made for her bedroom where she donned her dark-blue windbreaker, then exited the house.

The car that sat behind her car in the driveway with the engine running, and the lights out was unfamiliar to Ebony. Had she not known who was inside, she would have sworn that it was occupied by a body of officials from a higher agency, considering it had all the markings of a governmental vehicle with its safety guard rails on the front, strobe lights partially concealed beyond the grille, multiple antennas, and heavily tinted windows. Climbing in beside Rick, Ebony did a quick survey of the console, and realized that the car may have actually belonged to the government, which made her wonder...

"This is a government issued vehicle," she finally spoke as Rick was backing out of the driveway. "What happened to the last occupants?"

"I assume they had to find another vehicle to harass people in," he answered, not looking in her direction. "If you're worried about the GPS chip, it had already been taken out. We've had this car for over a month now."

"So, what if we get pulled over?"

"We'll be okay." He cast a quick glance over at her. "If we were to wreck, you'd probably fly through the windshield without the seatbelt around you."

Ebony glowered at him. "You and your riddles. Why can't you just ask me to put the seatbelt on?"

"Put the seatbelt on!"

"That's a command," she acknowledged.

Rick didn't reply. Ebony was not at all surprised. She'd grown accustomed to his lack of enthusiasm to argue back and forth with anybody, which is something she'd always found appealing in a man, but she already knew to fasten her seatbelt. After doing so, she allowed herself to relax on the soft cushion of her seat. It was quiet, save for the low moan of the engine, and the muffled sound of the tires grinding on the asphalt.

"So, where is he?" Ebony finally asked after a few minutes of gazing out the side window.

"His place," Rick answered keeping his eyes on the road.

"Is his girlfriend present?"

He nodded. "She is. There's also a baby."

"They have a child?" Ebony knew about the girlfriend, but this was her first time hearing of a baby.

"Everything is already in motion," Rick reminded, fixing her with a mere glance before redirecting his attention out the windshield. "If you're having second thoughts, I advise you not to entertain them. We did not enter the house wearing masks, so our identities are already compromised."

"I'm not having second thoughts," Ebony begged to differ. "Zachary brought on his own demise, and the girl chose the wrong time to be home."

"And the baby?" Rick asked not missing a beat.

Ebony directed her attention out the side window before responding. "I'll never give my consent to harm an innocent child."

She just knew Rick was going to purvey her with a million and one reasons as to why the child should suffer for what the father had done, but he didn't. In fact, he didn't respond at all, which was a big relief for Ebony. Taking this into account she chose not to mention anything else about tonight's mission. Better yet, if she could help it, she was not going to say another word for the duration of the ride. Although she anticipated asking him if the car's transceiver worked.

Momentarily, they were cruising down a residential street that boasted middle-class styled houses on each side.

Though they appeared to be homes of the well-to-do society, Ebony could see a slight reflection of her very own neighborhood with the model of vehicles, and the lack of the privacy of car garages. Rick parked in front of a house that had an older model Mecedes-Benz sitting in its driveway, then killed the engine and lights.

"Did you bring gloves?" he asked, unlatching his seatbelt.

Damn! Ebony thought, disengaging her own seatbelt. She knew she'd forgotten something but had no idea what it was until now. "I guess I was moving too fast," she offered looking out at the house they were in front of. "Is this the house?"

"No." He opened the glove compartment, pulled out a pair of black gloves, and handed them to her. "Put these on!"

With that, Rick, who had gloves on his own hands, dismounted, prompting Ebony to do the same. He crossed the street and as she fell into step with him, Ebony did another survey of the neighborhood to see if they were being watched, though she really couldn't tell for the bright streetlamps that seemed to play the obscurity game with her irises. Therefore, she just hoped that the coast was clear as they traveled up the walkway towards a house that seemed to no lights on, except for a dim glow that emitted from beyond the curtains of the front room. Upon approaching the front door, she thought that Rick was going to initiate some code knock in order for Bull or Anthony to let them in. Instead, he turned the knob and pushed the door open. After allowing Ebony to enter, Rick closed the door then led her into the living room where Anthony and Bull were seated on separate sofas clad in the same taskforce apparel as Rick.

In the center of the living room sat two chairs that were occupied by Zachary and his girlfriend, who were both bind to them by their legs. Ebony automatically assumed that their wrists were also secured by the same adhesive tape. One piece was over the girl's mouth. The house would have been completely quiet had it not been for the distant sound of the baby crying, which compelled Ebony to continue through the other exit of the living room that brought her to a small hallway. With only a mere glance into the kitchen, she followed the sound to the only door that was closed. With one of her gloved hands, she grabbed the knob, but seemed to linger a moment as if she expected to encounter anything other than an innocuous infant. After taking a deep breath, she entered the bedroom that was pretty much empty, with the exception of the baby's crib that sat in the middle of the room, and baby items such as bag of diapers, baby powder, baby oils, a set of bottles, and stuffed animals sprawled out in different sections of the floor. The pink wallpaper decorated with feminine cartoon characters was a vibrant addition to the room. It also let her know what gender the baby was. Approaching the side of the crib, she looked down upon the little girl that was clad in pink rompers and sitting in an upright position. Though she seemed to be actuating every *horsepower* that her lungs were equipped with, there was not a single tear on the child's face, nor in her eyes that were as clear as a sunny sky. Immediately upon seeing Ebony, she desisted her cry for help as easily as turning off a faucet and regarded her with enlarged pupils.

"You're already a good actress," Ebony said to the child that bore no resemblance to Zachary. "Do you know how many years it took me to perfect that tactic?"

In response the little girl held her arms out as if expecting Ebony to pick her up.

"I don't think that would be a good idea."

Ebony was in mid-reach of the child when Rick's voice reached her ears with great forewarning. Sensing it, she slowly withdrew her hands, but kept her back to Rick, whom she figured was standing in the threshold.

"It's bad enough that you're not wearing any kind of head gear," he resumed. "We can't afford to make the slightest mistake. In fact, we need to get this over with as quick as possible."

31

With only a slight nod, Ebony studied the child for another moment before making for the exit where Rick was standing holding a black revolver with a suppressor screwed into its barrel. Anthony and Bull were now on their feet when she and Rick re-entered the living room, but Ebony's main focus was on Zachary and his girlfriend, who were both giving her parallel looks of familiarity, though there were tears streaming down the woman's face. Ebony figured the tears were induced by the woman's understanding that she will not make it out of this situation alive, until the child resumed her cry for attention, and she saw the woman's shoulder slump with relief.

"I take that you two know who I am," Ebony said of their looks, now standing in front of them. "Yes, I'm the prosecutor you've seen on television. Why am I here? Well, someone in this room took it upon themselves to steal from me, a pound of marijuana to be exact."

Ebony watched as Zachary's eyes took on the size of half-dollars, and he frantically looked around the room at Anthony, Bull, and Rick, as if to make sure that this wasn't some kind of joke. Realizing that it wasn't, he reluctantly locked eyes with Ebony who after seconds into the stare down reached her left hand over her shoulder. Rick, who was standing behind her placed the heavy revolver into the palm of her gloved hand, then moved toward the window where he peered out before planting his back against the wall with his arms folded over his chest. Though Rick's visage was hard to read, Ebony could perceive the anticipation in his eyes. Even if she couldn't, she already knew that he'd been anticipating the day when she proved that she wasn't afraid to get her hands dirty.

"Do you know how it feels to have something taken from you, Zachary?" Ebony resumed, holding the weapon down by her side. "No? Well, let me show you."

Raising the revolver, Ebony shot Zachary's girlfriend in her left breast, intentionally aiming for her heart. The gun had a powerful kick, but the report was analogous to the purr of a ferocious kitten, though it managed to cause Zachary to flinch. With tears streaming down his face, he was now regarding his lifeless girlfriend, whose head was slumped forward as if she was napping with her eyes open. Then Zachary re-directed his attention to Ebony, giving her one of the most menacing looks she'd ever encountered.

"I know that look," Ebony said with narrowed eyes. "It's not tantamount to the look I had on my face when you made off with my merchandise, but it's close." She paused to gaze at her watch. "In most foreign countries, they would chop your hands off for such an act. Maybe even torture you for hours on end, which is something I wouldn't mind doing, but unfortunately, I don't have the time. Besides, you've already cost your girlfriend her life for the selfish stunt you pulled." Ebony bent at the waist, putting her face just inches of his. "Kind of makes you wonder what would become of your beautiful daughter after the deaths of her parents, huh?"

With that, she injected two slugs into Zachary's chest cavity, leaving him in the same manner as his daughter's mother. Though this was Ebony's first time committing the act of murder upon human beings, she did not feel an ounce of regret, nor the fear of possible consequences. Perhaps this was another trait she'd inherited from her father, or maybe what she'd done would haunt her dreams for many nights.

"What about the baby?" Bull questioned.

Evading her thoughts, Ebony regarded Bull for a few seconds before averting her gaze to Rick, who was still watching her from his position by the window. She'd just told him in the car that she would never give her consent to harm an innocent child, but why were her thoughts now contrarious to her earlier assertion? Could it be that she was sympathizing with the little girl that would probably lead a dysfunctional life without experiencing true unconditional love form her biological parents? Yes, that was definitely it. She moved over to one of the sofas where she retrieved a small pillow with cartoon characters stenciled into it and held it out to Bull.

"Get it over with!" She told him.

Chapter 4

Ebony had managed to make it to the courthouse a little earlier than usual, though she still didn't manage to beat District Attorney Barbara Hutchins, whose car was in its usual parking spot when she arrived. It's not that Ebony was having a hard time sleeping for what transpired on Friday, because she wasn't. Truth be told, it seemed as if she'd slept more comfortably in these past three nights than she'd done since the day she'd met Rick. This was quite odd, considering what she'd learned in her psychology classes. She had been anticipating nightmares of Friday's murders, but there weren't any. Whether it was because she'd welcome them with open arms, or she was genetically ensconced with the killer instincts; Ebony felt as though she will never know why she was reprieved of such normally uncomfortable conditions.

Entering her office, Ebony placed her briefcase, cell phone, and keys atop her desk before taking a seat and powering up her computer. As she watched the screen awaken like a newborn infant, she realized that she'd forgotten to stop by the breakroom for a cup of freshly brewed coffee that Barbara Hutchins would always have prepared for her subordinates along with a variety of bakes pastries. Figuring she would grab some on her way to the courtroom, Ebony got up and crossed over to her file cabinet where she retrieved today's court cases, then returned to her desk. Not postulating the extra time that she permitted herself by arriving early, she delved into the documents to refresh her memory. Ebony was over fifteen minutes into her files when there came a rap on her door. Before she could decide if she was going to bid the visitor to enter or not, the door eased open, and in walked Samantha Gordon clad in her black trench coat that was a replica of Ebony's, with her briefcase in one hand, keys and cellular in the other. Despite the fact that she'd been out for a week with the flu, Samantha showed no signs of it, whereas her make-up was flawless, her green eyes sparkled, and her smile was radiant with a joy that Ebony found contagious, being that she found herself smiling back at her best friend and clandestine lover.

"Hi, babe!" Samantha beamed, stopping in front of the desk, and looking down on Ebony.

"Welcome back, your sickness!" Ebony jested, with arched eyebrows. "It's good to have you back among the human race."

Samantha narrowed one of her eyes. "I don't think there's a better day than today to make a comeback, eh?"

"And why is that?"

"Are you kidding me right now!" exclaimed the redhead. "Did you seriously forget that the new prosecutor is set to arrive today?"

There was way too much enthusiasm in Samantha's tone for Ebony's liking, which is why she didn't care to respond.

"Did you pull him up on the government's employee site?" Samantha resumed.

Ebony made a face. "Why would I do that?"

"To be nosey," Samantha said in almost a whisper. "Besides, he's quite a hunk."

"Are you stalking this man already Sam?"

"Of course not!" she answered displaying a hurt expression. "I went on there to inspect his resume, which is impeccable by the way."

"He's coming from a big city," Ebony started, "so he'll probably look at us like we're some backwoods, bare feet, tobacco chewing hillbillies."

"Why would someone leave Fulton County for Linkton?" Samantha asked if she didn't share Ebony sentiments about the newcomer. "Wouldn't that be more like downgrading?"

"Maybe he's close to retiring," Ebony offered, "and wants to do the remainder of his time in a slower environment."

"Or maybe he knows that he has a better chance at making head D.A. in such a small county with a resume like his."

At that moment it seemed like the world stood still. Ebony's worry that Samantha may have already be obsessed with the new prosecutor was supplanted by her worry of being knocked out of the box for the district attorney's position by this outlander. If his resume is as consummate as her friend says it is, even if it's not his true intentions, he would still be the perfect candidate for the position. Yes, she was definitely worried.

"Good morning, Mr. Ragland!"

Ebony was pulled from her thoughts by the voice of Judge Carl Jackson who'd greeted the inmate that was escorted into the courtroom by Deputy Aaron Taylor. After nodding in response to the judge's greeting. Ragland shook the hand of his awaiting attorney, then took a seat at the defense table. Jackson's gaze seemed to linger on the young man with dreadlocks before regarding the documents in front of him.

"In the State versus Keyshawn Ragland," the judge proceeded, "the defendant is hereby charged with aggravated assault against one Donte Mathis, whereas defendant, by and through his attorney, has requested a polygraphed testing to prove his innocence."

Judge Jackson looked over to the defense table. "Ms. Kirkland, what I have before me is the polygraph consent document, signed by you and your client, Mr. Ragland. Do you have a copy of this?"

"I do," said the brunette, holding the document up for him to see.

"Is that your very own signature at the bottom of this form?"

She nodded. "It is."

Jackson shifted his gaze to the defendant. "Mr. Ragland, were you threatened, coerced, or bribed into signing this document?"

"No sir."

"You signed on your own volition?"

Ragland looked confused. "My own what?"

"Your own will," Judge Jackson rephrased. "Did you sign the Polygraphed Consent on your own will?"

"I did," he answered.

"Do you understand that by undergoing this procedure," Judge Jackson resumed, "you will be waiving your rights afforded to you by the First and Fourteenth Amendment of the United States Constitution?"

As if not fully comprehending, Ragland looked to his attorney, who only nodded. Regarding the judge, he said, "I understand, your honor."

"Do you also understand that the results from this testing will be considered accurate, and that there's no appeal process in this matter?"

"Yes, Your Honor."

Jackson cleared his throat. "Very well. On this twelfth day of February, I hereby grant defendant's request for an open-court polygraph testing, which will be conducted by Mrs. Hannah Swint. Will the defendant please take the witness stand?"

Getting to his feet, Keshawn Ragland made for the witness stand where he seemed to settle in comfortably. Then Judge Jackson bid the polygrapher to go ahead and set up the machine that was built into a panel on the side of the stand. Ebony watched the small, dark-haired woman for a moment before shifting her gaze to Aaron Taylor, who was leaning against the empty jury booth and to her surprise already watching her. Though she'd caught him watching her many times before, there was something totally different about the way he was evaluating her now. It's like his eyes were speaking a language that only she could understand, and if her mental Rosetta Stone was *Comme il faut*, then she was definitely fluent with this unspoken vernacular.

"All set, Your Honor." The polygrapher's voice brought Ebony's attention back to the witness stand where Keyshawn Ragland was already hooked up to the machine.

"Very well," Judge Jackson replied with a nod. "The witnesses to this proceeding are as follows: Attorney Pamela Kirkland from the public defender's office, Assistant District Attorney Ebony Davis, and me, Judge Carl Jackson. Today's date is the twelfth of February. The time is now nine fifty-seven A.M. Are there any objections from either party?"

"No, Your Honor," Ebony and the defense attorney answered in unison.

Judge Jackson regarded the polygrapher. "You may begin."

"Thank you, Your Honor." She faced Ragland holding a sheet of paper. "Mr. Ragland have you had any coffee or anything else with caffeine in it this morning?"

"No, I haven't," he answered, then looked down at the machine that began to hum softly at his response.

"Are you currently taking any medications?"

"No."

"It's routine that I start with warm-up questions," she apprised him. "So, bear with me. Is your real name Keshawn Raheem Ragland?"

"Yes."

"Were you born on the second of August of two thousand and one?"

"Yes."

"And that makes you twenty-two years old?"

"Yes."

She glanced at the polygraph's screen before going on. "Did you know Mr. Donte Mathis prior to this incident?"

"Yes."

"Did you see Mr. Mathis on November eighteenth of last year?"

"Yes, I did."

"At a nightclub?"

"Yes."

"Did you have an altercation with Mr. Mathis inside the club?"

"Yes," Ragland answered after lingering.

"Afterwards," the polygrapher resumed with another glance at the screen, "did you encounter Mr. Mathis outside of the same club?"

"Yes. In the parking lot."

It was Mrs. Swint's turn to linger as she watched the movement on the monitor. "On November eighteenth of last year," she began, "outside of this same nightclub, did you, Mr. Keyshawn Raheem Ragland commit assault against Mr. Donte Mathis by use of a firearm?"

***

It was shortly after twelve o'clock when Judge Jackson bid his court room and hour recess. Ebony already knew that she was going to have her lunch in the cafeteria but had to stop by her office to drop off her briefcase. The moment she opened her door to enter, she spotted a white, letter-sized envelope on the floor. Retrieving it, she extracted a folded piece of paper from the envelope that was a handwritten note from the head DA informing her of a meeting in their conference room at 5:30 today. Placing it and her briefcase atop the desk, she noticed the message indicator blinking on her office phone, and decided to go ahead and listen to them while she had enough time on her hands. The machine told her that she only had one message.

"Playing message," it announced before a familiar male's voice breached from the speaker: "Hello, Ms. Davis! This is Investigator John Pruden from the Department of Investigation. I know it's been a while since the last time we spoke, but there has been recent development in your case that need to be brought to your attention. In fact, this Saturday, at nineteen hundred hours, I'll be at the same diner where we met at for our last meeting. Ms. Davis, it would be in your best interest to show up."

Beep!

Ebony perceived the warning in his tone just as she imagined him raking his fingers through his hair half a dozen times while recording the message.

What could have possibly developed in the case of Jason's death? She thought as she exited her office, making for the elevators.

Surely, they couldn't have ascertained the identity of his murder, because the investigator wouldn't have wasted his time placing that call to her. Instead of raking her brains about it Ebony figured she'd find out in five days.

The cafeteria wasn't as packed as Ebony thought it would be, which made it easier for her to spot Samantha who was seated at a table alone tending to her lunch. Remembering that she told Ellen Martinez she would try the pasta salad, Ebony ordered that along with a bowl of mixed fruit slices, and a glass of sweet tea. After paying for her items, she sauntered across the room, acknowledging a few familiar faces. "What time did Richardson grant a recess?" Ebony inquired as she sat her tray down on the table and took a seat across from her friend.

"Eleven forty-something," Samantha answered, glancing at her watch. "I don't know why I didn't drive out to Lucky's Pizza Palace being that I've been craving pizza all morning."

"So, you settled for tuna on rye instead?" Ebony asked with a smirk on her face.

"Look who's talking!" Samantha retorted, smiling back. "Pasta salad and mixed fruit slices? What will it be tomorrow? Bird seeds?"

Ebony couldn't help but laugh at her friend's quip. "You scored big time with that one!" she commended. "So, how was your morning?"

"The usual," Samantha answered consuming the last bite of her sandwich. "Richarson had her panties in a bunch all morning. We constantly bumped heads as always. Hell, If I didn't know any better, I would think she has a crush on me."

Ebony was smirking again. "Imagine that."

Samantha waved a dismissive hand. "Whatever! Did you receive a notice from your boss lady?"

"About the meeting at five-thirty?" Ebony asked, forking a helping of the pasta salad into her mouth. "Whatever it's about, it better be worth holding me over past quitting time, and have you seen the new guy yet?"

"Of course," Samantha was smiling from ear to ear. "He and Barbara sat through one of my cases. Maybe she sat this meeting up so she could properly introduce him to everybody."

"That's not worth holding me over past quitting time," Ebony protested, helping herself to more of her pasta salad.

Samantha's infantile obsession with the new prosecutor was beginning to irk her,

"Or maybe it has something to do with that triple homicide that occurred over the weekend.

This had Ebony's full attention. "What triple homicide?"

"It happened somewhere on the south side," answered Samantha. "Two adults were shot, and their newborn was smothered to death, and I'm willing to bet anything that the man had some kind of ties to a gang or Mafia."

"Why would you say that?" Ebony asked in an uninteresting tone, taking a sip of her tea.

Samantha made a face. "They suffocated the baby, Ebony! This is not something a random criminal would do."

"I guess you're right," Ebony gave in ready to change the subject. "Have you heard anything from Albert?"

"Not a word." Now there was a hurt expression on the red head's face. "He's not answering his private phone, nor has he responded to any of my messages. The National Breast Cancer Awareness dinner is on the tenth of next month, and I have yet to receive an invitation."

"That's like a month from now," Ebony offered. "Maybe it's not time for—"

"Jennifer always sends her invitations out close to two months in advance," Samatha begged to differ, cutting her friend off.

"Well, maybe she doesn't have you listed on her automated invitation list."

"She and Albert shares the same invitation list," the red headed prosecutor persisted. "I've been seeing Albert for almost two years. I know when something amiss."

Ebony couldn't fault the woman's intuition. She should've expected Albert to cut her friend off after being blackmailed into *springing* Anthony from the situation he was in. Though she'd apprised him that Samantha was totally insensible of the video, Ebony thought Albert would at least maintain some kind of comity with Samantha, even if it was feigned. So, for the sake of her friend and the sake of being exposed as being the bane of the two love birds ongoing fling, Ebony knew that she would have to pay the governor a little visit. The big question is: how is she going to gain entrance to the mansion in order to speak with him?

Chapter 5

"It's too early in the week to determine, Mama," Anthony said as he pulled the Lincoln Innovator to a stop at a traffic light behind a community bus.

"Why am I getting the impression that you're avoiding me?" his mother's voice sounded through the speakers. He was using the car's Bluetooth feature.

"Why would I do something like that?" Anthony was shaking his head. He couldn't believe that his mother would actually think such a thing, knowing that he would lay down his very own life to save hers.

Carol drew a breath. "Things just haven't been the same since you've moved to Macon," she expressed. "It's almost like you're still in jail. Just last week, my pastor pulled me to the side and asked if you were incarcerated."

"Why would he ask you something like that?"

"I assume it was because he has yet to see the son I speak so highly of," Carol replied. "And I'm quite certain that some of the members are under the same impression, which is why I was hoping you would make it to the feast this weekend. Do you know how embarrassing it was for me to be the only person in attendance without a family member, or even a friend?"

"I really hate that you had to go through that, Mama," Anthony sympathized, switching lanes in order to pass the community bus. "Believe me if I could've made it, I would've been there, and you know this, Mama."

"Well…" Carol began drawing another breath. "I guess I'll have to sit my old self down and wait until you can find time to visit me."

"Don't say it like that, Mama," Anthony replied. "It's just that things have been kind of hectic lately. As soon as everything pans out, I'll be on the next thing smoking to Atlanta and that's my word."

Anthony knew that he had to make it up to his mother for the discomfiture she had to endure this past Sunday, and every other day she'd spent amongst her fellow church members, though all blame should be directed at Ebony who pretty much controls his every movement. It seemed as if she was enjoying assumed superiority over him, but Anthony had a trick for her this coming weekend. He was going to Atlanta no matter what!

Minutes after getting off the phone with his mother, Anthony pulled into the parking lot of Lester's Dry Cleaning Services and parked. He didn't see Rodney's car but noticed the older man emerging from the building clad in a huge overcoat that made him appear larger than his actual size. All Anthony knew about the man was his first name, if that was his real name, and that he was thirty-five years of age. He didn't care for any other personal information being that he wasn't interested in making friends with anyone.

"I had to pay those people to let me wait inside," Rodney confessed upon sliding into the front-passenger seat holding his hands over one of the vents in an attempt to warm them. "It's damn near below zero out here!"

"Where's your car?" Anthony inquired, looking around once more.

"My sister has it," he answered. "She had to go to the salon and grocery store, so I lent it to her. Plus, she didn't favor the idea of lugging groceries onto a community bus."

Anthony narrowed his eyes at the man. "Is that how you got here? On a bus?"

Rodney shrugged his shoulders. "Of course. What's wrong with that?"

"What's wrong with it!" Anthony wanted to assail him for posing such an obtuse question. "You're taking a big risk that's what's wrong with it! Do you know what'll happen if you get caught with that shit on a fucking community bus? They'll bury your ass under one of those Federal prisons!"

Rodney held a hand up. "Calm down, my friend! You're giving the cops a little too much credit."

"Am I?"

"Of course. Have you heard of anybody getting caught with drugs on a bus?"

Anthony hadn't heard of any, which was why he remained quiet.

"Well," Rodney resumed, "if it just so happens that I turn out to be the first you hear about, I promise to exercise my rights to remain silent."

Anthony didn't know if this clown intended to evoke laughter from his statement or not, but he didn't find it at all amusing. He didn't know Anthony's name, but one doesn't need to know a person's name in order to assist the authorities in a sting operation. He couldn't just not hand the package over to the man, yet it was his job to do so. Therefore, still skeptical about Rodney's transportation arrangement, Anthony pulled the saran-wrapped package from under his seat and handed it to him expecting the man to make his exit once he'd stuffed the package inside his coat, but he didn't. Instead, he dropped his hands into his lap and stared straight ahead as if expecting a ride to the bus station.

"Is there anything else I can help you with?" Anthony asked, thinking about his gun in the umbrella holder of the car's door. He didn't know what was on Rodney's mind.

"Did you hear what happened to Zachary?" he asked, maintaining his gaze out the windshield.

The question had come out of left field, which had Anthony on high alert, and attentively watching Rodney's every move. He knew that Rodney and Zachary were associates, but not the proximity of their friendship. He also didn't know what Rodney knew about Zachary's murder, which is why he had to tread lightly and choose his word carefully.

"I haven't seen nor heard from him," Anthony lied. "He hasn't contacted you?"

"He was at my house on Friday." Rodney was now looking at him. "We were shooting pool in the basement when he got a call from his daughter's mom. She was complaining about some kind of pain she was having and needed to be driven to the hospital." Rodney paused to look out the side window. "I guess it was a set-up because they found him, his girlfriend, and the baby murdered at their home that following day. It's been all over the news since then. You haven't seen it?"

"I did see the news," Anthony spoke carefully, "I remembered seeing that, but I didn't think it was Zachary and his family. I guess I was barely paying attention to it."

"You don't think Rick and Bull did it, do you?"

"Why would they—"

"Don't act like you don't know about Zachary running off with his last package!" Rodney cut in, now facing Anthony again. "And you're the drop-off man. You were probably the first to know."

"I don't think that I was the first," Anthony said in his own defense. "But I did hear about it. Yes, I'm the drop-off man, but that's all I'm required to do. Your job is to turn the product into currency. The big guys are to collect, and whatever else they do. I don't know if..."

"What about Chris?" Rodney intervened again. "He went missing on the day after Rick and Bull relieved him of his duties. His body was recovered last week. That was also on the news. Did you catch it? Or were you still barely paying attention?"

"What are you getting at?" Anthony asked, not liking his company's accusatory tone.

Rodney shrugged. "I don't know. Maybe it's just a hunch, but I think these guys have expiration dates on us."

Anthony narrowed his eyebrows but said nothing.

"Chris knew the exact date that he would be done working for them," Rodney continued, staring out the windshield again. "Maybe Rick and Bull killed him to prevent him from giving their names to the police if he should find himself in trouble with the law someday. Or, like I said maybe it's a hunch."

With that Rodney exited the car and made for the bus stop leaving Anthony wondering if what he'd said was really just a hunch or not. His summarization was logical but inconclusive. Yes, it would be a smart move to eliminate anyone that could unexpectedly lead the authorities to their doorsteps, but there's no proof that Rick and Bull commanded by Ebony, of course had murdered Chris for this reason, or were even complicit to Chris' murder. What if Rodney's theory turned out to be true? This would mean that he and the other workers would inevitably succumb to the same fate as Chris once their terms are up, which made Anthony wonder if he was exempt.

Chapter 6

"May I be a gentleman and escort you to your car?" Deputy Aaron Taylor asked as Ebony gathered her document into her briefcase preparing to make her exit for the day.

Ebony had already figured he would offer to escort her out, being that she'd intermittently caught him watching her throughout the day. It had gotten to the point where she had to muster up enough willpower to keep from looking in his direction, lest she give off the wrong signals. If given a chance, yes, she would sleep with him, but her mind wasn't on that at that moment. However, she could tell that he'd been building himself up to make whatever move he intended to make on her.

"That would be very sweet of you Aaron!" Ebony now said, securing the latches on her briefcase. "But I have a five-thirty meeting with the head honcho herself."

Aaron raised an eyebrow. "Are we in trouble?"

Ebony smiled. "Not this time. I think she want to introduce the new prosecutor to the rest of us."

"Well, that shouldn't take long, right?"

"It shouldn't."

He seemed to linger a few seconds before asserting, "I could wait if you want me to."

"I wouldn't recommend it." She was now facing him with her briefcase in one hand, keys, and cell phone in the other. "Besides, I know Samantha's dying to talk my head off about how her day went. Plus, you know how us girls like to fill each other in on the latest gossip while leaving work."

Aaron nodded his understanding but said nothing.

"Go on home to your family," Ebony told him. "I'll see you in the morning.

With that, Ebony made for the exit. She knew that she had probably struck a nerve by mentioning Aaron's family, but it was all she could come up with to make him *"pump his brakes."*

Aaron had already confessed that he and his wife were at odds, so Ebony was pretty much certain that she wasn't satisfying his sexual needs, but she was not yet ready to be his mistress. Maybe she couldn't see herself playing second fiddle to the woman he'd pledged his troth to. After retrieving her coat from her office, Ebony journeyed off to the small conference room that only boasted and oval-shaped table surrounded by eight straight-back chairs. Upon entering she saw that six of those chairs were occupied by District Attorney Barbara Hutchins, Corey Briggs, Samantha Gordon; the two state prosecutors, Rosely Holt, and Patrick Maynard, and the newest addition to the Linkton County District Attorney's office, Larry Hendrix. As if not wanting to start without her, everyone seemed to be absorbed in whatever they were doing on their cell phones, but stopped to watch her as she placed her briefcase on the floor and took a seat beside Samantha, who was— though Ebony wasn't surprised— seated next to Hendrix.

"Now that we're all here," Barbara Hutchins began, slipping her phone inside her tote bag beside her feet, "we can go ahead and start the meeting. Now as you all should have already deduced; I've assembled you here to properly introduce you all to the Assistant District Attorney Larry Hendrix. Mr. Hendrix, these are assistant district attorneys Corey Briggs, Samantha Gordon, Ebony Davis, Patrick Maynard, and Rosely Holt."

"It's nice to meet you all," Hendrix spoke, nodding to everyone in attendance, before bringing his gaze back to Ebony. "Mr. Davis, I've heard a great deal about your father, so it would definitely be an honor working with you."

Ebony only nodded in response.

"Does anyone have any quick questions for Mr. Hendrix?" Barbara asked.

Samanta took the initiative. "Why would you leave Fulton County for Linkton County?"

"To be close to my mother," he answered, drilling his ocean-blue eyes into Samantha's. "She resides in McRae, which is not too far from here. Once her doctor informed me that she's been diagnosed with cirrhosis, and would need in-home supervision, I tried to get her to move into my home in Riverdale, but she declined, not wanting to leave the house that she was raised up in. That's when I knew that I'd have to make the transition myself. Trust me, I would have never dreamed of leaving Fulton County for any other county. Plus, my wife and children are still having a hard time adjusting to their new surroundings. All in all, Linkton County seems like a decent place to continue my profession."

"It may not be as fast paced as Fulton County," Corey Briggs spoke, "but you could sometimes find yourself knee-deep in your work if you're not careful."

"I believe that" Hendrix answered with a nod. "And it seems as though you guys have become a primary venue for nondomestic high-profile cases. To be honest, I've never heard of Linkton County until one of my cases was transferred over to you all in 2017."

"The State versus Whitehead," Hutchins prompted, not missing a beat. "He was charged in the death of an off-duty police officer. I prosecuted that case myself."

"And you did an outstanding job," Hendrix commended.

"What are your ultimate goals, Mr. Hendrix?" Ebony inquired, hoping he didn't perceive the motive in her inflection.

He appeared confused. "My ultimate goals?"

"You have the ambience of someone who's always dreamed of becoming a judge," Ebony continued her ploy. "Is it true that you may become one of Linkton County's Finest?"

This made him smile. "I definitely like the sound of that. I mean, I haven't run across too many prosecutors that didn't have such dreams. However, I think I'd rather become Linkton County's Finest District Attorney someday."

Ebony's suspicion had just been confirmed. The account about his mother's ailment that prompted his migration may very well be true, but he was certainly taking advantage of this new-found opportunity. As Samantha had mentioned earlier, Hendrix probably knows that he has a better chance at attaining the D.A.'s position in Linkton County, than he did in Fulton, and whether he thought he was more advanced than the other presiding assistant attorneys or not, Ebony was sure that he was highly confident in his resume. Little did he know Ebony had no plans of letting her hard work go unrewarded.

Getting home, Ebony entered the house, voice-deactivated the alarm, then made for her bedroom without re-activating it. Anthony and Rick were to arrive at any minute. The conference had left her with little to no time to shower so, after relinquishing her pocketbook and briefcase, she re-entered the living room, carrying her handgun and two cell phones, in which she placed beside her once seated on the sofa, Ebony wasn't in the mood to watch television, though she did grab the remote control off the coffee table, and began slowly searching through the channels. After a couple of minutes into this, her pre-paid phone vibrated beside her, then fell silent indicating that her company had arrived. Considering this. Ebony shut off the tv, placed the remote back onto the table then sat the gun in her lap, keeping her index finger inside the trigger guard. Seconds later, Rick entered followed by Anthony who locked the door behind them.

"It won't fire on safety," Rick asserted as he placed the black pouch on the table in front of Ebony and stood there regarding her through mirror-tinted sunglasses despite the fact that the sun had descended hours ago.

"Did you two arrive in one care like I'd instructed?" Ebony asked, refusing to reveal how mad she was at herself for not checking to see it the gun's safety was off, and how Rick was able to see it from where he stood.

"Of course," he answered. "And don't be trying to change the subject."

With the gun still clutched in her right hand, Ebony got to her feet and tried to penetrate the mirror tint of Rick's sunglasses with her eyes. "The subject has been changed," she states with authority. "I appreciate your concern for my safety, but I don't need you to rectify every minor mistake I make. I'm human. Mistakes are inevitable."

Rick did not respond.

She turned to Anthony, who was standing behind, but to the right of Rick. "I hope you don't have any plans for this weekend.

"I'm driving to Atlanta to visit my mom," Anthony stated matter-of-factly.

"You can cancel that trip," Ebony told him. "I have a shipment coming in on Saturday, and you will accompany Rick and Bull when they go receive it."

Anthony looked as though he'd been offended. "They don't need me to accompany them. I'm quite sure that.."

"According to our agreement," Ebony cut him off, "I'm the one that gives the orders, and you're the one that has to follow them. Anything other than that would be a breach of contract, which will result in further actions being taken."

"Is that a threat?" Anthony questioned.

"Are you breaching our contract?" she returned.

Anthony seemed to linger in his response as he returned Ebony's stare, which had her wondering if she should go ahead and stamp an expiration date on him before he turns into a rogue elephant, and she no longer had any kind of control over him. Ebony didn't consider herself psychic, but she was taught to always go with her intuition and right now, her intuition was telling her that Anthony was slowly becoming rebellious. Just the thought of him revolting against her after putting her life and career on the line to emancipate him made Ebony want to shoot him dead right then and there as she unconsciously disengaged the safety lever on her gun.

"No," Anthony finally spoke. "I'm not breaching our contract. All I want to do is visit my mom. I haven't seen her in almost three weeks and there's no reason for me to make this trip with Rick and Bull when I've never made it with them before."

"There's a reason for everything Anthony," she told him. "Your reason for going is to introduce you the supplier and to familiarize you with the routine."

"But why?"

Ebony looked to Rick, then back to Anthony before answering. "Pretty soon, I'll have to let these guys go. Their contracts are almost up. By that time, you should be ready to take the reins. In case you haven't deduced, you'll be the new face of the operation. The supplier is already expecting you on Saturday. To him, your name is William, and you are Rick's nephew. Do you not agree with this arrangement?"

Anthony seemed to linger again as he diverted his gaze towards the front door. After a moment, he regarded her and asked, "How long am I to be the face of the operation? When is my contact up?"

"I saved your ass from the death penalty," Ebony reminded with narrowed eyes. "I bought you a house and car and provided you with a way to make more money than you've ever made breaking into toy stores. I mean, do I really need to answer your question?"

Anthony did not respond.

"You can wait outside in the car," she said dismissively. "I need to have a few words with Rick."

Apparently, they arrived in Rick's car because Rick handed his keys over to Anthony who studied them for a second then made for the door. Once he'd exited Ebony placed the gun on the coffee table, re-took her seat on the sofa, and crossed one leg over the other.

"It's like watching Tyrone Davis all over again with you two," Rick acknowledged taking a seat in the recliner. "And what's the word on that DNA testing?"

"It was still inconclusive the last time I checked."

"And when was that?"

"I'll call and make another appointment for next week," she used her dismissive tone again. "Right now, I'm a bit worried."

"About?"

Ebony drew a breath before going on. "I received a call from that investigator earlier."

"What'd he say?"

"It was a message he'd left on my office phone," she answered. "He wants to meet with me this Saturday at seven o'clock. Same diner. Said that it would be in my best interest to show up."

"So, this was more of a demand than a request, huh?" Rick spoke rubbing his chin.

"That's the way I perceived it," answered Ebony, "then there's the furtive threat."

"About it being in your best interest to show up?"

Ebony nodded. "Should I go?"

"Of course." Rick got to his feet. If you were being arrested, they wouldn't waste their time luring you into a meeting with an investigator. They would march you right out the front doors of the Linkton County Courthouse."

Chapter 7

"And this is our in-door track?"

Surveying the large, multicolored track reminded Ebony of the one she used to folic around on in middle school before becoming serious about running, though it was outdoors. Ebony's idee fix of indoor tracks were always of large, claustrophobic rooms with no windows, and dim lights besotted by multiples of insects, but this place was a big contradiction. She felt that the joggers should be able to enjoy the fresh outdoor air, instead of artificial air from air condition units, Ebony believed that in due time she would conform to the atmosphere. Now, after watching the handful of people that were now circling the track, she turned to the female instructor who given her the tour of the gymnasium.

"It's way better given than the one I'd seen in Linkton," she admitted, extending her right hand. "I guess I'm in."

"Great!" the woman exclaimed with a broad smile, shaking Ebony's hand with alacrity. "Let's get you signed up!"

It had only taken about fifteen minutes to fill out the necessary paperwork and to defray her membership card. Once this was complete, Ebony was back in her car and driving around Macon, Georgia with no destination in mind. Her meeting with the investigator was a little under 6 hours from now, which had her a bit angry that she couldn't think of one activity she could dally on until then. Maybe she wasn't trying to find something to do. Maybe she was too worried about the investigator's discoveries to do anything other than drive around in circles.

"Incoming call from Samatha," the car's Bluetooth system announced pulling Ebony from her abstract musing. "Do you wish to accept?"

"Yes," Ebony answered relieved to have someone to talk to though she was not going to tell Samantha about the meeting.

"Call is connected," the disembodied voice came back.

"Hi, babe!"

"I can't believe this!' Samantha's voice sounded through the speakers.

"What's the matter?" Ebony was expecting Samantha to lend her a shoulder to cry on, but it seemed like she was going to have to put her worries to the side and play comforter for her friend.

"I have yet to receive an invitation for the National Breast Cancer Awareness dinner," Samantha responded. "And Albert is still not answering his phone, nor responding to any of my messages. I'm tempted to drive out to his mansion and give him a piece of my mind."

"Which would be totally unprofessional," Ebony warned her. "Don't end up on the evening news as a crazy, deranged woman arrested for stalking the governor."

"A crazy and deranged woman?"

"That's how they'll display it to the media."

Samantha let out an exasperated sigh. "Well, what am I to do about this?"

"You definitely can't drive to the man's home and confront him," Ebony told her. "I'm quite sure he has a logical explanation for how things are currently going between the two of you. Maybe Jennifer's on to him and he's dodging you to prevent the whirlwind of trouble he'll find himself in. Who knows?"

"Or maybe he's found himself another courtesan," Samantha offered, doubt registering in her voice.

This made Ebony think about the housekeeper at the governor's mansion that resembled a younger version of Samantha. Yes, Ebony strongly believed that Albert Spires was *"making his round"* with the young and pretty creature, but she was not about to relay any of this to Samantha, which would definitely give her friend a self-justified reason to drive out the mansion and strangle the innocent woman. Considering this, Ebony knew that she had to be meticulous and choose her words wisely.

"Sam," Ebony began, "don't even torture yourself with such childish accusations. He didn't pledge his troth to you. He pledged it to Jennifer. She's the one he'd made a vow to be faithful to. So, if he's doing all of this to throw her off, then you'll have to sit back and wait on the outcome. Maybe he'll make contact once the coast is clear."

Samantha let out another sigh. "Maybe you're right."

"What's on your agenda for today?" Ebony changes the subject as she turns onto the expressway.

"Relaxation," answered Samantha. "A whole lot of it."

"Sounds good to me," Ebony told her. "I'm on my way."

"Really!" Samantha seemed to come alive.

"I can't spend the night Sam."

"Why not?"

"I just can't," Ebony offered. "I'll hang out with you for a few hours, then I have to be on my way."

"All right," Samantaha conceded. "Should I put on something sexy?"

Ebony smiled. "Your birthday suit."

***

5:47 P.M.

Rick pulled the rental car up to the small security booth that was occupied by a male in a military issued uniform and a burgundy beret looking cap atop his head. Despite the cold weather, he had the door to the booth standing wide open as if the bone chilling wind wasn't enough, a small fan was blowing on him. When Rick rolled down his window the smoke from the abnormally long cigarette dangling from the side of the security guard's mouth wafted in and managed to assail the nostrils of Anthony, who was seated in the back clad in a dark-blue dress suit he'd purchase for this occasion being that Rick and Bull (who were dressed in similar attire) had advised him to dress professionally.

"What is your business?" the guard questioned, voice conveying an accent Anthony couldn't quite make out.

"Veni, vidi, vici!" Rick responded.

The guard seemed to evaluate the occupants of the vehicle for an eon before exiting the booth and approaching the gate, in which he rolled back laterally on its wheels. Once it was wide enough Rick drove on through taking the extremely wide runway of the airfield at a slow pace while Anthony did his best to peer inside every hanger that they'd passed. The first hanger was occupied by a private jet of some sort that was being washed by three men with exceedingly long handle brushes. There was only an older white woman mopping the floor of the second hanger that was a little over two hundred yards of the first one.

"Do we need to go over anything?" Bull asked from the front passenger seat as they passed the third hanger that had its doors shut.

"That won't be necessary," Anthony answered knowing the question was for him.

Seconds later they pulled up to the fourth hanger, which was the last one. The doors were shut, but there was another man dressed in the same attire as the one in the security booth, seated out front in a steel folding chair. Anthony took notice of how the older man regarded them with a mere glance before getting up and sliding one of the large steel doors open. Anthony expected him to stand there and close the door back once they'd passed through, but he didn't. Instead, he walked ahead of them, pretty much using himself as a pacemaker causing Rick to inch the car along at a snail's pace until they reached the rear of two dark-colored SUVs that were parked parallel to each other. Their escort joined six other men that were standing behind the trucks, obviously awaiting their arrival. Five of those men were dressed as himself, but the one standing in the center of the group clad in a dark green dress suit, Anthony pretty much assumed he was the supplier.

"Let's get this over with fellas!" Rick said after shutting off the engine.

With that, the three of them dismounted; Bull carrying the briefcase containing the currency. Immediately Anthony took stock of the place as he had an overwhelming sense that there were people suspended from the ceiling, watching them through sighted scopes attached to assault rifles; but the only things hanging over their heads were different parts from small planes. There was a huge tank to the far right of them, in which he figured the loud diesel fumes were exuding from. Two heavy-duty forklifts were parked at odd angles further ahead of the two SUVs just beyond the pressure washer. Plus, there were more aircraft parts strewed about the place along with several industrial fans that were despite the weather blowing at a high intensity, which cause Anthony to tug at his black leather trench coat as Rick and Bull moved towards the front of the rental car where they stood facing the mob.

"Monsieur Frederick! Monsieur David!" The supplier stepped forward with arms wide open though he shook hands of Rick and bull with both of his hands. Then he regarded Anthoy with a raised eyebrow. "And you must be Monsieur William?"

"I am," Anthony answered accepting the man's ice-cold palms in a handshake.

"And I am Louis Napoleon," the supplier announced. "You are familiar with the name, no?"

Anthony pulled his hand from the man's unyielding grasp. "I can't say that I am."

There was a hurt expression on the supplier's face. "Why, Louis Napoleon was the nephew of Napoleon Bonaparte. He became president of the Second Republic in eighteen forty-eight. In eighteen forty-one…"

"So, that's not your real name? Anthony questioned, interrupting a history lesson he cared nothing about.

Napoleon shot an incredulous look over at Rick and Bull.

"He still has the mentality of a street dealer," Rick offered apologetically staring daggers at Anthony. "I myself was still naïve when I first started dealing on a bigger scale. I'm quite sure he'll come around."

"Well," Napoleon replied with a shrug, "we can't expect for the boy to be able to fill your shoes overnight, eh?"

"I appreciate you for being understanding Mr. Napoleon."

"Being understanding is what gets you far in this business, my friend," Napoleon let on. "But things are far more different back in Paris. A question like that, and your nephew would have been mistaken for an agent. Too many bodies were found in La Manche, and the Bay of Biscay. Too many, my friend." He drew a deep breath before going on. "Now, shall we do business?"

"Of course," Bull answered, handing the briefcase over to Rick who held it out to Anthony.

"And save the dumb-ass questions!" Rick chided Anthony in a low tone. "These guys won't hesitate to mail you home to your parents in a sardine can."

Anthony wanted to retort but couldn't think of anything to say. Besides he knew that to wrangle with Rick in front of the Frenchmen would be utterly unprofessional. Therefore, he accepted the briefcase and followed Napoleon to the rear of one of the SUVs where he opened the doors up to a carpeted compartment. The huge space was empty, except for a black briefcase akin to the one Anthony held.

"You can sit it right there, Monsieur William," the supplier Napoleon nodded at the case. "You first."

For some reason, when Anthony reached to open the briefcase, his hands began to tremble, which was something he couldn't truthfully ascribe to the cold weather. It was as if he was about to open a case containing a bomb instead of the currency to pay for the drugs. Well, truth be told, he didn't know what was inside the case. He was only assuming it was money, but why would there be anything other than that? After releasing the latches and lifting the top open on its hinges, Anthony found himself mesmerized by the rows of neatly stacked twenty dollar bills, which instantly jogged his memory back to the moment he's entered the vault of the First national Bank, in November of 2022, and encountered the extensive shelves that contained way more money than he'd ever seen in his entire life. That image was ensued by the image of him blowing Bo's brains out, then by the image of Marvin tossing the gas can at him temporarily impairing his vision.

"Greed will always be a man's downfall," Marvin's words echoed in Anthony's mind though the voice didn't match that of Marvin's. In fact, it wasn't as deep as Marvin's Plus, it was…non-American.

Anthony whipped his head around to face Napoleon who now regarded him with a blank expression. "What was that?"

"Greed will always be a man's downfall," Napoleon reiterated, then opened his own briefcase to reveal four brick shaped packages heavily wrapped in transparent plastic film. "Will you like to test the product?"

"It's the same shit, right?" Anthony asked not willing to taste test any kind of drug, but still wondering why this man would fix his mouth to say anything to him about greed.

Napoleon nodded. "According to my developers, yes."

"Will you like to count the money?"

"I don't think there's any need to."

"Then I guess we'll be on our way." Anthony secured the briefcase containing the drugs, pulled it from the truck, then held out his right hand. "It was a pleasure doing business with you Mr. Louis Napoleon."

"Likewise." The supplier took Anthony's hand in both of his.

"As I understand we will see each other again."

"Hopefully," Napoleon replied, locking eyes with Anthony. "Just remember what I told you Monsieur William."

With that, Napoleon gave orders to his men in their native tongue. Once one of his men took possession of the case containing the currency, and another secured the rear compartment of the truck, they all began climbing into the SUVs. Taking that as his cue, Anthony moves toward the rental car handing the case off to Rick before reclaiming his seat in the rear. When the older men joined him, Bull was in possession of the case.

"Just drop me off at my car," Anthony said as Rick made a U-turn and drove toward the entrance of the hanger.

"We're not done yet," Rick told him. "This stuff needs to be prepped and distributed."

"I'm already the distributor."

"You're one of the distributors," Rick corrected. "Today, you'll be doping a little more than passing out Girl's Scout Cookies. Don't think this preparation shit is easy because it's not. It's a man's game."

"So, I'm held hostage until I learn everything there is to know about prepping the drug?"

"I don't know what kind of agreement the two of you have," Rick replied, "but I'm doing as I was told. She had already explained to you the reason for all of this."

Anthony drew a breath. "You're right, but I'd still rather ride in my own car."

"I don't have a problem with that," Rick said then glanced over at Bull who only shrugged in response.

Once they were back on the main road, Rick turned on the radio and selected some ancient old song from his cellular that Anthony used to hear his mother and her husband, Leonard listen to while growing up. Thinking of Leonard's tragic death made Anthony realize how imperative it was that he make some kind of progress on his mission, in which he feels that he would already done had he not been working for Ebony.

It's true that he was making a decent amount of money while under her employment, but it was all time consuming and extraneous compared to what he really needed to do, but that was about to change. Anthony was still in his thoughts when Rick pulled the rental into the parking lot of the Langford Textiles Warehouse that was still occupied by vehicles belonging to the night shift workers. For some reason, he found himself smiling at how his own car sat inconspicuously amongst the others. Out of all the times he'd done this, Anthony had now come to realize that this harmless act was indeed an act of deception. There was nothing more to say between Anthony and the older men so, once the car came to a halt, Anthony quickly dismounted, activating his keyless entry to an engine start. While awaiting the air conditioner to disperse the remainder of its cold air, Anthony plugged his phone up the charger and programmed it to access calls through the car's Bluetooth system then he caught up to the rental just as it pulled back out onto the main road.

It was still daytime as Anthony drove keeping his Innovator at about two car links of the older men. By now, the heat coming from the vents had the interior feeling a bit warm prompting Anthony to maneuver out of his coat while maintaining control of the vehicle at thirty-two miles per hour. Tossing the coat on the seat beside him he activated his right turning signal, seeing that Rick was about to enter the expressway. Anthony already knew what his plans were, and they definitely didn't coincide with the plans Ebony had for him. It's not that he didn't appreciate her for trying to elevate him from a petty criminal to something of a drug lord because he appreciated it a great deal. It was just that the timing was all wrong. He also felt that she was endeavoring to force him out of his life and into the life of a total different person in which he found to be a bit scary; but how is that possible?

The Interstate 75 sign caught Anthony's attention informing him that they were nearing the conjunction. Whether Rick was going to continue on this interstate or take I-75, Anthony had no idea, being that he knew nothing about the destination he was being led to. Either way, he knew that what he was about to do would be as easy as cutting butter with a hot knife. Now, considering the proximity of the conjunction, Anthony eased his foot off the gas pedal allowing the evening traffic to casually breeze by him, and extending the distance between his car and the rental that he saw continue on past the bypass. For some odd reason, Anthony found himself smiling as he breached for I-75, keeping the rental car in his sight until he could see it no more, wondering if Rick had been watching the rear-view mirror at that time. Well, it really didn't matter because it was already done. There was no turning back now. He knew that he was playing a deadly game by adhering to old promises he'd made to himself, but the consequences meant nothing to him at that moment. If Ebony found herself wanting his head for this, then he would want her head for wanting his head.

Chapter 8

Ebony had managed to make it to the diner at 6:54 P.M. She'd only consumed a peanut butter and jelly sandwich for lunch, so she was a bit hungry, but for some reason, she couldn't bring herself to order anything from the menu she had been pretending to take interest in for the past fifteen minutes or so. Now, it was eleven minutes after seven and the investigator had yet to arrive. This made her look out the huge windows again at the parking lot, but the only movement outside was a couple rushing out to their car. The precipitation still showed no signs of letting up. The shrill laughter of one of the diners had gotten Ebony's attention, but before she could turn away from the window she spotted the gray, older model Buick pulling into the lot. At this point she didn't know if she should be relieved or disappointed because she'd been secretly hoping that something hindered him from showing up, a car wreck perhaps. Now, she watched Investigator John Pruden as he sauntered across the parcel, clad in a large overcoat and carrying that same burgundy briefcase in which she kept her eyes affixed to until it came down on the table in front of her with a loud thud. That's when she looked up in time to see him rake the fingers of his left hand through his damp hair.

"Ms. Davis," he said extending his right hand. "I'm glad you could make it. How have you been?"

"I've been okay," she answered accepting his hand. "Thanks for asking. How's life been treating you?"

"Oh, I can't complain." John began unbuttoning his coat. "Are you ordering?"

"I've already eaten," she lied, darting her eyes at the briefcase again.

"So have I."

Once out of his coat, John laid it across the opposite bench as if he had no intention on sitting there. This was confirmed when he flopped down onto the bench and scooted a little too close for Ebony's liking. Though she had on spandex pants under her jeans, she could feel heat emitting off the investigator's right thigh that was now resting against her left thigh. Not only was this awkward, but it made Ebony a bit uncomfortable.

"You've become quite a mogul since our last encounter," the investigator spoke, locking eyes with Ebony. "How does it feel to finally get the recognition that your father received?"

"I don't think I'll ever get the same recognition that my father received," Ebony responded.

John raised an eyebrow. "You don't?"

"Tyrone Davis had a surreal track record." Ebony was now gazing out the window. "Yes, I've always dreamed of being like him, but that would be highly impossible."

"I know you have more confidence in yourself than that, Ms. Davis."

Ebony regarded him with a blank expression. "Surely, you didn't lure me here to talk about my father. If I'm not mistaken, you claimed that there were new developments in my case."

"Oh! Yeah." He turned the briefcase so that the opening was facing him. Flipped the latches, then lifted the top.

After extracting and setting his recorder on the table, he held a manila envelope out to Ebony. "I thought you might be interested in these."

Accepting the envelope that felt empty, Ebony lifted the flap and removed a small stack on 7x10 photos from it, lying the envelope down in front of her. To say that she was taken aback by the photo that she was now looking at would be an understatement, but she couldn't fathom how a picture of her attending her grandmother's burial was any kind of development in the case of Jason's murder. However, it was confirmed when she moved to the next photo that was a close-up of Rick, who flanked her in his black suit and sunglasses. Knowing that the investigator was watching closely, Ebony made sure not to show signs of surprise as she moved on to the third photo that was a close-up of Bull as he opened the rear door of her Cadillac for her, as they prepared to leave the cemetery. Now, Ebony regarded John Pruden with another blank expression.

"Richard Carter and Alfonso Walker," he said, slowly holding her gaze. "I still can't figure out how a person of your stature could have a consortium with such common criminals. These guys are way too old for you."

"What does all this have to do with my fiancé's murder?" Ebony asked keeping her voice calm.

A smile slowly spread across the investigator's face. "Carter was picked out of a photo line-up by our star witness that saw him enter your home on that day carrying a bottle with a piece of cloth protruding from the opening of it, which was minutes before the fire started. I think this was also around the time you claimed to have left your house for your routine run."

Ebony remained silent.

"I've been doing this for quite some time now, Ms. Davis," he resumed, relieving her of the photos and began sliding them back inside the envelope. "I've interviewed a great number of battered and bruised women who were suspected of causing the demise of their male counterparts, so I'm pretty good at spotting your kind from a distance."

There was a pregnant pause as he now drilled his eyes into hers. "That's what I saw in you the moment I walked into this diner last year to interview you, a woman who finally relieved herself of an abusive relationship. The performance you put on with the crocodile tears. It was great, but redundant to a professional such as me. Now, what do you think is going to happen when I turn over my findings to the chief inspector, Ms. Davis?"

Ebony said nothing.

"I'm sure we both know the answer to that," he continued, letting his right hand drop down to her left thigh, which he began caressing. "Think about everything you have to lose Ebony. This is a capital offense, which automatically requires the death penalty. Don't think that Carter won't testify against you for a lesser sentence. He's done it before."

The investigator's hand was now between Ebony's thighs stroking her vagina through the fabrics of her leggings and jeans. "That would be the bane of your career Ebony," he went on. "Your life would definitely be over, but only you can prevent all of this. All you have to do is sleep with me, and I'll make all of this disappear. You won't hear anything else about it. I swear."

Ebony felt extremely vulnerable at that moment. As the indistinct chatter of the diners and the country music coming from the juke box continued in the background. All Ebony could think about was her grandfather, while this riff raff blatantly violated her, which was something she'd vowed to never allow another human being to do and get away with. Now, clearing her throat, Ebony gingerly grabbed his wandering hand and placed it in his own lap as she glanced around to see if anyone was paying attention, which they weren't.

"I'm gonna need some time to think about this," she spoke at a length, locking eyes with him.

"I think that's fair," John Pruden replied slipping the manila envelope back into his briefcase along with the voice recorder before closing it and getting to his feet. After donning his coat and retrieving his briefcase off the table, he raked his fingers through his hair while fixing her with a stern look. "You have one week. Next Saturday, I'll be at this same diner, same time. If you don't show, I'll turn in my findings that following Monday."

With that he turned on his heels and marched towards the exit. Ebony's mind was in a jumble as she watched the investigator cross the parking lot to his car. At a time like this, the average human being would be experiencing a high level of fear after basically being told that they were going to die in prison unless they perform some kind of unethical task. All Ebony felt at that time was hatred toward the government official. Though her mind was still unclear about how she was going to handle the situation, she knew that she was not going to be joining John Pruden in anybody's bed, which made her think about Governor Albert Spires' small and discolored penis. She was going to have to bring this to Rick's attention.

Chapter 9

Upon leaving the diner, Ebony placed a call to Rick telling him that he needed to rendezvous with her at her place as soon as possible but withheld the reason. Though she wanted to just drive around to try and clear her mind, Ebony knew that she had to hurry home to await the arrival of Rick, Bull, and Anthony who she assumed were still together. Rick had apprised her that *"we"* were still together at the preparation house and would be done shortly. Not knowing when they would arrive, Ebony decided to go ahead and take her shower knowing that Rick would use his key to gain entrance.

Ebony ended up staying in the shower for over twenty minutes. Upon exiting the bathroom, she peered into the living room to see if her company had arrived and was waiting for her, but they weren't. Therefore, already bundled up in one of her house robes she journeyed off to her bedroom where she donned a pair of jeans and a T-shirt. While standing at the vanity mirror reapplying her eyeliner, thoughts of the coitus she had with Samantha earlier invaded her mind. Samantha had really set her mind at ease before her meeting with the investigator. Perhaps, another sexual bout with the red head was what she needed at this moment. Although it would take her mind off of her current problems. Ebony knew that they would still exit. Something had to be done. The musical chimes of her doorbell pulled her from her abstract musing. Finished with the application of her cosmetic, Ebony made for the living room, wondering why Rick was using the doorbell instead of his key. Getting to the front door without giving it much thought she unlocked and pulled it open. At that moment she instantly became offended to see four of the Solid Nation members on her porch, all wearing large coats that were left unfastened, so their necklaces sported SN pendants were visibly on display. Though Rick once referred to them as TV thugs, a contrarious Ebony figured they would someday become a problem. Well, perhaps, this is the day she thought hating the fact that she unceremoniously opened the door as Rick had cautioned her against. Then her leaving the gun in the bedroom didn't make the situation any better, but she was not going to let the mere presence of these hoodlums daunt her.

"What?" Ebony asked, hoping that her visage was menacing enough to keep them at bay while standing with one hand poised on the doorknob and the other on her hip.

"Whoa, baby!" said the one standing directly before her holding his hands up in mock surrender. His dreadlocks cascaded past his shoulders and though it was dark outside, his mouthful of gold teeth that were in utter contrast to his dark skin seem to gleam as if reflecting off and invisible ray of light; being that the porch's light was off. "Despite our appearances, we're not here to cause any problems. That's not what Solid Nation is about."

"Well, why is Solid Nation standing on my porch at this time of night?" Ebony inquired feeling a bit at ease with the man's assertion of not being there to cause problems.

"We were hoping you could put us in with your boyfriend," he answered.

"Do what!"

This had definitely caught Ebony by surprise. She was really hoping that he wasn't talking about what she thought he was talking about. Well, of course he was talking about what she thought he was talking about. They're drug dealers.

What else would he be talking about, and she already knew he was referring to Rick when he said boyfriend.

In the moment of her shocked response, Ebony did a quick evaluation of the other members. The one standing to the left of the man she was speaking with was larger than the others, and also wore long dreadlocks. The one closest to him was dark complexioned with a diamond earring pierced in his nose, which Ebony was sure had gone out of style four decades ago. His hair was concealed under a black ball cap with SN stenciled on the front in gray letters. The last one had on an orange skullcap that matched his coat. He was light complexioned and appeared to be the youngest of the quartet. In fact, neither of them appeared to be over twenty-five years old.

"You don't have to play the innocent role with us sweetheart," the same man asserted. "We've been watching your house from the day you moved in. We're dealers, so we can pretty much pick up on the movements of another dealer and your boyfriend. He moves like clockwork. Plus, that black pouch he carries is a dead giveaway. Like I said, we're not here to cause problems. All we're trying to do is find another supplier."

"I think you all have the wrong assumption," Ebony replied, looking from one to the other. "And I'd appreciate it if you would excuse yourselves from my property."

"Cut the bullshit lady!" The bigger one decided to give it a try. You act like we're trying to rob or extort your old-ass boyfriend. We're trying to bring him some business."

"Sen-Tech," Ebony said over her shoulder. "Stand by for an emergency distress call. Sixty seconds."

"Standing by for emergency distress call," the disembodied voice returned from the monitor on the wall, several feet away from her.

"You now have approximately sixty seconds to deactivate or requested call will be forwarded to the local authorities."

73

"I think now would be the best time to get the fuck off my property!" Ebony voiced, done with playing nice with these thugs who were now regarding her with incredulous looks.

"It's not that serious to involve the cops lady," the initial speaker intoned, a look of hatred on his face. "I've already told you—"

"I think you're down to thirty seconds," Ebony cut him off, tilting her head to one side.

Ebony didn't have to look at the other members to know that they were regarding her with menacing looks akin to that of their assumed leader. The stare down lasted for another second or two before he turned on his heels and swaggered through the gap they'd made for him. Not knowing how much time she had remaining before her requested emergency distress call was routed to the police station, Ebony immediately closed and locked the door though she really wanted to watch them leave.

"Sen-Tech" she said as she passed the monitor en route to her bedroom, "disengage requested emergency distress call."

"Emergency distress call has been disengaged," the computerized voice responded.

Entering her room, Ebony retrieved her gun from under her pillow, switched off the safety, then returned to the living room where she peered out the window. She didn't see the gang members though she couldn't secure any kind of view from where she was standing. Therefore, she took a seat on the sofa placing the gun in her lap. The only sound that could be heard throughout the house was the constant hum of the heating system that periodically emitted a barely audible hissing sound, but the quietness of the house made it easy for her to hear the vehicle that sounded as though it pulled into her driveway. Momentarily, she heard two car doors close in tandem. While anticipating the sound of the third door, the sound of footsteps trampling on the front porch reached her ears followed by the sound of Rick's keys negotiating the lock on the front door. Seconds later, Rick entered, supervened by Bull, who closed and locked the door back.

"Where's Anthony?" she questioned as Rick placed the black pouch down on the coffee table in front of her.

"Everything's accounted for," Rick promulgated as if he hadn't heard the question. "The packages that were meant for Chris and Zachary are also in there."

"Where's Anthony?" Ebony tried again feeling like he was evading her.

The older men only exchanged glances.

"Am I speaking Chinese?" She asked now getting to her feet, holding the gun down by her side. "If so, feel free to let me know and I'd be more than happy to translate."

"He got ghost on us," Rick finally let on.

Ebony snapped her head back as if being physically struck. "And how in the hell did you lose him?"

"That's not what I said."

"I heard what you said," she replied, looking back and forth from the two. "Right now, somebody needs to be explaining to me how this separation came about."

Rick and Bull exchanged another glance before Bull took the initiative. "After meeting with Napoleon, Anthony asked to be taken back to his car, saying that he would follow us to the prep house. Somewhere along the way, on the interstate, he bailed out on us."

"Why would he do something like that?" Ebony wasn't feeling their accusations of Anthony just bailing out on them. "You all were on the expressway. Maybe he got lost in traffic. Did anybody even think to try his cell phone to find out what really happened?"

"There was no need to," Rick spoke up. "The traffic was light, which is how I was able to keep an eye on him through the rear-view mirror. I saw when he dropped back. Once I saw seventy-five coming, I'd already had him figured out."

"I see."

Re-taking her seat on the sofa, Ebony placed the gun on a cushion beside her, crossed one leg over the other and mulled over what she'd just heard. She already deduced Anthony's reason for taking Interstate 75 was to get to Atlanta as he has been hell bent on doing every weekend. Now, Ebony could understand how a person could love their mother dearly just as she'd loved hers, but Anthony was always a bit too anxious to get back to his hometown. It wasn't as if Ebony didn't know his true intentions. She knew that he was on the road to revenge, and it was eating him up that he was under her thumb when he could be hunting down the very people that had caused his pain and agony.

"What's the emergency you called us over here for?" Rick finally asked, pulling her from her thoughts.

Ebony cleared her throat, then lifted her eyes to meet his. "It's what that investigator revealed to me."

"And what's that?"

"He showed me photos of us at my grandmother's funeral," she answered. "Said that you were picked out of a photo line-up by a star witness that saw you enter my house carrying a bottle with a piece of cloth protruding from it on the day of Jason's murder. He was threatening to take us down for it."

"He's bluffing."

"Oh?"

"If he gonna take us down," Rick explained, "we would probably already be on death row. I mean, why wait?" Did he make any demands?"

Ebony lingered. She didn't want to reveal that part, but she knew it was essential to how the situation would be handled. "He said that if I slept with him," she spoke through clenched teeth, "he'd make the whole thing disappear."

Rick furrowed his eyebrows. "He actually said that?"

Ebony gave a slight nod. "That son of a bitch had the nerve to fondle me right there in the restaurant in front of all those people. He also warned me that you would testify against me for a lesser sentence. According to him, you've done it before. Is it true?"

Rick didn't respond.

"You gotta be fucking kidding me right now!" Ebony exploded fighting the urge to grab her gun off the cushion beside her. "You actually snitched on somebody?"

"It was a juvenile case," Rick spoke slow and deliberately locking eyes with her. "Burglary, I got caught inside a pawn shop I'd broken into with my aunt's boyfriend at the time. He had gotten away. I was only twelve. I knew nothing about the system, and how they played mind games in order to get confessions out of people."

"So, you were tricked into giving up a name of your aunt's boyfriend?" Ebony posed.

Rick remained silent.

"Was that the only time?"

"That was it," he admitted.

"So, how are we going to handle this investigator?" Ebony asked, a bit relieved that she'd gotten Rick's side if the story though she still planned to rifle through his files once she returns to her office on Monday.

"Well," Rick began, "that depends on how much time he gave you to make your decision."

"One week," she told him. "We're supposed to meet back at the same diner next Saturday."

"And he actually fondled you right there in the diner?"

It was Ebony's turn to remain silent. Rick appeared to be in deep thought as he rubbed his chin.

"He will definitely have to die for that," he voiced. "But there's something strange about his approach. I mean, don't they get bonuses or qualification for rank when they crack cases of this magnitude?"

"I think so," answered Ebony.

"Then why would he sacrifice those things just to have sex with you?" Rick asked. "It doesn't add up."

"So, what do you suggest?" Ebony was tired of going back and forth with this. Yes, she was all for the demise of the investigator. Now, all Rick has to do is come up with a plan of execution.

"I think you should call the Department of Investigations," Rick said, then held up a hand to silence her protest.

"Get the chief investigator on the line and ask him for an update on your case. Now, from watching *First 48,* when I was younger, I learned that all cases have deadlines. If they're not solved before that deadline, they're automatically closed, only to be opened when there's new developments."

"Well," Ebony started, "that's exactly what he said he has, new developments."

"Pictures of us at your grandmother's funeral?" There was a sheet doubt in the older man's voice. "Really?"

"That's what he—"

"Call the Department of Investigations," Rick cut her off now looking at his watch. "Find out everything you can from the chief investigator. Whatever he tells you will determine how we handle this situation. Until then, get some rest.

Easy for you to say, Ebony thought as she watched them leave closing the front door behind them. She immediately thought about the Solid Nation members which for some strange reason had her mentally bracing herself for the sound of gunfire as she remained rooted to the sofa, left hand absently rested on the gun beside her. The sound of the two car doors slamming had finally reached her ears, supervened by the engine starting. After listening to the roar of the engine fade off as the car drove away, Ebony grabbed her gun, locked the front door, set the alarm, then was about to make for her bedroom when she spotted the pouch on the coffee table. She had totally forgotten about the money. Retrieving the bag Ebony entered the kitchen where she placed the gun and bag on the table before pushing it along with its four chairs closer to the back door. Using her designated butterknife to unwedge three planks from the floor, Ebony retrieved the duffle bag from the cavity of it and placed it on the table beside the smaller one. She didn't bother with taking a seat because all she had to do was transfer the bills from the smaller bag to the bigger one, return the bigger bag to the floor, then try, and get some rest as Rick had advised. Upon unzipping and dumping the contents of the smaller bag onto the table, and seeing two wrapped packages of crush, all thoughts of climbing into bed had quickly vanished. Suddenly, Ebony's heart rate seemed to double as she ran her hand over the smooth plastic wrappings of one of the packages that was the size of a standard bath soap. Not only was she now perspiring, but Ebony was so caught up in her thoughts, she didn't know at what point she actually pulled one of the chairs out and sat in it. Why was she still holding the butterknife?

At this moment, all kinds of bells were going off in Ebony's head whiles she now drummed on the package with the knife in in a mercurial cadence, but what were the bells for? Were they warnings? Were they rewarded of what she'd stumbled upon? Well, whatever they represented, Ebony knew that whatever she did with the drugs would be her very own decision. Isn't that why Rick brought the remainder of the shipment to her? The drugs belonged to her just like the stack of rubber banded bills that also tumbled from the black bag. It all belongs to her.

Allowing her mind to adopt this illogical pretext, Ebony took the knife and perforated the package she's been molesting for the past couple of minutes. Pulling the knife back out she found herself staring at the white powered substance that seemed to glitter at the tip of it. Suddenly, a smile slowly spread across her face. It had been almost eight months since she used the drug and considering that she should be on her way to prison the rest of her life, Ebony felt as though she needed something to mitigate her worries pro tempore.

Chapter 10

Anthony extinguished the lights before pulling into his mother's driveway and parking behind her car. It was only 23 minutes after 8, but Anthony was almost sure that his mother was preparing for bed, or already in it, considering she has church services in the morning. He already knew that once he makes his unceremonious presence known, she was going to be hell bent on dragging him along with her, which is why he brought two dress suits along with other articles of clothing and shoes he'd packed before driving to meet with Bull and Rick.

Now, killing the engine, Anthony surveyed the dark neighborhood that was lit by streetlamps and porch lights, which always brought back childhood memories. Though he hadn't been under his mother's roof for more than ten years, this was always considered home. This is where he'd always felt tranquility, where his heart will always lie. Anthony didn't know how long he would be staying there, but he planned to make the very best of it.

After retrieving his two tote bags from the truck, Anthony used his own keys to gain entrance to his mother's home where he reset the alarm before moving through the quiet house to his old bedroom. The only lights left were of the kitchen, and the bathroom, which were sure signs that Carol Anne Jenkins had already *"called it a night."*

Entering his old room, Anthony was surprised at how his mother had re-decorated it to look the same way it did when he was just a child. There were even stuffed animals and toys strewn about, which was how he would always leave it before going to bed. This would've been the perfect picture of his childhood had these items been of his era. Though Anthony was lost to the identities of the toys and stuffed animals, he was highly familiar with the animated character on the bedspread only because he found himself watching the cartoon with his son on several occasions.

Being that he was already exhausted, and in need of some rest himself, Anthony deposited his things on the floor beside the bed with the intent to put them properly away the following day. Exiting the bedroom, he was about to enter the bathroom that was just beyond the door when he heard his mother laugh, which caused him to stop in his tracks. The constant flicker of light from the television shining under her bedroom door now had his attention. Of course, this wasn't strange because she'd always slept with the set on. It also wasn't strange that she was still up at this hour. So, why did Anthony have this strange feeling that something was amiss? Surely if his mother had a *friend*, he'd be the first to know right? With that thought in mind, Anthony changed course and marched toward his mother's bedroom where he lightly rapped on the door before turning the knob and pushing it open. While mentally preparing himself for an image that would be embedded in his memory bank for the rest of his life. To his satisfaction, she was lying in bed, alone with the covers pulled up to her chest, and a startled expression on her face that slowly gave way to a huge smile.

"You're here!" she expressed breathlessly.

"Of course," Anthony replied, entering the room. Nearing the bed, he bent down to accept her warm embrace. Now, standing upright and looking down at her he said, "I'm surprised you're still up."

"I was doing my hair when *Self-Made Women* came on," Carol explained. "I'm just catching the re-run of it and why'd you come so late? The weekend is almost over."

"It's always better late than never," Anthony replied glancing over at the television mounted on the wall. "Besides, I had a lot to catch up on that had me tied up until earlier. So, being that I have a few days to myself, I decided to pop up."

"Well, I hope you decide to *'pop up'* at church service tomorrow," she stated with a smile.

Anthony reciprocated her expression. "Of course, Mama. First, I'll need a good night's rest."

"Okay, baby. Goodnight."

"Goodnight, Mama."

With a peck on his mother's forehead, Anthony exited closing the door behind him. More relieved that he didn't catch her with some strange man. He let out a sigh as he entered the bathroom where he first drained his bladder, then rinsed his hands. He'd always kept an extra toothbrush there. After retrieving the toothpaste from the medicine cabinet, he was about to reach for his toothbrush when he spotted a third one lodged in the toothbrush rack, where there had always been two, supervening Leonard's passing.

However, the third one was that of a of a child's with designs of the same cartoon character he'd seen on the bedspread in his old bedroom. Too tired to try and make some sense of this, Anthony brushed his teeth then returned to his room where he shed his coat and tossed it upon the dresser. After removing his shoes and pants, he extinguished the light and climbed into bed, ensconcing himself under what seemed like seven layers of blankets.

***

It seemed like Anthony had just dozed off when the sound of pots and pans clanging together reached his ears, followed by the aroma of fried bacon assailing his nostrils. Being that he's accustomed to living alone, the noise startled him for a split second. For all he knew, within the 13th of a minute, someone could have broken in, with the intent to harm him for something to do with Ebony, or her ancient-old goons; but he was safe. He was home. Now, hearing his mother tap lightly on the bedroom door, Anthony closed his eyes to give off the impression that he was still asleep.

"Anthony?" Carol's sweet voice reached his ears in almost a whisper.

"Mmm." Anthony put an exaggerated stretch as he sleepily opened his eyes to see his mother slowly approach the bed carrying a plate of food in one hand, and a glass of orange juice in the other.

"Breakfast baby," she announced, sitting the beverage on the small table beside the bed. "Sit up! And I hope you got some clothes on."

"Don't act like you never seen me naked before," he teased with a smirk on his face as he sat up, planting his back against the headboard.

Carol narrowed her eyes. "That's when you were a baby. Plus, you were way cuter."

Anthony feigned hurt. "You don't think I'm cute anymore?"

"Definitely not!" his mother expressed. "In fact, I think your ugliness is beyond repair."

This tickled Anthony. "That's a good one! I wonder which one of your favorite TV shows you stole that from."

"You just eat your food," she replied before sauntering toward the door in her housecoat. Reaching the threshold, she stopped and turned to face him. "I didn't know which of your suits you were gonna wear, so I ironed them both. They're still in my room."

"Okay."

Carol left, closing the door behind her. Anthony looked down at the plate in his hand that contained grits. Eggs, toast, and bacon. Being that the bacon's aroma is what sparked his hunger upon awakening, he quickly shoves one of the strips into his mouth and chewed with his eyes closed. Swallowing, Anthony opened his eyes and was about to take hold of his fork when he noticed how different the room looked now compared to how it looked the following night. The stuffed animals and toys that were cluttering the floor were nowhere in sight. There was also no sign of his luggage, nor the coat and pants he's taken off before climbing into bed. Maybe his mother had come in and cleaned up while he was asleep, which was something she'd done pretty much every night when he was a child; but why did it seem so eerie to him now?

Anthony tried to contemplate this while tending to his meal. But thoughts of Marvin and Janelle kept encroaching his mind. He's been doing his best to track them down in the course of the time bidded by Ebony which wasn't much, but for the first time since he'd been out of jail Anthony was beginning to feel as if he was very close to doing so. Maybe he was feeling this way because he'd finally emancipated himself from Ebony's bondage, but he didn't plan on staying away from her forever. All he wanted to do was to avenge himself for all the pain and suffering he had to endure ever since the day of the bank robbery in Atlanta. This would at least set his mind at ease so he could concentrate on being whatever it was that Ebony was trying to make him out to be. He was sure she'd understand, or maybe he was hoping she'd understand.

Concluding his meal, Anthony gulped down the remainder of his orange juice and set the dishes on the small table before throwing the covers off him and swinging his legs over the side of the bed, planting his feet on the plush carpet that seemed to add to the comfort of his already comfortable socks. That's when he finally realized that the top spread had been changed. There was no more Phantom Man. This made Anthony ponder how hard he's been sleeping as he crossed the room to the dresser where he figured his mother had stored his clothing. If she was able to pull the thick cover off him and neatly replace it with another while he was *'counting sheep'*, then he was vulnerable to the attack of anybody while in that state. Suppose Ebony decides to send her henchmen after him for breaching their contract?

Anthony tried not to think about that as he retrieved a T-shirt and a pair of boxer shorts from the dresser and made for the bathroom. His mother's bedroom door was closed, so he figured she was getting dressed. Upon entering the bathroom, he let the lid down and placed his underwear on top of it before tampering with the knobs on the shower. Once the temperature was adjusted to his liking, Anthony moved to the sink to rid his mouth of morning breath comingled with the contents of his breakfast. Before he could open the medicine cabinet for the toothpaste, he noticed that there were now two toothbrushes in the toothbrush holder, when he was certain he'd seen three just last night. It wasn't surprising that the one decorated with the animated character just so happened to be the one that was missing.

Now, Anthony was really perplexed because he was beginning to feel as if he'd only imagined the toothbrush, toys, stuffed animals, and cartoon-stenciled bedspread; but he knew better than to give in to that sentiment. There was no way he imagined these things. After his shower, Anthony clad only in his T-shirt and boxers headed back to his bedroom where he immediately noticed that the dishes were gone and his two suits were lying across the already made bed, but his mother was nowhere to be found. Either she had become a magician, or he had somehow slipped into the matrix. Of course, neither of those assumptions were true and to prove this, Anthony made for the closet where he was sure his mother had stowed the toys and stuffed animals.

"How long do you plan on staying?"

Stopping in his tracks, Anthony turned to see his mother standing in the threshold of the door, clad in a peach-colored Sunday dress, matching heels, and carrying a pair of men's dress shoes that were black in color. Her make-up was flawless; her hairdo was impeccable. The fragrance of her perfume had already permeated the room. Anthony was always awed by how her face managed to retain its youthfulness, but right now, he was a bit addled by her question. "Huh?" he asked as if not hearing correctly.

"I see you've packed a lot of clothes," she explained, looking around the room as if they were visibly spread about. "Are you moving back in?"

Anthony smiled. "No, Mama, but it's possible that I may be staying for a week. I mean if it's okay with you."

"Boy, you know you can stay for as long as you want," Carol let on. "Did she grant you a vacation?"

"Something like that."

Carol wavered a bit before speaking again. "Well, I guess you were rushing and forgot to pack your dress shoes."

"Yeah, I guess I did," Anthony agreed as realization kicked in. He shifted his gaze to the shoes in his mother's hand.

"These were Leonard's." she purported holding the highly-polishes shoes up as if presenting them to a potential buyer. "The only other shoes I have are mine, and I don't think you would…"

"Don't even go there!" He cut his mother off, smiling as he crossed the room, and gently relieved her of the shoes. "I'll make do with these. You can keep those shoes that were passed down to you by Mary."

"Mary who?"

"The one that gave birth to Jesus."

Carol gasped, though she was still smiling. "Boy you know better!"

"Don't act like she didn't babysit you when you were a baby," Anthony pressed, knowing how his mother felt about him making a mockery of her religion. "And don't act like that wasn't Jesus standing behind you in your class graduation picture."

"Oh! You're too much!" Carol was laughing hysterically now. "I gotta make sure the whole congregation pray for you today."

She was still laughing as she left the room, closing the door behind her. Anthony was still smiling, but his smile slowly faded when his eyes fell upon the shoes he was now holding. He could vividly remember Leonard smiling bright as the patent leather on those shoes he'd always worn to church services on the Sundays that he was home from active duty. Quickly shaking those thoughts, Anthony mind reverted back to the mission he was on before interrupted by his mother. Placing the shoes atop the dresser, he spun on his bare heels, and resumed his course towards the closet. Yes, he was definitely about to prove to himself that none of the things he'd seen last night were fabricated by his psyche. Grabbing both handles in his hands, Anthony pushed the doors laterally on their tracks, and almost swore out loud.

This was another one of his mother's "junk rooms", where she stored what seemed like memorabilia from the past of every member of the family. It seems as though everything was accounted for except for the items he was in search of. Did his mother hide them in another part of the house? Well, of course, she did but why? It was patent that the things belonged to a small child, but what child? Had she been babysitting one of the neighbor's children? A child of one of her church members? No. Neither of those seemed to sit well with him. There was something strange going on, and Anthony was determined to find out what.

Chapter 11

It was almost 12 in the afternoon when Ebony was finally able to pull herself out of bed. She didn't have a headache, but the sunlight shining through the curtains she'd forgotten to close was quite exasperating to her retinae at that moment. Plus, the rays seemed a little too bright for the middle of February.

Wiping her eyes with the back of her hands, Ebony slid her feet into her house shoes and looked over at the nightstand. It was still cluttered with paraphernalia of her personal previous day soiree, which contained a half empty bottle of cognac, a plate with a rolled-up bill and the breached package of the drug she thought she'd consumed an excessive amount of. It looked as if she'd barely touched the drug, though Ebony clearly remembered voraciously stuffing her nose with it until falling into a drug induced sleep.

Looking at the drug now, sparked an unabated urge that Ebony could not resist. She used the fingernail on her pinky that was over a millimeter long to scoop some of it from the package, and dump it in the plate, where she made two lines with her government's identification card. Then she sniffed a line into each nostril through the rolled-up bill. The usual stinging sensation that followed was a bit mild, being that the walls of her nose were already numb. Once again, accustomed to the after effect.

Ebony's first duty of the day was to shower, in which she took her time doing, returning to her bedroom almost an hour later. Donning one of her jeans suits and a pair of black boots, she journeyed off to the kitchen where she poured her favorite coffee beans into the coffee maker and began the brewing process. As always, the coffee maker signaled its finalization, seconds after she'd raked her scrambled eggs onto a saucer. For some reason, the drug has never diminished her appetite, so Ebony didn't have a problem devouring her meager breakfast.

Returning to her bedroom Ebony stuffed her drug paraphernalia into the drawer of the nightstand, leaving the bottle where it was. Then she retrieved her keys, cell phone, and pocketbook before heading for the front door, activating the alarm on her way out. Despite the springtime like rays emanating from the sun, the forty-something degree wind that immediately assailed her told another story that corroborated that of the bare trees lining the yards of the neighborhood which once again, had her longing for the 'protection' of a car garage. It was bad enough she'd forgotten to start her car by phone before leaving out. Therefore, Ebony had to brook with the remainder of the cool air that blew from the vents, while connecting her phone to the car's Bluetooth system.

"SkyFone," Ebony spoke, watching an elderly woman make her way up the street, clad in mountain of coats and skull caps. "Call Samantha."

"Calling Samantha," the disembodied voice boomed through the speakers.

Satisfied with the warm air now blowing from the vents, Ebony pulled out of her driveway and made for the main road.

"Hello?" Samantha's voice sounded anything but happy coming through the car's sound system.

"Girl, what's wrong now?"

Samantha exhaled before responding. "I give up."

Ebony smiled. "Well, can we at least have sex one more time before you jump off the Eiffel Tower?"

Samantha remained quiet on the other end.

"Okay, I'm sorry baby," Ebony cooed making a left on Cooper Road. "Are you gonna tell me what's wrong? Does it have anything to do with the dinner?"

Her friend exhaled again but didn't respond this time. Ebony slowly shook her head. "Sam," she began, "we've already talked about this. I know there's nothing I can say to get your mind off of Albert, which is why I'm on my way to pick you up."

"You are?"

"Of course," Ebony replied. "We're going to a daytime bar. There's one in Savannah that I've looked up on the web. They have a classic soul food menu that I wouldn't mind checking out.

"And you want to drive all the way to Savannah to eat classic soul food?"

"It's really not that far," Ebony contended, sniffing back the drainage that threatened to exude from her nostrils. "In fact, it'll be like a small road trip. We can sing songs and gossip all the way there.

"Are you sure you're up for it?" Samantha questioned. "You sound as if you're coming down with something highly contagious."

This made Ebony smile. "Very funny! Just be ready when I get there."

Ebony pressed the disconnect button, knowing what she had to do. This outing with Samantha would only get her friend's mind off of Albert for today and being that she was the reason for all of this, Ebony was highly determined to bring her friend some closure.

"SkyFone," she spoke, "call the International Comedy Agency."

"Calling the International Comedy Agency."

"You have reached the International Comedy Agency," a female's voice sprouted through the speakers. I'm sorry there's no one here to take your call at this time, but if you would leave your name, number, and your reason for calling, someone will get back to you as soon as possible."

Beep!

"Please have Lance Stephens to call Ebony Davis at her office," she relayed. "It's very important."

Ebony disconnected. She had another call to make but couldn't make it on that phone. Thankful that she was held up at a traffic light, she fished her other cellular from her pocketbook on the seat beside her. Not knowing when the traffic light would change, Ebony speed-dialed Anthony's number only to acquire his voicemail. Leaving a message was definitely out. Therefore, she redialed, getting the same results just as the traffic began to resume. She was able to speed-dial another number before moving along with the other vehicles.

"I'm listening," Rick's voice penetrated the earpiece.

"Have you tried to contact Anthony?"

"Several times," Rick told her. "He's not answering."

"Yeah, I see that." She sniffed back another drainage.

Rick didn't miss a beat. "How do you want us to handle this?"

"Accordingly," she replied. "He's now considered a traitor, and you know how I feel about traitors; but he will get what's coming to him in due time. He's in Atlanta and is probably expecting me to send the calvary to collect him at any moment."

"So, you think he's hiding?"

"No, I don't think he's hiding," Ebony replied. "But I can assure you that he's being extremely cautious and won't hesitate to kill you and Bull on sight."

"Any idea on why he just took off like that?" Rick asked as if her statement didn't faze him.

"He's on a mission," Ebony told him, remembering what her grandfather had said about her being on the road to revenge, on the night he committed suicide. "And given his current mind state, he's not gonna let anyone interfere with it, no matter what."

"So, we just wait?"

"For the time being." She wiped her nose with the back of her hand. "I'll let you know when to move."

Chapter 12

"It's good to finally meet you."

Church services were over, and Anthony's mother must have introduced him to every member in attendance, which seemed like close to eighty people. Now, they were standing in the church's parking lot being battered by a strong wind, while Carol introduced him to a woman by the name of Helen, who seemed to have a genuine liking for his mother. Though she didn't look the part, it was clear that she was his mother's contemporary. Her gold tooth and multi-color coiffure were evidence that she was not yet ready to succumb to her true age.

"It's good to meet you also," Anthony now replied, shaking the hand of the woman who didn't bother to take off one of her gloves.

"This is my daughter, Rene," Helen offered indicating the woman standing with her accompanied by a little girl who looked to be about seven years old, "and my granddaughter Rachel."

"Hello ladies!" Anthony shook the hands of both the mother and daughter.

"Rene is also single at the moment," Helen promulgated with a large smirk on her face.

"Mama!" Rene's caramel complexion seemed to redden at the cheeks, while her daughter regarded him with a broad smile and expectant eyes.

"It's true," Helen retorted, sharing a knowing look with Carol.

"Sometimes, that's the best way to be," Anthony insisted, locking eyes with the woman of whom he felt his mother had ulterior motives to link him up with. "I'm enjoying the single life myself.

"Really?" Rene seemed impressed by his assertion.

"Of course." He offered a warm smile, despite the weather. "I feel nothing should be forced. When something is meant to be, God will be the one to make all the connections."

"And I agree," Rene responded, regarding her mother with narrowed eyes.

"Whatever!" Helen said this with a dismissive wave of the hand before diverting her attention back to Anthony. "So, Anthony we've heard a lot about you. What made you move all the way to Macon?"

"I needed a change of scenery."

"You moved all the way to Macon for a change of scenery?"

"Helen!" Carol intervened.

"Girl, I'm just making conversation." Without waiting for a response, she resumed her interrogation. "And how long are you back in Atlanta for?"

"I really can't say," Anthony purported, now feeling uncomfortable with the line of questioning, "but it's possible that I'll be here for at least a week."

Helen's eyebrows were raised in mock surprise. "That's wonderful! I think your mother would really enjoy a full week with her long lost son."

Carol giggled. "Very funny, Helen! Don't you have a dinner to prepare?"

"Oh, absolutely!" she answered. "I'll prepare it, but Rene will be getting her hand dirty today. What do you two have planned?"

"Well," Carol began shooting a look of uncertainty at her son. "I guess I'll be getting my hands dirty also."

"Just make sure you call me before you go to bed."

"Don't I always?"

Helen raised her hands in a surrendering gesture. "Okay. Don't shoot." Then she turned to Anthony. "Again, it was nice meeting you."

"Likewise."

Anthony nodded to Rene and Rachel while his mother bid them farewell with embraces before departing. Being that Anthony had started his car by phone upon exiting the church, the interior was nice and warm when he and his mother climbed in.

"So, how'd you like the service?" Carol asked, applying her safety belt.

Anthony shrugged his shoulders while pulling out of the parking spot. "I really can't say. For some reason, I felt like the pastor was talking to me throughout the whole sermon."

"A person only feels like that when they're guilty of something," she offered, now regarding him. "Are you guilty of something?"

"Am I guilty of something!" Anthony mentally exclaimed.

This is not the response he expected, but her response had him feeling as if she'd told the pastor, and possibly the whole congregation, a little too much about him. Why else did he choose today to speak on crime, punishment, and revenge? Clearly the pastor was aware of Anthony's prior crime sprees and convictions, but is it possible that she could have revealed his retribution toward Janelle and Marvin? No, of course not. That would be mere speculation on his mother's part, being that Anthony had never mentioned anything to her or anybody else about retaliating against the people that have wronged him, but was it that hard for her to sense this in someone of her own flesh and blood?

"We are all guilty of something," Anthony now responded to his mother's query, keeping his eyes on the road. "We all have secrets, skeletons in our closets."

Carol remained silent. In fact, she was quiet for the duration of the ride back to the house, which was alright with Anthony. He was pretty sure that the conversation would veer off in a direction he did not want to go in.

Getting to the house, Anthony offered to assist with preparing the meal in which Carol had declined, claiming she would use the time to "talk to God about some things". Not wanting to bother her, Anthony retreated to his bedroom where he deposited his keys and cell phone on top of the dresser before doffing his dress clothes and slipping into a pair of jeans and a sweater.

Then, he flopped down on the bed with his phone to check it for missed calls, and just as he expected there were two from Ebony. There were no messages, which had him wondering if she'd already dispatched her goons to do whatever she paid them to do.

Now, he was wondering if he should call and explain everything to her, but as he thought about it, the idea of explaining his actions to Ebony didn't seem all too alluring, being that he didn't explain his actions to his own mother. So, if she's that sure about his unexpected departure and feels as though she wanted to resort to violence, then Anthony was going to make sure he's fully prepared. He just hopes she doesn't stoop so low as to involve his mother, which would be a line she would fully regret crossing.

Chapter 13

Monday

"Are there any existing cases to support your claims, Mr. Tanner?" asked Judge Jackson from his bench.

"Yes, Your Honor." The dark-haired attorney that was already on his feet at the defense table, began sifting through his notes while his jail-attire dressed client nervously fidgeted with his fingers in his lap. "In Reynolds versus the State," the attorney resumed, regarding the judge, "the defendant has been convicted of a felony prior to his arrest in two thousand and twenty for aggravated assault, which is also a felony. In this particular case, the State moved to recidivise the defendant under section 17-10-7; subsection C, which did not conform with the standard rules of the recidivist statute. Plus, the State failed to provide a timely notice of intent to seek said punishment, which brought on a dismissal of this case via writ of habeas corpus. At this moment, the defense is trying to preclude—"

"Your Honor," Ebony intervened, getting to her feet, and sniffing back another drainage caused by the dosage of crush she'd enjoyed in her office before making for the courtroom this morning. "The defense's argument is irrelevant at this time, being that this is a pleas and arraignment. Yes, The State is seeking the recidivist punishment against Mr. Tony Nash, in which he is wall qualified for under Section 17-10-7; subsection A, where a defendant meets criterion after being convicted of one felony, then subsequently committing another felony. In Reynolds versus the State, a blind man could see how the prosecutor mishandled the case with incompetence and unprofessionalism to a degree that—"

"Ms. Davis!" Judge Jackson cut in with an all too serious look on his face. "Could you please refrain from making detractive remarks towards government officials?"

"Yes, Your Honor," Ebony replied, knowing that the drug had her in a foul mood, where she was subjected to lash out at any moment. "However," she resumed, "the defendant, a one-time convicted felon, is currently charged with theft by taking a motor vehicle, which is also a felony; but that's neither here nor there at this moment. Right now, at this date and time, the defendant is here to make a decision of accepting the State's offer of five years to serve or taking his chances in a trial by jury."

The judge looked over at the defense table. "Is the defendant interested in accepting State's offer?"

"No, Your Honor," Attorney Matthew Finch answered after looking down at his client, who was already shaking his head. "However, the defense is asking the court to consider setting a reasonable bond for the defendant, who's the father of two young children, and the son of a mother who's currently suffering from cirrhosis."

"Would that be all from the defense?" asked the judge.

"Yes, Your Honor."

Judge Jackson turned to Ebony. "Any objections from the State?"

"Always," Ebony replied, sniffing back another drainage, and wiping her nose with the back of her hand. "Being a parent and dealing with ailments in the household, like every other household in America doesn't reprieve anyone of sin, nor the breaking of any man-made laws. Mr. Nash broke the law by committing a second felony, which proves that he's a habitual violator with no respect for the laws. Its makers, nor its enforcers. Therefore, The State prays that the court considers the defendant's irreverence for its rules and regulations and retain him without bond until a trial date is set."

"Your objection is duly noted, Ms. Davis," the judge acknowledged. "But do you have any substantial reasons why Mr. Nash should not be granted a bond?"

"For one," Ebony spoke, not missing a beat, "this is a plea and arraignment, not a bond hearing. If the defendant wishes to make such request, a motion for a bond hearing should be filed by and through his attorney in order to make it proper before this court."

Judge Carl Jackson was slowly nodding. "That law did change a few years ago. Mr. Finch I'm going to deny your invalid request for bail at this time. However, being that your client is not in favor of the State's offer, and wishes to be tried by a jury, we'll go ahead and get the first part out the way, which is the signing of the indictment."

After all parties signed the indictment, Judge Jackson granted an hour recess, which Ebony had been waiting all morning for. She didn't have much of an appetite. Therefore, going anywhere near the cafeteria was totally out of the question. Besides, she declined Aaron's lunch invitation upon entering the courtroom that morning. She's been feeling bad about it ever since then, which is why she'd been reluctant to make eye contact, or even look in his direction all morning.

Making it to her office, Ebony locked the door, deposited her briefcase on top of the desk, then flopped down into her chair, and took a moment to relish the heat blowing into her vents, being that the corridors of the ancient building were void of such. That's when she noticed the message indicator glowing on her office phone. She pressed the review button before digging her pocketbook out of the bottom drawer of her desk.

"You have two messages," the computerized voice apprised, followed by a beeping sound. "Message one: 'Hello, Ms. Davis!'" a familiar masculine voice came through the small speaker. "I received your message. However, if you really wish to contact me, I mean, it doesn't take a rocket scientist to know that the best time to do so is within business hours." He chuckled at his own joke. "Anway, my extension is 1123. I'll be waiting to hear from you. Ciao."

Beep.

By this time, Ebony had fetched from her pocketbook a vial that belonged to her grandmother. What once contained some kind of medication that kept her grandmother alive, now contained Ebony's drug of choice, which she was now inhaling a grain of into her right nostril from the tip of her fingernail, just as the first message ended.

"Message Two: 'Hello, Ms. Davis!'" An unfamiliar feminine voice spouted. "I am Lisa Wortham from the Banner and Associates law firm, and I'd really like to speak with you concerning the death of your grandmother, Mrs. regina Davis. If it's not inconvenient to your schedule, could you call me as soon as you get this message? I would really like to meet with you before returning to Texas. My private number is…"

Ebony quickly jotted the phone number down on a manila folder that was lying on her desk, as she wondered why some attorney from another state was interested in her grandmother's demise. Whatever her reasons were, Ebony clearly discerned the urgency in the woman's voice, which actually had her anticipating this encounter; but first things first. She though as she dialed the phone number to the International Comedy Agency actuating Lance's extension.

"Lance Stephens," he announced over the speaker phone just as Ebony was feeding the drug to her other nostril.

After sniffing the drug further into her system and doing her best to wipe whatever residue that may be visible with her thumb and index, she said, "It's me, Ebony Davis."

"What a pleasant surprise!" Lance expressed. "To what do I owe this call?"

"I'm calling you about the National Breast Cancer Awareness dinner," she told him. "Are you scheduled?"

"Yes, but I'm bringing an amateur comedian to stand in for me. You know, let him get his feet wet."

"What about a date?" Ebony ventured, getting to her reason for calling. "Are you bringing one of your lady friends?"

"I don't think I've ever taken a date to any event," he said slowly. "Why'd you ask?"

"I was hoping that I could accompany you as your date for the dinner."

It was quiet on the other end.

"Are you there?" Ebony tested.

"You're joking, right?" Lance finally responded. "I'm quite sure you and Samantha Gordon have been invited. Hell, it seems as though you two have a comity with the governor and his wife."

If only you knew, Ebony thought, but said, "Samantha is the recipient of those invitations. I'm always the plus one. However, Samantha has just decided that she's not going. I've already brought my dress for the event, and really had my heart set on sharing a cocktail with Dorothy Stockholm."

"Yeah. I just can't seem to get enough of hearing how she survived breast cancer," Lance replied. Then after a pause, he asked. "And you want to tag along as my date?"

Ebony could tell he was elated by the idea though he did his best to conceal it. "Only if you'd have me as your date," she said as sweetly as she could.

"I'm okay with that," he said, cooly. "Where will we meet up? At the mansion?"

"Perhaps, I'll call you back with the arrangements." Ebony told him before handing up, then dialing the number written on the manila folder.

"Hello?" the attorney answered shortly.

"Lisa Wortham?" Ebony asked, knowing very well it was her.

"Thanks for calling, Ms. Davis," the woman replied, a hint of relief in her tone. "As I've said in my message, I'd really like to meet with as soon as possible."

"Give me one reason why I should grant you this request," Ebony demanded, fighting back another drainage. "And why is some lawyer from Texas all of a sudden interested in the death of my grandmother, who died seven months ago?"

"Well…" The attorney lingered. "I may have proof that she didn't die from natural cessation of heartbeat due to her disease."

This had Ebony's full attention. "What are you saying?"

"I'm saying that Mrs. Regina Davis may have suffered an unjustified death."

Chapter 14

The wind immediately assailed Anthony the moment he climbed from the comfortably warm interior of his car. Thankful for the skullcap that kept his ears, and the top of his head warm, he zipped up his large coat, stuffed his hands into his pockets and looked out at the house he'd parked in front of.

Anthony was not surprised at how the place still looked the same as it did when he first started visiting as a teenager. Despite the curtains in the window, the house looked abandoned with its weather damaged paint and unkempt lawn that was cluttered with discarded household appliances, vehicles parts and toys. There were also two ancient looking cars in the yard that were stripped of their tires and engines with the axles partially buried in the earth.

Anthony smiled at the subterfuge as he entered the yard walking past the cars and circumventing the discarded items. Clearing the side of the house, he trailed the dip in the ground that led to the door of the basement, where he was met by a white, over-sized pit bull that charged at him, growling, and bounded by a huge chain that looked like it should be attached to a boat's anchor.

"Shut up, Lucy!" Anthony intoned.

Hearing her name, the dog's demeanor quickly switched from menacing to affectionate, with her eyes enlarging with anticipation, ears dropping back like levers on a forklift, and tail wagging so hard, Anthony could hear the whomp,

whomp, whomp sound as it sliced through the air. His friend had the dog trained to not jump up on people unless attacking, so she waited impatiently on the ground for Anthomy to scratch her in place she loved to be scratched in. As he did, Lucy ardently trailed him to the door, dragging the chain with her.

"Stay!" he demanded, and the dog immediately sat on her haunches, tail still active with excitement.

Anthony turned and was about to knock on the wooden door with the large four-sectional window when he heard the locks being disengaged. Moments later the door creaked open on its hinges, and there stood Blue, one of Anthony's childhood friends.

Clean-shaven as always, Blue didn't look as if he'd aged a bit as his 6'4" frame towered in the doorway, clad in a large jumpsuit that was tucked inside fleece-lined boots and a black skullcap pull real low over his head. Usually, Blue would greet him with his gap-tooth smile and a warm embrace, but right then, he wasn't smiling and there was nothing warm about the look he was giving Anthony.

"It's good to see you, too," Anthony tested, now feeling a bad vibe about his extemporary visit.

"I saw that shit on the news," Blue stated, drilling his eyes into Anthony's. "If there was any truth to anything they said, then there's no way in hell you're standing in my yard right now. You'd be on your way to death row, and I haven't seen anything on the news about you escaping."

Anthony knew exactly what his friend was thinking, which is what he himself would think had he been in Blue's shoes. Such a thought is hard to relinquish when one is fully aware of the reality of it. Therefore, Anthony knew that it was going to be an impossible task to try to change his friend's thoughts. But for the sake of his reason for being there, he knew he had to put forth some kind of effort.

"I know what you're thinking," Anthony finally responded. "Hell, I'd be thinking the same thing if I were you, but that's not the case Blue. You know me better than that."

Blue raised his eyebrows. "Do I?"

"Come on Blue!" Anthony reasoned. "Do you really believe I would try to set you up? We've done too much illegal shit together. Do you really think I'd be working with the very people we hate?"

"So, how'd you get out?" Blue asked, now leaning against one side of the doorframe. "I know damn well they didn't just drop the case."

"Hell no!" Anthony dug into his pockets, an endeavor to warm them. "Believe it or not, but I've been out for over six months now, and I still don't know how it happened. Maybe, the jail's computers had started fucking up again. That's the only reason I could come up with and if that's the case, I know it won't be long before they figure out I've been released by mistake and come after me."

"So, where you been all this time?"

"In Macon, Georgia," he answered. "I've been having limited contact with my mom and Janelle just in case they're already after me. Blue, I don't plan on going down without a fight. Especially when I know they intend to kill me anyway."

Blue didn't respond. He had diverted his attention to Lucy, who'd set out after a bird that had landed in the yard far beyond her reach, considering the length of the chain. After realizing she couldn't get to the bird that paid her no attention, Lucy began sniffing around the yard as if in search for food. Periodically, she would stop fast in her tracks, and look back at the bird to make sure it didn't try to sneak up on her.

"I was forced into this situation," Anthony replied. "I'm just hoping it doesn't play out the way I think it's gonna play out. Plus, I have some business that need to be taken care of as soon as possible."

"And this is not a sting operation?"

"You know me better than that Blue," Anthony reminded him, though he noticed some of the suspicion was gone from his friend's voice. "Besides, it's not like you're El Chapo, or some shit like that."

Blue finally displayed his gap-toothed smile, obviously amused by the statement.

"Can a friend come in out of the cold?" Anthony inquired, feeling his body temperature drop for a second.

Blue seemed to ruminate on this for a few seconds before stepping aside to allow him entrance. Just like the front yard, Blue's room, which was the basement, was still in the same exact order it's always been in. The concrete wall was poorly decorated with posters of Blue's favorite athletes, musicians, actors, video girls and a 57-inch television. The sofa bed that Anthony rarely seen the sofa part of was unkempt as always. The dresser that sat against one wall was cluttered with remnants and trash form various restaurants as well as the coffee table that sat between the sofa bed and two metal folding chairs, in which Anthony took a seat in one of after leaving his boots by the door.

He'd never understood why his friend was so adamant about preventing people from tracking dirt onto his carpet but didn't care as to how much the rest of the room resembled a pigsty.

"You might wanna leave your coat on," Blue asserted after locking the door and perching on the edge of the bed. "My bird -brain mom chose to spend her money on drugs instead of the gas bill, but it should be back on in another hour or so."

"How's she doing anyway?" Anthony asked, blowing his breath into his cupped hands, then rubbing them together for warmth, though the coldness of the metal chair didn't make things any better.

"She's still here," Blue answered. He extracted a cigarette from the pack on the table, then lit it. After holding in smoke for what seemed like eternity, he blew a thick cloud into the air before saying, "I wanna hear how shit went down, because the news people had that shit sounding like something from a movie script and what the fuck possessed you and Bo to knock over a bank?"

Anthony was slowly shaking his head. "That shit was crazy Blue," he answered. "I didn't think Marvin would turn on us like that."

Blue furrowed his eyebrows. "Who the fuck is Marvin?"

"Some white dude I met on my last bid," Anthony explicated. "He was my cellmate. At lockdown, he would always tell me stories about how he robbed restaurants and corner stores. Then one night, he told me about his plans of robbing the First National Bank. Said he had been casing out the place for about two months before being arrested for driving under the influence."

"And you asked him to let you in on it." This was a statement.

"Not immediately," Anthony replied, defensively. "After hearing his plans, I spent nights picturing myself pulling something like that off. On the night he was called to be released, I got his phone number and asked if he would hold off until I got out."

"So, Bo lost his life because you trusted this dude," Blue said, grounding his cigarette out in the ashtray on the table.

Anthony looked Blue square in his eyes. "Like I said, we didn't think he would turn on us like that."

"You're always supposed to expect the double-cross when it comes to shit like that," Blue lectured. "Especially when you snatch hundreds of fucking thousands from a bank's vault! How the hell did he get the drop on you two anyway?"

"We had made it to the spot where we had another car stashed," Anthony explained. "I was to transfer the money from the truck to the car while Marvin got the gasoline can so we could torch the truck."

"And at that time what was Bo doing?"

"At that time, he was the look-out."

"The look-out!" Blue scoffed. "In the woods? What the fuck was he looking out for? Deer?"

Anthony did his best not to scowl at his sarcastic friend. "I was bagging the second bag of money from the truck when I heard the shot. I looked up just in time to see Bo falling to the ground and Marvin aiming his gun in my direction. On instinct, I ducked behind the truck and pulled my own gun. We had a shoot-out that didn't last long, being that we were already short on ammo. That's when I charged at him not thinking about the gas can in his hand until he threw it at me." Anthony was slowly shaking his head. "When that shit got in my eyes, I just knew I was gonna die, but I ended up waking up in Grady Memorial Hospital with a concussion, handcuffed to the bed and Atlanta police all over the place."

"He knocked you out and left you with a small portion of the money, so the police would know for sure that you were involved in the robbery," Blue summarized.

Anthony said nothing.

"Is he the 'business' you claim needs to be taken care of as soon as possible?"

Anthony nodded.

"Do you know where he is?"

"Not at the moment," answered Anthony. "But I'm after his ass like a bounty hunter."

"What about the money?" Blue wanted to know. "Are you still interested in your share or only his life?"

Chapter 15

"Who is it?"

It's been almost thirty minutes since Ebony had concluded her phone call with attorney from Texas. Since then, she'd been mulling over the attorney's speculation of her grandmother's death, which really wasn't all too surprising to Ebony, being that she was suspicious from the moment Regina Davis breathed her last breath.

Especially when she'd always looked at her grandmother as one of the strongest and perennial women to ever walk this side of the planet. There was no way that some mere complication of the heart had easily subdued her like that. So, maybe there's some truth to the attorney's assertion.

"It's your best friend in the whole wide world," Samantha's voice came back at her beyond the door.

Quickly tossing the vial containing crush back into her pocketbook, Ebony did a once-over of her desk, to make sure there was nothing out of place, before getting up and crossing the room to the door wiping her nose with the back of her hand. She opened the door to a smiling Samantha whose presence is always welcomed, but she didn't expect for her friend to be accompanied by the new prosecutor, Larry Hendrix, who seemed a little too happy to be Samantha's shadow. He too was smiling in which Ebony found notably annoying.

"What's the matter?" asked Samantha, her visage turning from happiness to concern.

"Oh! Nothing," Ebony quickly recovered with a plausible smile, realizing she's allowed her facial expression to display how she was currently feeling about the scurrilous picture before her. "What are you two up to?"

With a relieved look on her face, Samantha said, "We're on our way to the cafeteria and were wondering if you'd join us."

"Sure," Ebony responded without thought. "Give me a second."

Closing the door, Ebony donned her coat and locked her pocketbook in the bottom drawer of her desk. After slipping her phone onto her pants pocket, she grabbed her keys and made for the door, coercing the muscles in her face to form another gay expression for the sake of Samantha and Larry Hendrix who were not standing in front of her door when she opened it. She didn't see them until she stepped out into the hall to lock her office up. They were standing farther down the hall, in front of the elevators, both regarding her with expectant looks.

"So, what've you two been up to all day?" Ebony asked upon joining them.

"Ms. Hutchins had us studying the Bailyn case," Samantha answered as Hendrix rung for the elevator.

"And she wants Mr. Hendrix to assist you at the trial," Ebony surmised.

"Well..." Samantha lingered, shooting a quick glance at him. "I thought it would play out in that manner, but the Queen of the Damned wanted it the other way around. So, I'll be the assistant clown at the circus."

Ding!

"Did you have to refer to it as a circus?" Hendrix asked as he allowed the women to enter the elevator before joining them and ringing for the first floor.

Samantha scoffed. "Don't tell me you've never referred to a trial as a circus before."

"Of course," he replied. "It's just that, I guess I just feel bad about being handed a case that you've worked so hard to prepare for."

"Well..." Samantha shrugged. "It's not your fault, Besides, you can pretty much expect Ms. Hutchins to make such whimsical decisions."

"I see," Hendrix was pensive for a few seconds before going on. "But, if it makes you feel any better, I'll be the assistant clown at the circus."

"You'll let me lead the trial?" Samantha asked with incredulity as the shaft landed on the first floor. "What about Ms. Hutchins?"

"What about her?"

"She'll be there," Samantha pointed out.

Hendrix regarded her with a conspiring grin. "Great! That'll be your chance to prove to her that you're a better prosecutor than I am. It'll be a chance for me to watch you at full throttle. I'll be like your personal cheerleader, cheering you on from the sideline."

"God, what a cornball," Ebony muttered, rolling her eyes. She trailed behind Hendrix and a now blushing Samantha.

It's not that she couldn't see why her friend was falling head over heels for the drop-dead handsome prosecutor with his mesmerizing ocean-blue eyes, because it was highly evident. Maybe, she was too possessive of Samantha and felt that Samantha shouldn't openly flirt with men in her presence, which was disrespectful to their implicit arrangement. Or was it the crush that had Ebony's mind charged with malicious thoughts? Whichever it was, Ebony knew that she was starting to hate Assistant District Attorney Larry Hendrix by the second.

Upon entering the partially crowed cafeteria, Ebony immediately spotted Deputy Aaron Taylor sitting at a table alone. Though his facial expression was inscrutable as he watched them approach the serving line, Ebony felt a pang of guilt for declining his lunch invitation, which caused her to avert her eyes away from the blank stare of his. Was he thinking that she rejected him just to have lunch with Samantha, or could he be thinking that she was attentively avoiding him for fear of things escalating between them? Though the latter was partially true, Ebony knew she had to assuage his mind of such thoughts immediately, which is why after the three of them received their orders, she led the way to the table he was occupying.

"Do you mind if we join you?" she asked.

"Help yourselves," Taylor responded, gesturing to the three unoccupied chairs. "I'm about to head on out anyway."

"Already?" Ebony feigned a hurt expression as she took the seat beside him, taking a gander at his tray that contained an empty cup, and discarded edges of sliced bread.

"You mean to tell me that you're leaving without having your favorite dessert?"

Ebony didn't give him a chance to respond. While placing her order of chicken salad and iced tea, she made sure to include two slices of apple pie, seeing from across the room that his tray was void of a saucer which indicated that he hadn't helped himself to any of the various pies or cakes. Remembering what her grandmother has always said about getting to a man's heart through his stomach. Ebony decided to test the axiom, which was why she now placed a saucer containing a slice of pie and a plastic fork onto his tray.

"Aww!" Samantha cooed from across the table. "That is so sweet!"

Taylor regarded her with a disconcerted look on his face. "How are you, Ms. Gordon?"

"I'm fine, Mr. Taylor," she replied, with a mischievous grin then indicated Larry Hendrix, whom she was seated next to. "Have you met Assistant District Attorney Larry Hendrix? He's the newest addition to our office."

"No, we haven't been properly introduced," Taylor asserted, nodding to Hendrix. "I'm Deputy Aaron Taylor. It's nice to meet you."

"Likewise, sir," Hendrix returned the greeting with a nod.

"So," Taylor went on slicing into his pie," I hear you came all the way from Fulton County."

"I did." Hendrix was now pouring Ranch dressing on the salad he ordered.

"How do you like Linkton so far?"

There was a hint of a smile on his face. "It's gonna take some getting used to, but I do like how you all have pretty much everything in the same building. In Fulton, we'd damn near have to cross the Pacific Ocean to access the evidence room. Plus, the cafeteria is a great accommodation also."

"I guess you didn't expect that from us hillbillies, huh?" Ebony sneered, chunking a forkful of salad into her mouth.

"Ebony!" Samantha chided.

"No, it's okay." Hendrix was regarding Ebony with a smile more suitable for a disobedient child. "Don't let where I come from cause you to pre-judge me, Ms. Davis," he told her. "Despite your sentiments towards me, I'm not here to judge, not supplant any of you. If it wasn't for my mother's illness, I'd still be in Fulton County. Trust me, I'm a prosecutor, and Linkton County seemed like a decent place to continue my profession. So, here I am, and I come as a team player, hoping that you all would accept me as such."

He sounded sincere, but Ebony was nobody's fool. From the beginning she felt that Hendrix was out to acquire the district attorney's position and she was sticking to her guns on this one. For some reason, the story about his mother being sick was starting to sound equivocal to her. Now, she was wondering if she should do a little investigation of her own.

***

It was a few minutes before five o'clock when Judge Jackson relieved his courtroom for the day. While Ebony gathered her things to make her exit, Aaron Taylor managed to make his way to her table, offering to accompany her to her car. She gladly accepted, being that she had intentionally wanted to dodge Samantha, and figured that she could use the time to 'make amends' with Taylor.

"The winds are expected to pick up over the weekend," Taylor informed as he and Ebony now crossed the parking garage. "It'll be in the low twenties with the winds blowing at a hundred and sixty miles per hour for the next couple of weeks."

"Well, at least you have someone to keep you warm for the cold nights to come." Ebony knew that her statement would strike a nerve in Taylor, which was why she didn't dare look in his direction when she spoke.

She was using Law 43 from Robert's Greene's *48 Laws of Power*, and this particular law offers advice on how to work on the hearts and minds of others, though she didn't need the instructions of a book to assist her with such. She did fully understand why it was her father's favorite book.

"Things are not always what they seem," Taylor responded, now looking off in the opposite direction.

"I know what you mean," Ebony told him. She was studying the side of his face. "But, if this is something she's chosen, then she's the one that's missing out. Like they say: 'You won't miss something until it's gone,' and she would definitely miss you whether you believe it or not."

This made him jerk his head in her direction and Ebony could see a sign of hope, commingled with a twinkle in his eyes. Therefore, she put the 'icing on the cake' by offering a smile for added measure. They made it to her car that she'd automatically started by her cellular before exiting the building. She turned to face Taylor, expecting him to reply, but he seemed nonplussed which made Ebony smile inside because she just knew his heart was doing all kinds of somersaults at the moment.

"Well, I guess I better get going," she decided to break the ice.

Taylor cleared his throat. "Yeah, me too," he finally spoke still holding her gaze. Then, after a pregnant pause, he asked, "Do you have any plans for Saturday?"

"Not that I know of."

There was another pause before he went on. "If it's okay with you, I'd like to take you to see a movie. I mean, I know it's gonna be cold, but—"

"What's playing this weekend?" she interrupted, smiling at his coyness.

He shrugged his shoulders. "Honestly, I have no idea, but I'm quite sure we would find one worth watching."

"Sounds good to me!" Ebony expressed. "But what about her? I'm quite sure—"

"Let me worry about that," he cut her off. "Tomorrow we'll come up with a time and which restaurant we'll have lunch at." With that he leaned in and planted a soft kiss on her cheek. "Goodnight, Ms. Davis."

"Goodnight," she said to his back as he made for his own car.

Truth be told, Ebony did not expect Taylor to go that far. Perhaps, he was using the shy tactic in order to get her to drop her guard, and as reluctantly as she hates to admit, it worked. But what if that wasn't the case? What if she was reading it all wrong? Maybe Taylor had managed to build enough courage in the end to plant the innocuous kiss on her. Ebony pondered this until she pulled her car into the parking lot of Daila's Diner, which wasn't at all full. Parking, she sat for a moment, mentally preparing herself for whatever the attorney from Texas had to reveal to her. She was highly familiar with how people were conned out of money by people posing as lawyers, in such cases like this, which is why she looked the attorney up and memorized her face just in case the woman she was meeting was arrogating Attorney Lisa Wortham's selfhood.

Upon entering the restaurant, the face that Ebony committed to her memory from the screen of her computer was the first face she spotted. She was seated at the rear accompanied by a male, who had his back to Ebony. She saw that they were both well-dressed as she approached with butterflies in her stomach. For some reason, she was now wishing this whole thing was a rouse because the mere presence of the white woman with her sandy-brown hair pulled into a long ponytail had Ebony in a state of uneasiness. Plus, the butterflies seemed to multiply when she reached the table and was greeted by two pairs of expectant eyes.

"I'm here," Ebony intoned, looking from one to the other.

"Thanks for coming, Ms. Davis!" Wortham said, holding out her hand in which Ebony had to remove one of her gloves to shake. Then the attorney indicated the seat beside her. "Please have a seat."

Ebony complied, placing her cell phone, keys, and gloves on the table that contained a manila folder that sat in front of Wortham and some dark-colored, durable folder that sat before her male companion. There were also two cups of coffee with steam wafting from them as if they were just ordered.

"You already know who I am," Wortham went on, then held her hand out in presentation toward the older man seated across from them. "I would like you to meet Doctor Khomeini, the initial researcher in this case."

"Hi!" Ebony held a hand out to him.

"It's nice to meet you, Ms. Davis," Khomeini spoke with an accent that Ebony couldn't pick up on, shaking her hand with one of his frail and partially wrinkled ones. "Thank you for joining us."

Ebony nodded.

"Can we order you something?" the attorney offered.

"No, I'm fine."

"Okay," Wortham replied, opening the folder up in front of her. "Do you have any questions before we present our case to you?"

"Did you really come all the way from Texas to talk to me about the death of my grandmother?"

"Well," she began, "we actually had seven other clients to see in the Georgia area while in the course of doing so, we were informed about you. So, instead of having to make a subsequent trip, I had your file faxed to me from the office, which is why we're pressed for time right now. Our flight leaves at 7:20."

Ebony nodded her understanding. "Okay, I'm listening."

"Are you familiar with a drug by the name of Xycobin?"

This made Ebony think about the vial she had tucked inside her pocketbook on the front passenger seat of her car. The same vial that once contained her grandmother's heart pills but was now a compact carrier for Ebony's drug of choice, which made her feel a twinge of guilt. "I've heard of it," Ebony responded.

The attorney referred to the documents in front of her. "Well, according to my notes, this medication was ordered for Mrs. Regina Davis, on June 3 of last year from a newly established pharmacy out in Wisconsin. This same medication has caused the death of Mrs. Davis and a great number of other people, which is why we're endeavoring to bring a class action suit against Pharmacy of America Laboratories." She paused, locking eyes with Ebony. "Ms. Davis, we really want you to apprehend the seriousness of this. Though your grandmother was diagnosed with an erratic heart disease, she was still a victim of wrongful death due to the mismanaging of a lethal experimental drug. All we're asking—"

"I want proof," Ebony cut her off, now thinking about Dr. McAdams, who'd ordered the drug and the doctor at the hospital who'd pronounced her grandmother dead on July 25, 2023. "Prove to me that my grandmother died a wrongful death. Validate your lethal experimental drug claim."

Attorney Wortham looked across the table to her concomitant, "Doctor?"

He nodded before opening his folder and plunging into his documented notes that were outlined with illustrations. "On September 9th, 2022, Mrs. Regina Davis suffered from a heart attack, which is a life threatening episode of a heart disease that can result from a blood clot or advance atherosclerosis in the coronary arteries and occurs when the flow of blood to the heart muscle itself is cut off or severely impeded as to cause destruction of cardiac tissue."

He flipped over to the next page. "After undergoing treatment at the Linkton County Medical Center, physicians prescribed Lipitor to Mrs. Davis, which includes anticoagulants that prevent unwanted clotting and vasodilators that widen the blood vessels. Xycobin was produced to replicate Lipitor, but also contained acetaminophen to reduce pain and fever." He turned to the next page, but his dark eyes were on Ebony as he continued. "After conducting and autonomous research of the copy-cat drug, we deduced that it lacked the potency of its predecessor, which renders it inadequate to sustain any form of heart disease."

"What about the FDA?" Ebony posed. "I'm quite sure this drug had to undergo their inspection and approval."

Dr. Khomeini averted his gaze to Attorney Lisa Wortham, prompting Ebony to do the same.

"The FDA representatives are tight-lipped about their involvement concerning the drug," Wortham let on. "And it's hard to tell if they had any involvement at all, being that the drug is ordered from the laboratory and shipped directly to the patient in containers that only display the pharmacy's appellative, and the name of the product, no FDA stamp. Once this case is properly brought before a court, we'll file a motion to produce and send out additional subpoenas to whomever is complicit to making and-or distribution of the drug in question."

"And you're absolutely positive that Xycobin is the cause of my grandmother's death?" Ebony asked as she slowly took in the fact that her grandmother had actually been murdered.

"Yes," Wortham slid her opened folder over to Ebony, then produced an ink pen lying it on top of the documents. "All you have to do is read and sign these and we'll do the rest."

Chapter 16

"Look who finally decided to show up."

Upon leaving Blue's house, Anthony had lunch at Chili's, then drove around Atlanta trying to mentally form some kind of plan of action, being that he had not once thought of how he was actually going to deal with Janelle or Marvin, once encountering them. He'd never thought about recovering any of the bank robbery's money from Marvin, until Blue mentioned it earlier. He still didn't know exactly how much they'd taken, but he was quite sure that Marvin hadn't spent it all by now. So, maybe he should, indeed, inquire on the remainder of the currency, and then kill him.

Now, it was after five o'clock, when Anthony returned to his mother's home, and entered the living room, where she was seated in her recliner, accompanied by her friend Helen and Helen's daughter Rene. Carol was still in uniform, being that she'd just returned home from the hotel she does housekeeping for. Helen and Rene were both clad in the same uniform, indicating that they too shared the same employment.

Considering all the things going through his mind, Anthony was not up for entertaining guests, but since he didn't plan on being in their presence for no more than a couple of minutes, he managed to put on his best award-winning smile as he removed the skullcap from his head.

"Hello, ladies!" he greeted.

"Hi, Anthony!" Helen replied as Rene waved her hand in response. "How are you?"

"I'm fine, Ms. Helen," he answered. "How are you?"

"I'm blessed baby," she responded, shooting a quick glance at Rene, who was seated beside her. "Still trying to find a good husband for my daughter."

"Mama!" Rene protested, though she was smiling.

"Girl, you need to stop!" Carol mustered through a fit of laughter.

"I can't believe you find that funny, Carol," Helen asserted a hurt expression on her face. "I am serious."

"I know," Carol said, still laughing. "That's why it's so funny."

Disregarding her daughter and best friend, Helen diverted her attention back to Anthony. "Anthony, at least take her to see a movie, or something. I'll pay for the date myself."

"That wouldn't be necessary, Ms. Helen," Anthony assured, casting a glance at Rene who didn't look like the type of woman that would have any problems getting attention from men, nor women for that matter.

"So, you'll do this one little favor for your mother and I?"

"Sure," Anthony said, before realizing he had spoken without giving it any thought.

After logging his cell phone number into Rene's phone, Anthony excused himself then made for his old bedroom where he closed the door and lay back on the bed without taking his coat off knowing that he had to go back out after a while.

His meeting with Blue was at eleven o'clock, which gave Anthony approximately six hours and fourteen minutes to prepare. Later that night after lying under the covers, fully dressed just in case his mother decided to peer in and check on him, Anthony was astir putting on his all-weather boots before donning his skullcap. His handgun and keys were the last items he retrieved as he exits the bedroom with chariness, tucking the gun in his waistband, and holding his keys tightly in his hand to prevent them from jingling, alarming his mother if she was still awake.

Upon exiting the house, Anthony reset the alarm, thankful that his mother's income wasn't sufficient to afford the luxury of high-advanced Sen-Tech model where she could be sneaky to call up his location on its monitor to see if he was still inside the house instead of peering in the bedroom. Plus, Sen-Tech Corporations kept records of the functions of their many devices, incontestably to keep tabs on their customers' ins and outs, just in case authorities inquired on whether one of their customers had left their residence at a certain time.

Yes, at that moment, he was very happy that her home wasn't equipped with this incriminating brainchild.

Anthony's first destination was an urban neighborhood he'd visited earlier while formulating his plan upon leaving Blue's home, which didn't take no more than twenty minutes. Knowing that he had to be inconspicuous while meandering about the community, he chose an adjacent street that was a dead end, flanked by overgrown trees and shrubs. Plus, there were three streetlamps in which only two seemed to be hanging on to dear life, as their faint flow did no kind of justice to the areas they were to illuminate.

Thankful that it was dark at the end of the street, Anthony parked, retrieved his small flashlight from the umbrella holder in the driver's door, and walked a short distance back up the street until he came upon a piece of plywood he'd left earlier, which reminded him of where he found the scanty pathway that would gain him access to the neighborhood.

Though the flashlight was small in size, it produced enough illumination to avail Anthony as he trotted upon unkempt earth for a good two minutes, before coming out to the rear of two houses that were too close for his liking, but he was glad there were no fences, nor dogs that would blow his cover with their alarming barks. As he approached the gap between both houses, his eyes darted back and forth from the two, checking the windows to make sure he wasn't being watched. Lights were on, and he could hear indistinct chatter from within the walls of both homes. Plus, he saw periodic movement beyond their curtains.

Ruminating how early it was, Anthony did not expect for the residents to have called it a night by now. In fact, he'd mentally prepared himself for some kind of encounter. Finally clearing the sides of both houses, Anthony stopped and actually sighed out loud as he stared across the street at the red Chevrolet pick-up, genuinely relieved that the truck was still there.

Now, shifting his gaze to survey the area, he saw that there were only two men out. They were both drinking beer as one was leaning against a car, and the other stood before him, running his mouth about something Anthony couldn't make out. Their proximity to the truck was about ten yards, which didn't matter one bit to him because his feet were now back in motion.

While making for the truck, Anthony watched the men from the corners of his eyes, seeing that they were now watching him. Even the loquacious one had ceased with his babbling. Nearing the truck, he twisted off the cap at the bottom of his flashlight, revealing its Loc-Tite component, in which he slid into the lock on the driver's door and pushed on the button to activate. The device vibrated and hummed inaudibly as it molested the lock. Seconds after it started, the humming and vibrating stopped, and the device shut off on its own. Wasting no time, Anthony twisted the flashlight, feeling and hearing the lock disengage.

Pulling the door open, he casually climbed into the driver's seat and was now able to keep an eye on the men from the rearview mirror as he worked the Loc-Tite on the ignition. So far, they hadn't made any attempt to stop him. Perhaps they didn't like the owner of the truck, Anthony thought and were glad that someone was stealing it. Thinking of this made him smile, as he now turned the switch, bringing the engine to life. The radio also came on at a high volume with a song by the known rap artist, Hundun Da Don, pumping from the speakers. Easing the gear into drive, Anthony pulled off, casting another glance at the two men while singing along with one of his favorite rap artists from Thompson, Georgia.

It was seven minutes before eleven, when Anthony finally pulled the truck up in front of a house that appeared uninhibited. There were no signs of light, nor movement within the house. Though the land didn't look uncared for, there were still no vehicles of any sort to indicate someone actually resides there. Anthony knew that he was at the right location, being that he was accustomed to how his friend operated. Therefore, he killed the lights, turned back the damaged keyless ignition to shut the engine off, then dismounted, tucking his gun inside the waistband of his pants as he looked about the neighborhood. He didn't see anything out of place. As far as he could tell, there wasn't anybody watching him from any of the nearby houses, nor parked vehicles. Rounding the front of the truck, Anthony walked dutifully toward the house. Before he could reach the front door, it opened slowly on its hinges. Now, he could see the faint glow of some lighting source emitting from another room, further in the house, but not the person who opened the door.

Clearly, they were standing behind the door, which didn't intimidate him. Highly conversant with the procedure, Anthony entered the house, and stopped short of the door, keeping his hands where they could clearly be seen by the small group of men standing to the far right of him in the darkened living room that was spared about 1.2 percent of the light coming from what seemed like the only illuminated room that was further down the hall, which didn't do him any good, being that he couldn't make out any features of the three figures to his right, not the one standing behind him, who immediately closed the door upon his ingress. He could see the silhouettes of the three assault rifles aimed in his direction.

"How many guns do have on you?" the man behind him spoke in gruff voice.

"Just one," Anthony responded, maintaining his position.

"Where is it?"

"Tucked in front of my pants," Anthony told him, leery of his line of questioning.

Before Anthony knew it, he felt the man's masculine hand breach the bottom end of his coat and worm its way around his side to his stomach, where his weapon was securely tucked. He'd been through this several times with the law, but for some reason, Anthony was feeling beyond violated by this particular search and seizer.

Once the man relieved Anthony of his gun, he used his free hand to frisk Anthony for any other weapon. Finding nothing of importance, he stepped around Anthony and made for the hallway. "This way," he instructed.

Anthony didn't have to look back to see if the other three goons were trailing him. He could hear their shoes on the thin carpet. The room that held the only glow in the house, turned out to be the kitchen, which was lit by an orange lightbulb hanging above a table containing multiple handguns and assault rifles. There were four metal folding chairs surrounding the rectangular-shaped table, whereas one was occupied by Blue, who was clad in dark apparel, topped with a state-of-the art bullet-proof vest. There were also two other men standing around the kitchen dressed in the same fashion as Blue. Upon entering the kitchen, Anthony finally realized that they were all dressed as though they were anticipating a war.

"He had this," Anthony's predecessor apprised, holding Anthony's gun up for Blue to see.

Blue apathetically eyed the piece as he exhaled tobacco smoke from his mouth. "Vehicle?" he finally asked.

"Red pick-up," the henchman answered. "Look like a Chevy."

Still holding a lit cigarette in one hand, Blue grabbed the hand-held radio transmitter off the table with the other. "Red pick-up," he spoke into it, now regarding Anthony with a blank stare.

"Came in about three minutes ago," a male's voice responded through the radio's speaker.

"Company?"

"None so far."

"Good," Blue replied. "Remain on post. Keep your eyes peeled."

"I'm on it."

Placing the radio transmitter back onto the table, Blue took a long drag on his cigarette, while maintaining eye contact with Anthony. After grounding it on the edge of the table and leaving it there, he switched his gaze to the man standing closet to him. "I'll take it from here," Blue asserted. "Get your men back on post!"

With a simple nod the man did as he was told, gesturing for his men to move along as he trailed them, still in possession of Anthony's gun. Anthony wanted to protest, but knew it wouldn't get him anywhere, considering how tensed Blue and his men seemed at the moment, which is the first time he'd seen his friend conduct business in such a manner.

Thinking this made him regard the two remaining goons who were watching him and holding their weapons as if they were anticipating him doing something that would give them reason to use them.

"Let's do business," Blue said, gesturing to the chair at the other far end of the table.

"I've never seen you with this many men on hand," Anthony acknowledged as he sat. "Is there a storm coming?"

"I don't know yet," Blue answered, locking eyes with Anthony. "But we're prepared to shoot it out with whoever. Jail is not an option."

Anthony did not respond. He already knew what his friend was implying. This only confirmed that he hadn't succeeded in swaying Blue's mind about the bunk incident, which resulted in Bo's death and his own spontaneous release from confinement. Blue's sentiments were acceptable. Anthony didn't blame him for proceeding with extreme caution but couldn't say that it didn't bother him as to how his friend now treated him like an outsider. Certainly, the love and respect were no more.

"This is all I could get my hands on at the moment." Blue apprised, pulling Anthony from his reverie, indicating the arsenal before them. "If you're looking for anything other than these, you'll have to give me a little more time."

"I'm not looking for anything in particular," Anthony told him. He picked a short-barrel 9 millimeter up off the table and studied it for a few seconds before placing it directly in front of him. The next gun he chose was a Stockholm .357 revolver that fit snugly in the palm of his hand, with its rubber, palm-imprinted handle. Placing that beside his first choice, Anthony had to lift his behind from the seat in order to reach the gun he'd had his eyes on from the moment he entered the kitchen, which was the Larson and Mann P. 98 sub-machine gun; the only model of its kind, manufactured with a suppressor and cooling system.

"I'll definitely need this one," he stated, marveling at the military-issued weapon.

"And you just want those three?"

"For now," Anthony stood, still holding the gun. With his free hand, he extracted a wad of folded bills from his pants pocket and held them out to Blue.

"How much is that?" Blue queried, with furrowed eyebrows.

"Twelve hundred."

Blue jerked his head back as if being struck. "Twelve hundred! That P.98 costs fifteen by itself."

"This all I have right now," Anthony lied, he had more stashed at his home in Macon, Georgia. "Come on, Blue. You know my situation. You know that once I get everything in order, I'll make up the differences."

Blue now had a pensive look on his face.

"Do it for an old friend," Anthony prompted. "You know I've always been a man of my word."

***

Upon leaving the house with the three weapons he'd chosen, plus ammunition, Anthony made a forty-five-minute drive to a neighborhood that he was highly familiar with. As he cruised slowly down Rosewood Drive, he made sure to survey the area to make sure that no one was out and about. He'd already taken risk encountering the two men while purloining the truck. An encounter of any sort would be chancy at the moment. His final task for the night was a bit different, but whether someone was out or not, Anthony had already made up his mind that his plan has to be executed tonight. Making it to the other end of Rosewood, Anthony chose the driveway of one of the houses to turn the truck around and head back in the opposite direction, only passing four houses. He parked in front of the fifth one and quickly cut the engine and lights. Anthony wasn't one hundred percent sure if he wasn't being watched by someone beyond the walls of any of the houses, but he was certain no one was outside at that time of night, in that cold weather, doing the 'neighborhood watch' thing.

Now, watching the top of the street from whence he'd come, Anthony found himself wondering how his son was doing. Did he constantly pester his mother about the whereabouts of his father? He was sure that his son misses him just as he misses his son. Anthony still couldn't fathom how Janelle just made such a selfish decision to uproot Alex from his life. Did she know that such a stunt could be deleterious to a child's psyche? Did she even care? How could—

The chrome wheels glinting off the streetlamps caught his attention just before the black Dodge SUV turned onto the street, and slowly moved in Anthony's direction with the lights off. His newly acquired guns were lying on the seat beside him. Reaching for the .357, Anthony fondled it in his gloved hands while endeavoring to make out the number of occupants through the windshield of the truck that was now about twenty yards out and closing. Though he's already loaded the gun, Anthony still ejected the cylindrical chamber for a terse inspection.

The SUV finally came to a halt in front of a house on the opposite side of the street at almost twenty yards away from Anthony's location, which was expected. The occupant's routine has been the same for years. He parks in front of the same house, then treks through the small wooden area behind the house which brings him out into the backyard of his very own home.

Anthony had anticipated waiting for him just inside the wooden area, but quickly curbed that thought, being that this particular residence had two large dogs in their backyard that would bark their hearts out as long as they knew that he was in the vicinity but, they were highly familiar with their trespassing neighbor from the next street over.

The driver's door of the Dodge swung open, but the driver seemed preoccupied with whatever things he had to gather before dismounting. This was Anthony's cue. He climbed from the truck, pushing the driver's door up without letting it snap shut. Then he marched in the direction of his target with the gun visibly swinging at his side. This guy was very cautious, so Anthony knew that it was going to be impossible to approach unnoticed, but he was prepared for a gunfight, which is something he expected while formulating this plan. When Anthony got withing ten yards of the SUV, the driver alighted, stepping out from around the open door with a handgun of his own down at his side as he regarded Anthony with a blank stare. By this time, Anthony had the revolver raised as he quickened his steps to close the gap between them.

"I wouldn't entertain that thought if I were you," Anthony stated, stopping several feet away from his old friend, gun aimed at his face. "I'm surprised you let me get the drop on you like this. Maybe you've become too comfortable with this routine over the years."

"Maybe," Blue finally spoke maintaining eye contact with Anthony. "Or maybe I became too comfortable with ignoring the snakes in the grass instead of exterminating them."

Anthony cocked his head to one side. "Are you calling me a snake?"

Blue remained silent.

"I've demonstrated nothing but loyalty to you ever since we've known each other," Anthony went on to point out.

"And now?" Blue queried.

It was Anthony's turn to remain silent.

"Don't think for one minute I believed what you said about the bank incident," Blue continued. "You tried to pull a double-cross by killing BO and the other guy, but the other guy outsmarted you. It's easy for one snake to recognize another, right?"

Blue was taunting him, and Anthony knew it. He also knew that it wouldn't do either of them any good if he lashed out at Blue, who was only showing bravado because he knew that he was about to expire. Truth be told he expected this out of his long-time friend. "Okay," Anthony spoke at a length. "I did kill Bo, but don't act like you drew that conclusion on your own. I was charged with his murder. Hell, I was caught with the gun that he was murdered with. The media made sure that the whole world knew this, Einstein. Anyway, I have to get going. Any last words?"

A smile slowly creased Blue's face. "Of course. Fuck you!"

Anthony saw it coming. Blue's arm shot upward as he simultaneously peddled back in an attempt to secure an aim with his gun and escape the impact of one aimed at his face. Anthony, who'd already expected this, squeezed the trigger of the .357 caliber before Blue's gun was high enough to acquire an aim. The bullet slammed into his left eye and exploded from the back of his head, accompanied by a spray of bone, mucus, and brain matter. Before Blue's nerve system crashed, it sent out one last impulse through his body causing his finger to jerk back on the trigger of his gun discharging it. When Blue's body made contact with the ground, his gun clattered against the pavement and skittered inches away as his lifeless eyes stared up at nothing. Dropping the .357 beside the deceased friend, Anthony turns and headed back to the truck.

Chapter 17

Tuesday

"Have you come up with a time and place we'll have lunch before catching a movie?" Deputy Aaron Taylor asked upon approaching the State's table where Ebony was standing gathering her belongings, preparing to exit the courtroom.

"I haven't really given it any thought," Ebony admitted, now connecting the latches on her briefcase. "Which theater are we going to?"

"I was thinking of the one out in Warner Robins."

Of course, Ebony thought. *As far away from his wife as possible.*

"Unless you have one in mind," he added, hastily, apparently ruminating on her delay of response.

"No," she answered, with a smile. "Warner Robins is fine. We have enough time to come up with a rendezvous place."

Taylor nodded. "You're right."

"Ah, Ms. Davis?"

Ebony looked at Judge Jackson, who was still seated on the bench. "Sir?"

"I want those documents before me the moment you step foot in this courtroom tomorrow morning," he demanded.

"Yes, sir!" She checked her watch before reverting her attention to Taylor. "I'm really in a rush."

"It's okay, I'll see you in the morning."

Quickly making her exit, Ebony rushed toward the elevators and managed to catch one that arrived at the same time she did. She didn't need anything from her office, Ebony took the elevator down to the garage, hoping to exit the building without running into anyone who would slow her down, which was something she could not afford at the moment. Putting a little more pep in her step than usual, Ebony entered the parking garage wondering for the millionth time today what she was getting herself into as she neared her car. Surely, Rick had told her to call the chief investigator of the Department of Investigators but being the obstinate individual that she's always been, Ebony decided that she would 'drop' in on him instead. What if he's already retired home to his family by the time she arrives? Did she have a contingency plan? Well, of course. Instead of attempting this same dim-witted stunt tomorrow, she would place a call to him on her lunch break. Saturday was getting dreadfully close, so this chat was highly imperative. She was just hoping not to run into John Pruden.

Luckily for her, the DOI's headquarters was only about a thirty-five-minute drive in which she'd managed to cover in twenty-three minutes. As she'd expected, their parking lot was almost deserted with only four vehicles present. Ebony just hoped that one of them belonged to the person whom she sought, while gingerly easing her Cadillac into a spot belonging to Lieutenant Alvera Fruitrail, according to the metal plate attached to a steel pole dug into the ground.

"Sorry, Lieutenant Fruitrail," Ebony mumbled, cutting the engine. "I just need to borrow your spot for a few minutes."

Though she parked directly in front of the building, at a good twenty feet away from its entrance, Ebony was still not in favor of leaving the warm console of her car so soon, but this was something that had to be done. She still wasn't sure if the chief investigator hadn't already gone for the day. Considering this, Ebony dismounted with only her keys and cell phone in tow making for the glass front door that was mirror tinted. Only taking a couple of seconds to regard herself in the glass, Ebony pulled the door open and marched dutifully up to the front desk where the receptionist was standing, donning her overcoat. Stopping mid-preparation, she now regarded the woman standing before her desk with a look of uncertainty.

"Are you here to pick someone up?" the young woman asked, dubiously.

"No," Ebony knew that it wouldn't be wise to take umbrage, being that she was pretty much encroaching, "I'm here to see Chief Investigator Livingston."

"At this time of the hour?" the receptionist posed. "Look, ma'am, if you've missed your appointment, we could get you another one set up. Right now, we're thirty-two minutes past quitting time."

Ding!

They both looked in the direction of the elevators to see a middle-aged male and female emerge and move in their direction. Ebony's heart dropped to her stomach at realization that this could be Ted Livingston on his way home for the evening. There's no way he would bid her a few minutes of his time when he's already on his way out of the front door. Therefore, she would have to—

"Goodnight, Haylee!" the older woman said in passing.

"Goodnight, Mrs. O'Neal!" the receptionist responded, then nodded to the woman's concomitant. "Mr. Blankenship."

"You just make sure to get some rest, young lady," the heavy-set man chided, maintaining stride with his co-worker. "I don't wanna see you nodding off at your desk again."

"Yes, sir!" The receptionist genuflected. After watching the two investigators exit, she looked back at Ebony then began tapping keys on her computer's keypad. "I can log your information in right now but won't be able to set you another appointment until I get in tomorrow."

"That won't be necessary." Ebony was done with playing nice with the little girl. "Right now, you need to get Mr. Livingston on the phone and convey that Assistant District Attorney Ebony Davis would like to speak with him at once!"

The girl's pupils seemed to enlarge. Perhaps Ebony's title had garnered this reaction. Surely, the receptionist was now under the impression that her supervisor was in some kind of trouble. She was visibly frightened but did as she was told. Putting the desk phone's receiver to her ear, she dialed four digits and waited.

"And please, don't sugar-coat my words," Ebony stated for added measure.

Haylee gave a slight nod before speaking into the receiver. "Yes, Mr. Livingston? There's an assistant district attorney by the name of Ebony Davis, who insists on seeing you immediately. Yes, she's standing before me right now, and she doesn't look too happy. She didn't say sir. I'm on my way out. What do you want me to do with this visitor? Well, I guess I really don't have a choice." She hung up the phone, then regarded Ebony with a plausible smile. "He wants me to escort you up."

"Thank you!"

It had only taken another minute for the receptionist to gather her things. Without another word to Ebony, she rounded the desk with a large pocketbook hanging off her shoulder and a pink cellular in her hand making for the elevators. Ebony followed, admiring the red pumps on the young woman's size seven feet. They were knockoffs and Haylee didn't make them appear more than that. There was not an ounce of sexiness in her strut, which had Ebony wondering if the girl was still a virgin.

Lucky for them, the same elevator that the two investigators had arrived on was still stationary. Getting on, Haylee pressed the button for the floor that they were headed to causing the steel door to close immediately. Now, standing beside the younger woman, Ebony could tell that she attentively affixed her eyes to the floor numbering indicator overhead in an endeavor to avoid engaging in small talk with someone who may be responsible for sending one of her relatives to prison. This made Ebony smile to herself.

Ding!

The succinct ride to the second floor, which was the top floor, was over. Before the door could roll all the way back, Haylee was high tailing it out of the elevator as if to reach her supervisor's office ahead of Ebony, to make sure he'd concealed anything be used against him in court, or maybe she was just in a rush to get home to whomever was awaiting her arrival. Whatever it was, Ebony couldn't careless, but she did follow further behind the receptionist at a slow pace as they moved along the corridor that was analogous to the district attorney's floor in size. There were office doors lining both sides of the hall. They were all closed, except for the one at the far end in which Haylee stopped in the threshold of.

"Here's your visitor," she promulgated, indicating Ebony who was still about eight feet behind and closing. "Signed, sealed, and delivered."

Haylee stepped aside to allow Ebony to enter the office where the chief investigator sat behind a desk cluttered by souvenirs and small framed photos that surrounded his computer and desk phone. Plus, the stench from the freshly smoked cigar that Ebony had been inhaling since getting off the elevator, reigned supreme in the small room. It didn't help that his window was closed tightly against the bone-chilling air haunting the exterior of the building.

"Mrs. Davis," Livingston spoke, lugging his bulky but tall frame from the comfort of his soft leather chair, hand extended.

"It's *Miss*," she rectified, accepting his hand. "I didn't make it past the engagement."

"Oh! I'm sorry!"

"It's okay."

"May I go home now?" Haylee intervened from the doorway.

Livingston regarded his secretary. "Sure, Ms. Romberg. I'll see you in the morning and thanks!"

"No problem," she responded, feet already in motion towards the elevators.

"Please, have a seat!" The burly man indicated the chair across from his desk. Once Ebony was seated, he squeezed back into his chair. "You'll have to excuse the cigar smoke. This is like the best time that I can really enjoy a good smoke. The wife hates it and forbids me from smoking anywhere near our property, and she'd have a heart attack if she finds out I do it anywhere near the kids." He paused to take a breath. "So, to what do I owe this visit?"

"I'm seeking an update on my case," Ebony spoke slowly choosing her words carefully. "The death of my fiancé, Jason Towns. He died in a housefire, July 19th of last year."

"You know what?" Livingston replied, a look of recognition on his face. "I thought you looked familiar. I remember your face from the news. I remember the case. In fact, it was the first time I'd heard of zodine, and if I remember correctly, outside of initial findings, there were no new developments."

"What were the initial findings?" Ebony ventured.

"I'll have to refer to the file," he said getting up from his chair again. After retrieving a manila folder from his file cabinet, he returned to his seat and opened it up in front of him. "According to the file," Livingston resumed, "my investigator coagulated reports from a fire inspector by the name of Suzan Parrish and a medical examiner by the name of Russel Pilkington, which is routine. Several neighbors were questioned. Neither of them produced anything substantial. Then there's the summary from your interview." He looked at Ebony. "The case was closed on the twenty-seventh of July."

"So soon?"

The chief investigator drew a breath. "Look, Ms. Davis, I had one of my best investigators on your case, whose judgement I would never second guess. She took pride in her work and would never turn over her findings until she was sure that she'd left no stones unturned."

"She?" Ebony inquired, figuring he was looking through the wrong folder.

"Of course," he answered regarding her with furrowed eyebrows. "Investigator Rachel Weaver was handling your case. You don't remember being interviewed by her?"

"I was interviewed by investigator John Pruden." Now she was sure he was looking through the wrong folder.

"That can't be right," Livingston countered, sifting back through the documents. H estopped when he found what he was looking for. "You know what? I apologize. Pruden had done the interview because Weaver had become ill after visiting a chemical plant, but the interview was all Pruden had conduced to the case. After a couple of days of resting, Weaver was back in the saddle. This was her case. She concluded it."

"Where is she now?" Ebony wanted to know.

"She retired for medical reasons back in November," he rejoined, closing the folder. "I'm sorry that we couldn't solve your case. Most cases we get are like that. It happens."

"Is it possible that John Pruden could still be working to solve the case?" Ebony feigned naïve.

"No, that would not be possible."

"Why not?"

"He no longer works here," Livingston informed. "He was terminated for committing acts unbecoming a peace officer which is something I am not at liberty to discuss."

"When was he terminated?" Ebony asked, feeling the blood inside her boil over.

"In December."

Chapter 18

"That's some weird shit!" Bull offered after Ebony relayed what she'd ascertained about John Pruden to him and Rick.

"And the chief wouldn't tell you why this dude was terminated?" asked Rick, who was seated beside Bull on the sofa, as Ebony paced back and forth on the other side of the coffee table with her hands behind her back.

"He claimed that he was not at liberty to discuss it," Ebony answered still pacing with her hands behind her back and eyes to the floor. "I assume it was some kind of sexual exploitation involving a co-worker or client."

"That could very well be true," Rick offered, "but what he did is irrelevant. Right now, we should be coming up with a way to deal with him and it must involve death."

"I'm definitely with that," Bull added.

Stopping to face them, Ebony sniffed back a drainage before asking, "Does anyone have any ideas?"

"Not at the moment," answered Rick. "But you won't be meeting with him on Saturday."

"I won't?"

"Of course not!" Rick got to his feet stretching. "Once we come up with something, I'll let you know and what's the word on Anthony?"

Truth be told, Ebony hadn't given the situation with Anthony any thought for some time now. It was clear that he'd blatantly thumbed his nose at their agreement.

139

Therefore, he deserved whatever penalty she deemed appropriate to impose on him. So, while Rick and Bull were colluding the demise of John Pruden, she was going to have her hands tied with the concoction of Anthony's.

"He'll get what's coming to him," Ebony now answered.

"Let's deal with John Pruden first, and I'd rather he be dead by Monday, just in case he does have a way to re-open the case presenting those photos to the chief investigator. I'm not interested in finding out if he's bluffing or not."

"He'll definitely be dead by Monday." Rick asserted before moving towards the front door.

Bull got off the sofa to follow. As he did, Ebony caught the way he regarded her body with lustful eyes, which wasn't the first time, but Ebony couldn't see herself being mad at the older man for wanting something younger and prepossessing as herself although his actions were indecently unprofessional. Plus, the look in his eyes always sent out some kind of warning sign to her sixth sense. As if he has ulterior motives that he's still indecisive about acting on. It was the same look that her grandfather used to give her before bringing himself to violate her innocence.

Well, Ebony thought while closing and locking the door behind them, *if Bull attempts to act on his intentions, he'll be joining Terrence Davis in hell.* "Sen-Tech," Ebony spoke while enroute to her bedroom, "activate the alarm!"

"Alarm activated," she heard the disembodied voice respond behind her.

Entering the bedroom, Ebony flopped down on the edge of her bed, and looked down at her nightstand, where she'd left a saucer containing crush, a rolled-up bill, and her driver's license. Grabbing her license, she divided the powdered drug into two lines, then snorted one into each nostril. Lying back on the bed, she closed her eyes, and allowed the drug to plague her mind with surreal images until everything went dark.

Ebony's alarm clock sounded like it was hooked up to an amplifier when it came alive causing her to wake with a start, and jolt upward in a sitting position which brought on a severe case of dizziness. She didn't expect to fall asleep in the same position, still fully dressed, and she definitely didn't expect to fall asleep without taking a shower. She now made haste to do right after silencing the clock.

Ebony had inadvertently spent 37 minutes in the shower after getting caught up in the sensation of how the soothing hot water caressingly pelted her skin. Upon returning to her bedroom, she realized that she hadn't lain out any clothes for today, nor done anything with her hair, which would consume more of her time and make her much later than she already was. Therefore, Ebony grabbed the first pantsuit she stumbled upon in her closet, combed her hair into a ponytail that she deemed public worthy, and managed to make it to work at 8:46, but she didn't catch any flak from Barbara Hutchins nor Judge Jackson which was surprising.

"State," Judge Jackson spoke, pulling Ebony from her reverie for the umpteenth time that morning. "What's your offer?"

Ebony got to her feet at the State's table. "Your Honor, being that this is Ms. Patterson's second forgery charge and she's still on probation for the first one, the State is offering ten years to serve, without the possibility of parole."

"Your Honor," Attorney Ellen Martinez spoke from the defense table, where she was seated with her Caucasian client. "You and I both know that my client doesn't deserve ten years without the possibility of parole. Yes, this is her second forgery charge, but the statute doesn't imply such a stiff punishment."

"According to the statute," Ebony countered, now regarding the older Spanish woman, "any person charged with the offense of forgery may receive punishment from one to ten years in confinement."

"Which may also be probated, Your Honor," Martinez came back, reluctant to look in Ebony's direction.

"Which was already probated, Your Honor," Ebony rectified. "But Ms. Patterson wasn't grateful to the courts for reprieving her physical confinement, which is why she chose to return with another violation of the same charge, violating her probation in the process. That alone constitutes ten years without the possibility of parole."

The judge regarded Ellen with a tired look. "Does your client wish to accept the offer or not?"

"One moment, Your Honor."

While Martinez conferred with her client, Ebony took a seat and sifted through her documents to see how many more cases she had for the day. Once confirmed, she leaned back in her chair and shifted her gaze over to Aaron Taylor, who was standing off to the side of the judge's bench with his hands tucked inside his coat and bald head tucked snugly under his matching skullcap that had LCSD stenciled on it in yellow, block letters. She wasn't at all surprised to see that he was watching her, which seemed like all he ever does. Ebony already knew that he wanted her sexually, but lately he'd been displaying hunger as if he'd been divested of such pleasure for a long period of time. Ebony knew the feeling because she hadn't been with a man since Jason.

Maybe, that'll change this coming Saturday.

"Your Honor," Martinez finally spoke, "my client will gladly accept the State's offer if it came with the eligibility of parole."

The judge looked to the State's table. "State, is there any way that you could reconsider and reconstruct your offer to include parole eligibility?"

"No, sir."

Judge Jackson sighed. "Would both counsels approach the bench?" Once Ebony and Martinez were standing before him for the private conference, he asked Ebony in almost a whisper, "Is there a particular reason why you're so hell-bent on making sure that the defendant is sentenced without the possibility of parole?"

"Is there a particular reason why you are so opposed to the State's recommendation which is in accordance with the statute handed down by its legislators?" Ebony recriminated with arched eyebrows. "I'm doing my job, which is to ensure that the punishments of all criminals are within the guidelines of state and federal laws and are proper before the court. Your job is to—"

"I don't need you telling me what my job is, Ms. Davis!" the judge hissed with a menacing look on his face. "I can do your job, blindfolded, which is why I'm on this bench. You may want to remember that."

"The State's recommendation still stands," Ebony stood her ground maintaining eye contact with him.

After a few seconds, Judge Jackson shifted his gaze to Ellen Martinez. "Ms. Martinez, we've been at this for too long. The State is not relenting."

"Well," Martinez said with a shrug. "My client won't accept if it doesn't come with parole."

"Then its settled," he replied. "Now, we have to get it on record."

The women returned to their respectable seats.

"If we could pick up where we left off," the judge continued, "the State was asked if it could reconsider and reconstruct its offer to allow the defendant a chance at parole, which the State refused. Am I right?"

"Yes. Your Honor," Ebony answered.

He shifted his gaze to the defense table. "At this time, the State is unmovable. Does the defendant wish to accept the offer of ten years without the possibility of parole, or not?"

"Yes, Your Honor," Ellen Martinez answered. "My client accepts the offer."

"And the court is in acceptance of the defendant's plea of guilty," Judge Jackson replied, in formality. "Once the indictment is signed by all parties and is proper before the court, I'd like to call an hour recess."

After the indictment was signed, and the detainee was escorted back to the holding cell, Judge Jackson gave everyone instructions to return to the courtroom in an hour. Ebony used this time to journey to her office, but instead of going straight to her office upon arriving on the floor, Ebony make for the break room to see if there were any coffee and doughnuts left over from that morning. Upon entering the small room, she encountered Roselyn Holt, one of the two state court prosecutors seated at the small table, helping herself to a doughnut and a cup of coffee. As always, the slightly overweight woman had her hair pulled into a bun and way too much red lipstick smeared onto her lips. Just as Ebony entered, she was stubbing out her cigarette in a makeshift ashtray. After taking a quaff of her coffee she regarded the superior court prosecutor with a broad smile.

"Hi, Ebony!"

"How's it going Rosie?" Ebony replied making for the refrigerator, stifling a cough brought on by the heavy cloud of tobacco smoke.

"I can't complain," said Holt. "My husband got his job back as a truck driver, so he's back on the road. Emily just turned sixteen and I think she's already a lesbian."

"What makes you think that?" Ebony inquired. She placed two doughnuts on a paper towel, sat them on the table, then moved toward the coffeemaker.

"It's too obvious." Rosely Holt took a bite of her doughnut before continuing. "Her best friend Debbie is a dead giveaway. Not only does she dress and look like a boy, but she walks around grabbing at her crotch as if she was born with the male organ. Hell, if I didn't know her, you couldn't pay me to believe she's a girl."

"Well," Ebony started, now leaning against the counter with a cup of coffee cupped in both hands. "Maybe Debbie is a certified butch, but that's not concrete enough to convict Emily of lesbianism."

"True," There was now a sinister grin on Holt's face. "That's why I saved the essential evidence for last."

Ebony couldn't help but be amused by the woman's mock theatrical presentational tone of voice. "I'm listening," she assured.

"Now," the state court prosecutor proceeded, "whenever Kelsea comes over to the house, they would sit in Emily's room with the door standing wide open, but whenever Debbie comes over, they'd be in the room with the door closed and locked." She held up a finger as if she knew that Ebony was about to dissent. "After developing the notion that Emily and Debbie were an item, I began snooping around. I would listen at the bedroom door. It was hard to decipher what they were saying because they spoke quietly, but on several occasions, I'd hear kissing sounds and moaning."

"So, you're convinced they're having sex."

"I wasn't born yesterday," Holt stated, then narrowed her eyes at Ebony. "And speaking of sex has anyone sampled the new sirloin streak yet?"

"Hendrix?" Ebony asked, knowing good and well that the round woman was referring to the new prosecutor.

"Hell, yeah!" There was a huge smile on Holt's face. "That man has a nice set of buns in his back pocket!"

"I am not having this conversation with your horny ass," Ebony said through her laughter, grabbing her doughnuts off the table. "I have phone calls to make."

"Well, if you and Samantha Gordon decide to sample the goods," Holt said, "I'll hold his ass down."

Making it to the threshold of the breakroom Ebony stopped and looked back at her. "I think that would be rape."

"That's why we'll have to kill him and skip town." Rosely Holt's laughter was ringing in Ebony's ears as she made for her office, doughnuts in one hand, cup of coffee in the other.

Though Ebony wasn't in the mood for laughter, she should have known that Holt was going to bring it out of her as always, being that she was their very own 'office clown'. The laughter did bring her temporary relief from the heated confrontation she'd had with Judge Carl Jackson a moment ago, and the worries of how things were going to play out over this coming weekend.

Entering her office, Ebony used her foot to push the door closed then moved over to her desk where she placed her coffee and doughnuts down before taking a seat. That's when she realized that she'd forgotten to warm her doughnuts up in the microwave.

Dammit! she thought as she unlocked and retrieved the Nu-Tel cellular that Rick had given her from the bottom drawer.

After powering the phone up and seeing there were no messages from Rick or Bull, she fished her SkyFone from her coat's pocket and perused her contacts until coming upon the phone number she was looking for, in which she dialed in on the Nu-Tel. Placing the SkyFone atop the desk, Ebony took a bite from one of the doughnuts, then leaned back in her chair listening to the ringtone, hoping the guy was even awake at this time of day.

"Yo?" the familiar masculine voice answered.

"May I speak to Zoe?" Ebony asked just in case it wasn't him.

"Who else would be answering my phone shorty?" he queried, apparently taking umbrage. "And who is this, any-damn-way?"

"Sophia," she answered, remembering the name she'd given him. "We met back in July at the—"

"July!" he exclaimed, cutting her off. "Shorty that's damn near eight months ago. It doesn't matter where we met, I hope you don't expect me to remember you. Why'd it take you so long to call me?"

"Well," Ebony started, "at the time we met, I had just started my own business. I had intended to call you shortly afterwards, but I got caught up trying to get everything into motion and making sure that my business stayed afloat. I had to hire and train employees. Plus, I had to oversee the shipment of product and supplies."

"What kind of business is this?"

"It's a small bakery," she answered quick on her toes.

"In what part of Atlanta?"

"It's in Macon."

"Why Macon, shorty?"

"That's where I live."

"So, you moved to Macon?"

"I've always lived in Macon."

Zoe lingered a few seconds before asking, "So, you just remembered my number?"

"Actually," Ebony began retrieving her cup of coffee off the desk, "I was strolling through my phone for one of my employee's number when I spotted yours. That's when I realize you may be the man for the job."

"Job!" he cried out. "Shorty, I don't bake cakes and shit. Well, not those kinds of cakes."

Ebony sipped her coffee then replaced the cup. "My sister's husband is in Atlanta," she let on. "She suspects him of having another family there but can't prove it which is why she can't file for a proper divorce. We're looking for someone who can follow and monitor his movements."

"Shorty, you can't be serious," he told her. "I'm a criminal, not a fucking detective. Tell your sister to hire a private investigator. They get paid to snitch. It's their job."

"She can't take the findings of a private investigator to court."

"Why not?"

"They'll say she violated his privacy rights," she lied, hoping he didn't know much about the law. "We're willing to pay you. Just name your price."

Chapter 19

Anthony had awakened in a cold sweat around 5A.M. from a nightmare he was having. In this frightening dream he was being haunted by Blue's murder, but as it played out, he was the one being murdered after being chased through a seemingly endless graveyard in the dark by Blue who was accompanied by Marvin. After running for what seemed like eternity, Anthony tripped over some unforeseen object and landed on top of a grave that had his name inscribed into the tombstone. By the time he rolled onto his back, his pursuers were already standing over him, both aiming handguns at his face. From that position, Anthony could clearly see the night's sky through Blue's head where his left eye used to be before being blown out by the .357 caliber. Blue was visibly fuming, but his accomplice was slowly shaking his head with a simper plastered on his face.

"You just wouldn't listen," Marvin taunted. "Greed had you thrown in jail. Now it's brought you straight to your own grave." That's when they both opened fire forcing him to escape the disturbing dream.

Upon awaking, Anthony just lay in bed staring at the ceiling and wondering about his own demise. Would Marvin be the one to murder him, or would his death be orchestrated by Ebony? She already knows where his mother lives. Therefore, its incontestable that she could have men posted outside at any time, ready to carry out her orders, but the big question is: Would she take it as far as to bring harm upon his mother for what he'd done?

Anthony heard his mother's alarm clock sounding off at 7:15. The house was completely quiet, so he could pretty much hear every movement after silencing the clock. Though it seemed alienated, Anthony closed his eyes and tried to envision his mother as he listened to her move about the house preparing to leave for work, which actually helped to get his mind off of the nightmare and its apparent implications. His eyes were still closed when his mother opened the bedroom door and peered in on him before leaving the house.

After waiting for fifteen to twenty minutes to see if his mother would re-enter upon forgetting something, Anthony got out of his bed feeling the effects of an interrupted sleep that was taking toll on his body as well as his mental, but a hot, hour-long shower seemed to rejuvenate him. Re-entering the bedroom Anthony finished drying off, got dressed, then made the bed up. He didn't plan on exiting that early, but he had to get out of that house.

Now, Anthony looked at his watch to see that it was 1:49P.M. He'd been parked in front of the vacant house for almost four hours, which was the same house he'd sat in front of for four hours on end ever since returning to Atlanta. When he befriended Marvin, while being detained at the Fulton County Jail for burglary a while back, he remembered Marvin talking about growing up and still residing in this same neighborhood in the Buckhead area. He just wished he knew which one of the beautiful houses lining both sides of the street he would end up paying a visit to.

Has it ever crossed Anthony's mind that Marvin may have taken the money from the bank heist and moved away? Well of course, but Marvin didn't come off as the type that would spend money just because he has it. In fact, it seems as though Marvin would need a perfectly good reason to just up and leave such a nice neighborhood. It's not like he was aware of Anthony's miraculous release. That would definitely be a good reason to pack up and move to another state or another continent. A car drove by pulling Anthony from his abstract musing. It was an older model Nissan wagon that pulled into the driveway of the house right next to the one he was parked in front of. The older white man had left almost two hours ago. Now, the man dismounted, clad in stonewashed jeans, a large corduroy coat, and a red ballcap pulled tightly over his head. If the man wasn't beyond fifty years of age, then the silver bush protruding from under his hat and matching beard that had grown several inches away from his face seemed to tell a different story. Shutting off the engine Anthony got out and made sure to keep his hands in plain sight as he traveled up the driveway and approached the man, who had begun pulling bags of groceries from the rear compartment of the car. He had stopped what he was doing to regard the stranger.

"Good afternoon, sir!" Anthony spoke with respect hoping to put the old man's mind at ease."

"How may I help you?" questioned the man who was now holding a paper bag full of groceries.

"I'm inquiring about Ms. Maxine Whyte," Anthony purported, quoting the realtor's name he'd seen on the For Sale sign planted in the front yard of the house that his car was still parked in front of.

"The realtor?"

"Yes."

"What about her?"

"I've set several appointments with her this week to look at this house," Anthony resumed his play, gesturing toward the adjacent home, "and she's cancelled every last one of them."

"I see." The older man looked over at Anthony's car. "I was wondering why you've been parked there every day, but it's understandable why Ms. Whyte would cancel appointments."

Anthony just listened.

"She's one of the most prominent realtors in the Buckhead area," the man went on to explicate. "Plus, she has another office in Savannah, Georgia, where she also sells houses and commercial properties. So, she's a very busy woman. Perhaps, you've been in contact with her secretary."

"Perhaps," Anthony replied looking back at a passing car making sure to get a look at the driver, which was a young white woman.

"But she's a good person. She does good business."

"So, I've heard." Anthony directed his attention back to the older man ready to play his card. "I was referred to her by my old friend, Marvin Harris."

The older man now evaluated Anthony with furrowed eyebrows, in which he hoped was a sign of recognition to Marvin's name and not that he'd finally recognized Anthony's face from the news reportage of the bank robbery that took place over a year ago. If it turned out to be the latter, Anthony knew he would have to make a quick executive decision. He also knew that the murder of the old man would bring a lot of heat upon the neighborhood, which was something he could not afford at the moment.

"Are you talking about Louise Atkins' boy?" the old man finally inquired.

"Yes," Anthony answered, relieved. He didn't know Marvin's mother's name but hoped that the old fart was putting him on the right track. "We've been friends since high school," he added. "Is he still around?"

"I haven't seen Little Marvin in ages," he answered, stifling a sneeze. "But Louise still lives in the same house. We still talk but for some reason, she refuses to talk about him. If he's back in jail, I can only assume he'd done something she's ashamed of because she gets really emotional whenever someone mentions his name. In fact, the last time I saw him was almost a year ago. That was when he bought her that truck."

Anthony looked in the direction he nodded in. It wasn't hard to spot the house that sat four houses down on the opposite side of the street. The truck he was referring to was a black 2022 GMC Denali: Luxury Edition which Anthony knew started at sixty thousand dollars. Sitting in the driveway behind the SUV was the red sedan that just rode by driven by the blonde, who'd just dismounted and was moving toward the front door. She was wearing a leather trench coat and black boots with heels that made her look as though she was about 6'2". "Who is that?" Anthony asked, watching the woman use her own keys to gain entrance to the home.

"I have no idea," the older man answered. "She comes by once or twice a week. I've seen her take out trash, so I assume she's the cleaning lady, but I've never questioned Louise about her."

"Well," Anthony started making a show of checking his watch. "I guess Maxine cancelled another appointment, but thanks for your time, sir."

"Are you giving up on the house?"

Anthony looked as if he was pondering the question before saying, "I guess so. Maybe I'll try the Conyers area."

"Well, good luck, son!"

"Thanks!" Making it back to the car, Anthony started the engine, then took another look at the house where the blonde was now carrying a trash bag out to the lime green plastic bin at the curb just as the old man had informed. She'd doffed her coat revealing a black turtleneck sweater that bared down on her large breast and blue jeans that visibly flaunted her curvaceous figure. She seemed very attractive from Anthony's vantage. Even the old man was now ogling her, which made Anthony smile as he made a U-turn and drove away.

It was almost after 4 o'clock when Anthony returned to his mother's house. With nothing to do he made for the living room and tried to occupy his mind by watching television but for some reason, his eyes kept darting from the screen to the array of pictures his mother had all over the place. Most of the time his eyes would land on a picture containing Leonard, who'd been there since Anthony's birth. The only father that Anthony has ever known. It was sad just how he'd lost his life fighting a war that had nothing to do with him.

Shifting his gaze, Anthony studied different pictures of his son at various stages of his life. There were pictures of him holding Alex when he was just an infant. Janelle even accompanied them in some of the photos. The smiling faces of he, Janelle and Anthoy of how happy they were as a family, but Janelle ruined that image when she decided to run off with the intent to keep him from seeing his son again. For what? Because he'd incurred charges that were sure to land him in prison for the rest of his life? The thought caused the ill feelings that he has for his son's mother to resurface. He just knew that she'd run off with another man, who'd play father figure to his son. Images of another man watching Alex's favorite cartoons with him brought on the image of how his old bedroom had looked when he showed up at his mother's house last Friday. It was incontestable that the bedspread and toys belonged to Alex, which was why his mother had crept into the room like a thief in the night while he slept and displaced the items.

Shutting off the television, Anthony stood and peered out of the window to make sure his mother hadn't made it home yet. Then he made off towards her bedroom. Wasting no time, he entered immediately feeling as if he was invading her privacy. He was sure he hadn't imagined the items, but he had to know for certain. If she'd hidden them in her room, then Anthony knew that they were in her closet, and he was right. Upon pulling the door to the closet open, he saw the bedspread folded up on the floor amidst her boxes of shoes, and the toys sitting atop the shelf. There were also a few brand-new, unopened toys amongst the old ones.

After taking in what he came to see, Anthony exited, leaving his mother's room the same way he found it, and made for his old bedroom when he began packing his belongings. This revelation had given him an idea, in which he intended to immediately act upon. He was already packed and back on the living room sofa pretending to be interested in some TV show when his mother, who was accompanied by Helen and Rene, entered the house.

"Are you leaving?" Carol questioned, immediately noticing the two bags sitting on the floor beside the coffee table.

Anthony stood, facing the three women, who were all regarding him with parallel looks of disbelief. "I have to get back to Macon," he promulgated. "It's urgent."

"Is something wrong with Ebony?" There was a genuine look of concern on Carol's face.

"I don't know any details," he answered, hating to lie to his mother. "I was only told to return immediately."

"So, I guess you don't know when you're coming back, huh?"

"I can't say at the moment," Anthony told her. "But I'm leaving my suits, so I'll have something to wear to church whenever I do come back." He regarded his mother's friends. "It was nice meeting you, Ms. Helen, Rene, you can call me any time."

After saying his goodbyes, Anthony made his exit. He didn't have his plan fully mapped out, but his destination was Buckhead, where he would acquire a room at one of the cheap motels not far from his, nor Marvin's mother's home. Once that task was complete, Anthony walked to a nearby fast food restaurant where he ordered to go, choosing to eat his dinner in solitude. After consuming his meal, he laid back in the bed staring up at the ceiling as he mentally formulated his plans for tomorrow and Friday, especially Friday.

Anthony hadn't realized he'd fallen asleep until he was awakened by the selected ringtone of his cellular phone lying next to him. Upon opening his eyes, he saw that the room was dark, being that it was now nighttime. The only light visible was shown through the thin curtains from the sundry lights of the night, and the cellular, in which he picked up and looked at the screen before answering.

"Hello?" His voice came out groggy.

"Did I wake you?" Rene voice sounded through the earpiece.

"No," Anthony lied, stifling a yawn. "But I am tired. What's on your mind?"

"I just called to make sure you made it home safe," she purported. "Is everything all right with whatever situation you had to rush back home to?"

"It's getting there."

There was a pregnant pause before she asked, "So who's Ebony?"

"A woman that I work for."

"Your mom seemed very concerned about this woman you work for.

Anthony found himself smiling. "Do I detect jealousy?"

"Maybe."

"How's Rachel?" He changed the subject, not knowing if she was joking or not.

"She's doing fine," Rene answered. "She's also been asking about you."

"Really?" Anthony sat up, rubbing the small of his back.

"I think she's already crazy about you," Rene said with a chuckle. "She asked me if we are getting married."

Anthony also found this funny. "That little girl is too much," he offered.

"Yes, she is."

"And what's the story on her father?"

Chapter 20

Friday
February 23rd

Anthony was finally able to drag himself out of bed at 11:56 A.M. Though he was clad in thermal undergarment and a sweat suit, he was still cold, being that the room's heating system wasn't working. The temperature outside was in the low forties. He made a mental note to complain about the heater to the front desk upon leaving for the day as he made for the bathroom to take a shower. While allowing the soothing hot water to pelt his tensed body, Anthony's mind was on Rene thought it should've been on Janelle and Marvin. He couldn't believe how he'd driven to Atlanta with retribution on his mind and ended up getting involved with the dark-complexion beauty. He knew that it was inevitable, considering his inexorable mother, and her tag-team partner Helen. However, Rene's down to earth and has a keen sense of humor that the average man couldn't resist. In fact, after talking to her for hours on the phone last night, Anthony promised himself that at the conclusion of his mission, he would spend ample time getting properly acquainted with her daughter.

Well, first he would have to reconcile with Ebony. Now, clad in a black jean suit and ballcap. Anthony donned his leather coat before exiting the motel room, heading for the main office. As the weather predicted, the temperature was still in the low forties and the wind was moving at about fifty-five miles per hour, howling as it bullied and assaulted everything in its path. Anthony didn't mind the force of it. What bothered him was how the wind molested the insides of his ears making him wish that he'd worn a skull cap instead of the ball cap.

"Good afternoon, sir!" a white male around the same age as Anthony greeted him when he entered the small office that seemed equipped with a state of the art heating system, considering how comfortably warm the place was. "It feels like a blizzard out there, huh?"

"Yes, it does," Anthony answered reaching the desk. "It almost feels the same way inside that room that you all rented to me."

The clerk made a face. "Don't tell me that your heater is out."

"It is."

"What room is this?" he asked, grabbing a walkie-talkie from atop the desk.

"Eight."

"Front office to maintenance," he spoke into the device.

"Go ahead for maintenance," came the reply.

"The heater in unit eight needs to be fixed, immediately."

"Once I *immediately* fix the one in unit twelve," the custodian came back, voice saturated with sarcasm, "I'll *immediately* skip down to unit eight."

"Smart ass!" the clerk said to Anthony replacing the radio. "The retard fuck can barely read. In fact, he's the perfect example of what happens when a man decides to impregnate his own sister, but he's good at what he does. So, if you could weather the storm just a little while longer, he'll be at your door in no time."

"I'm on my way out right now."

"Well, it'll be fixed by the time you return."

Exiting the office, Anthony jammed his hands into the pockets of his coat and began his trek towards the car rental place, which was about six blocks out. At this time, he'd pushed Rene to the back of his mind and was focused on his mission. He'd already determined Marvin's fate but was still indecisive of how he was going to handle Janelle, though he felt that he was closer to finding Janelle that he was Marvin.

It had taken almost twenty minutes to reach the rental place. Anthony face was numb, and it felt like his toes were longer attached to his feet. Already knowing he needed something that would blend in with everyday traffic, Anthony took it upon himself to peruse the lot, instead of lobbying assistance from any of the employees, which didn't take a full minute. With his selection in mind, he entered the establishment, and approached the desk that was occupied by a young, white female.

"Hi!" she beamed. "Welcome to Buckhead Rentals. Do you need help finding what you're looking for?"

"I've already found it."

The older model Audi was dark blue in color. Plus, it was a commonly sighted vehicle, considering its affordability. Anthony pulled the rental into the motel's parking lot, parking beside his car making sure to back into the slot aligning its trunk with that of the Lincoln. He took a second to survey the lot, which was not surprisingly empty of human life. The utility cart was parked in front of his room, so he assumed the maintenance man was inside tending to the heater.

Actuating the trunks of each car by their remotes, Anthony dismounted and retrieved the black bag containing the 9-millimeter, and Larson & Mann P.98 submachine gun he'd purchased from Blue and transferred it over to the Audi. Before closing the trunk, he extracted the 9-millimeter from the bag, holding it down by his side as he climbed back into the driver's seat and pulled off, placing the gun inside the glove compartment.

Now that he'd completed the task of acquiring another car, Anthony was ready to put something on his stomach. The drive-thru of a fast food restaurant was his best choice, being that he was trying to be as anonymous as much as he could while still stalking his part of Georgia. After consuming his meal in the restaurant's parking lot, he made the short drive to Richard Street. Parking in front of the abandoned house was totally out of the question, being that he revealed himself to the old man who turned out to be quite an observer. Therefore, he drove on, riding past Marvin's mother's home. Her truck wasn't in the driveway, which had him wondering if he should break in and wait for her to return but what would he do then? Force her to call and lure Marvin to the house? No. That would only subject her to the same fate as her son, which wouldn't be fair to her.

The digital clock on the dashboard read: 3:17P.M. Being that Anthony wasn't familiar with Marvin's mother's daily routine he had to remit his task of finding Marvin for another day. Leaving the neighborhood, he decided to drive out to his mother's locale after filling the gas tank at a nearby Quick Trip. He knew that it was risky parking several houses up from his mother's, but it was the only way he could do a proper surveillance on her place. He just hoped that the residents of the house he was now sitting in front of didn't heckle or call the police on him. Not wanting to draw any more attention to himself, Anthony cut the car off to extinguish the visible fumes blowing from the exhaust pipes of the car, then reclined his seat as far as it would go. The interior of the car was still warm but as he listened to how the wind pummeled the exterior of it, Anthony knew it wouldn't be long before the warmth dissipated, and he was sitting in the cold. He shuddered at the thought.

At almost thirty minutes later, Anthony's mother drove past him, pulling into her driveway. Helen's car wasn't trailing behind, which meant that she and Rene didn't stop by to gossip before heading out to their own home for the night. Now, Anthony watched as his mother gathered a few grocery bags from her car and made haste to the front door. Within seconds she was inside, slamming the door behind her. The Audi was still retaining its heat, but Anthony could tell that it had declined a little. Other than the occasional resident returning home from work, there was no other movement on this particular street.

After another hour had gone by, Anthony began thinking that he miscalculated his feigned departure. Perhaps he should have done it this past Monday, or maybe he should have waited until the following Monday. Either way would have given his mother ample time to…

A dark gray, mid-sized SUV drove by pulling Anthony from his reverie. Though it was not yet dark, the brake lights of the vehicle shined brilliantly as the driver bared down on the pedal to decelerate. Figuring it was another resident returning home, Anthony disregarded the vehicle to look down at his watch, figuring he would stay put until nine o'clock. By that time, he was certain that his mother would be in bed and not expecting company. This meant that he had a little over three hours before—

"Slow down, Alex!"

Though the voice sounded distant and muffled, due to the airtight windows of the Audi, there was no mistaking who it belonged to nor the name of which he'd heard. Anthony sat up in his seat just in time to see his son take heed to the admonishment of his mother, who was just rounding the SUV carrying Alex's overnight bag. Alex, in a large coat that almost seemed to swallow him up with the hood pulled over his head, had actually stopped to wait for his mother. As Anthony watched Janelle, who was clad in a long leather coat with her red micro-braids pulled into a ponytail, he began experiencing mixed emotions. Yes, he still had love for her, but the hatred lingered over his heart like a dark cloud.

At that time, Carol, who was incontestably expecting them, appeared in the doorway still wearing her work uniform. Then as if his mother hadn't scolded him almost a minute ago, Alex sprinted towards his grandmother, who scooped him up into her arms and drowned him in kisses. Once Janelle approached and the women began talking, Anthony wondered if his mother had informed Janelle of his release. Well, of course, he concluded. A blind man could see that these two women were in collusion. Janelle was hell-bent on keeping Anthony from seeing his son and being that Carol hadn't said anything to him about Alex coming over, she was just as guilty. So, how could Anthony not feel ill will towards his mother for what was playing out in front of him?

Now Anthony watched as Janelle handed the overnight bag over to Carol, kissed Alex on the cheek, then headed back to her car as Carol disappeared inside the house with Alex. He was already readjusting the seat as she mounted her vehicle. He waited until she pulled away from the house before starting the car and following her, totally unaware of the car that was parked further back down the street before he arrived and was now trailing behind him.

Chapter 21

Saturday

"So, did it hold to your standards?" Aaron Taylor asked Ebony as they exited the movie theater amidst the other movie goers.

As planned, the two of them rendezvoused on the outskirts of Linkton County before taking Ebony's car to Warner Robins, where they had lunch prior to selecting a movie. The movie turned out to be a great one, but Ebony couldn't fully focus on it because of the meeting with John Pruden at seven o'clock, which she would not be attending. Rick didn't tell her how he and Bull intended to 'handle' the investigator, but she knew better than to doubt them. Especially Rick, who'd shown his ability to eliminate problems on several occasions. He'd also cautioned her to watch her surroundings just in case Pruden was still following, and now taking pictures of her.

"It was better than I expected," she now answered his question. "I just hope that never occurs. We have enough violence going on as it is."

"Indeed," Aaron replied. They had just entered the lobby. "I just didn't see that ending coming. Them accidentally killing each other was highly unexpected."

"It was quite ingenious," Ebony commended, stopping in her tracks, causing him to do the same. "Do we have enough time for me to visit the ladies' room?"

Aaron gendered at his watch. "Hell, we have enough time to do whatever. I'm in no rush."

"Great!" She ran the back of her hand along his jaw.

"Don't let one of these women steal you away while I'm gone."

With that, she sauntered off, leaving the older man standing in the same spot blushing. This made Ebony smile to herself, knowing that she probably gave him an erection. Hell, she hadn't been with a man since Jason, and there's no telling when the last time Aaron had been intimate with his wife or any other woman for that matter. Who knows? Maybe they'd both get lucky today.

Entering the restroom, Ebony entered one of the stalls making sure to slide the bolt into place, securing the door. After wiping the toilet seat with a Santi-Wipe, she sat on the stool and retrieved the vial from her pocketbook. Seeing that it was almost empty, reminded her that she needed to get her hands on another batch asap, but for now, she intended to 'medicate' herself with the dose that she'd been craving all morning. After using her fingernail to feed her nostrils, she returned the vial, closed her eyes, and listened to the voices of the other women moving about the restroom. Most of them raving about a movie they'd just seen.

"I thought I'd have to send a rescue team in there after you," Aaron, who was still standing in the same spot, said as Ebony approached.

"Was I gone that long?"

He looked at his watch. "Almost twenty minutes."

"I think I stood in line for ten of those minutes," she lied, looping her arm through his and leading him towards the exit. "So, what are we to do now?"

"Well," Aaron started, "we've already done what we planned to do."

"That doesn't mean our date has to end," Ebony replied, smiling up at the man, who was thirteen years older than herself.

Aaron regarded her with a suspicious look. "What do you have in mind?"

"I saw a midday bar up the street from here," she told him. "Shall we?"

"I'm just along for the ride," he responded, as they exited the building, stepping out into the extremely cold weather, with her arm still looped inside his. "In fact, I consider myself kidnapped at this moment."

"Be careful!" she warned, playfully. "Some kidnapped victims end up being sexually abused."

Aaron couldn't help but laugh at the comment. Ebony could tell that he wasn't sure if she was joking or not, which she wasn't. Despite how cold it was, Ebony insides were burning with passion and the crush that now coursed through her system wasn't helping at all. In fact, the drug amplified her hormones, sending them into overdrive. She didn't know how she was going to pull it off, but Ebony had made up in her mind that she was going to have sex with Aaron today. First, she had to get him to loosen up. Perhaps, a little alcohol would do the trick.

The bar was a few blocks up from the theater, which had only taken them 7 minutes to reach. The atmosphere was warm and filled with the aroma of various cooked foods. A handful of customers were perched on stools at the bar, while others were seated at tables, eating, drinking, and conversing amongst one another. There was also a small group of people out on the dance floor having what appeared to be a dance-off to some old rap song coming from a jukebox sitting in one corner.

"That song has to be like a hundred years old." Ebony said as they settled in at the bar. "It came out around the same time you were born, right?"

"Are you saying I look a hundred years old?" Aaron posed with narrowed eyes.

"No." There was a hint of a smile on her face as she evaluated him from head to toe. "You look thirty. I guess you just have the air of a centenarian."

"I don't know if I should take that as a compliment or an insult," he confessed.

"Are you guys ordering?"

Ebony turned to face the bartender, who approached with her hair braided up into a wild mohawk, dyed pink which matched the color of her lip gloss and fingernail polish. Ruminating the warm atmosphere, she had on a blank tank top that was stretched against her large breast. She didn't have on a bra, so Ebony could clearly see the imprint of the woman's pointed nipples, which added fuel to the fire of her already heated hormones.

"Sure," Ebony answered the woman's question, looking directly into her eyes. "We'll have two cognacs with just a touch of lemon."

Aaron protested. "At this time of day?"

"Of course," Ebony replied, still holding the woman's gaze. "That's two each."

"Coming right up."

The bartender darted her eyes at Aaron, once, but proceeded to place four drinking glasses before them. After filling them all halfway with alcohol, she squeezed lemon extract into them, then decorated the rim of each glass with a slice of lemon. Ebony didn't waste time. She removed the slice of lemon from one glass, downed the liquid, then bit into the slice, separating the edible part away from the peel.

"Whoa!" exclaimed Aaron, displaying a look of disbelief. "You do know you're driving right?"

"I hope you don't think that exiguous amount of alcohol would impair my ability to operate a motor vehicle," she asserted, in a tone that she would normally use in the courtroom. "Besides, the first cup is always to the head." She nodded at the other three glasses. "It's your turn. I mean, that's if you're not scared."

Aaron maintained his look of disbelief but said nothing.

"Will you two be ordering anything from the food menu?" intervened the bartender who hadn't budged.

"Not right now, babe," Ebony answered. "Whenever we decide on anything, I'll make sure to flag you down."

"Or you can flag down one of the others."

Ebony smiled benignly at the woman. "I think I'll stick with you."

"Are you okay?" Aaron asked Ebony once the bartender made off with an amused look on her face.

"Sure, babe." She squeezed his knee, then slid one of the glasses closer to him. "Bottoms up! You only live once, and we're not getting any younger. Come on, Aaron! Show me the spirit you had at those parties back in the 15th century."

Aaron laughed as he scooped the glass off the counter. "You are something else," he told her before swallowing the alcohol in one gulp, then biting into the lemon slice.

"Oh, you haven't seen anything yet," she said standing.

"Look, I left my Cash Card in my pocketbook. I'll be right back."

"I'll pay for the drinks," Aaron protested.

"You paid for the lunch and the movie," she pointed out. "Let me handle things from here on out."

Aaron took hold of her elbow, stopping her in her tracks. "You don't think I should go out there with you?"

"Do I need a bodyguard?" she reconstructed his question. "I doubt it. I may not be trained in any form of fighting, but I do know how to run and scream like a suburban white girl if I'm being attacked. Now, relax. I'll be back in a sec."

With that, Ebony exited the building, bracing herself for the torturous wind, which really didn't seem so cold, being that her insides were warm from the shot of cognac she'd taken which was now commingled with the dosage of crush still streaming through her system. Ebony didn't leave her credit card in the car. She only used that as a pretext to journey over to the small motel that was right next door to the bar. She just hoped they were not full.

"Welcome to the Lambert Inn!" an older white female with long, red hair greeted Ebony from behind the desk. "Would you like to rent a room?"

"Do you have any available?" Ebony asked, sniffing back drainage.

"Sure do," the woman answered, a suspicious look on her face.

On her way back to the bar, Ebony made sure to retrieve her pocketbook from the car before re-entering the building where Aaron was still in the same spot. She noticed that he'd taken off his coat, which was folded on an empty stool beside him, and was turned in his seat, sipping from his second glass of cognac, smiling while watching the same group of people out on the dance floor make a mockery of various dances.

"Did you get lost?" Aaron questioned when she approached.

"I tend to do that from time to time." Instead of retaking her seat on the stool, Ebony place her pocketbook on top of it making sure to squeeze herself into the small space between hers and the one Aaron occupied intentionally brushing against him as she took hold of her second glass, taking a sip. "Are you ordering anything from the food menu?"

He now regarded her without a hint of discomfort to her proximity. "I'll have to take a raincheck. We have the grandchildren over for the weekend, and they highly insist on pizza and hot wings tonight."

"So, that means I'll have to get you home at a decent time, huh?"

"I would appreciate it." He ganders at his watch. "We probably should be on our way back now."

"It's still early," Ebony protested, taking another quaff of her drink. "Besides, I have a request."

"Which is?" Aaron inquired, now regarding her askance.

"This," she replied, nonchalantly, gripping his penis through his pants, a bit surprised to find it already fully erect.

***

6:57 P.M.

They'd been parked across the street from the diner for over ten minutes. The mom and pop hardware store had already closed for the day, so the Ford was the only vehicle in the lot, with the engine running, and exhaust fumes billowing from the rear. The humming from its idling engine and the whistling of the wind muted by the car's manufactured insulation were the only sounds they could hear while monitoring the goings of the informal restaurant, awaiting a sign of the man described to them by their boss. Bull grunted, shifting in his seat.

"What's bothering you?" Rick inquired, keeping his eyes on the diner. They were clad in their black taskforce like apparel.

"What makes you think something's bothering me?" Bull shot back, aggravation lacing his tone.

"You've been in a foul mood all day," Rick pointed out.

"Just have a lot on my mind is all."

"Like?"

Bull sighed before answering, "We're getting too old for this shit, Rick."

"Yeah, I know."

"I can't believe we're back doing the same things we were doing over eighteen years ago."

Rick now looked over at his associate. "This was your call, remember? You're the one who got arrested and insisted that I contact her. You made a deal with her that, unfortunately, included me. She held up her end. Now we're holding up ours."

"I really didn't plan on holding up my end," Bull admitted.

"Yeah, I figured that." Rick looked back toward the diner. "So, what changed your mind?"

"I knew you were gonna stick to the plan no matter what," Bull answered. "Truth be told, if it wasn't for you, I'd be on death row right now. All she did was provide you with information. You're the one who risked your freedom to make sure I got mine back. If I owe anybody, it's you. Fuck Ebony!"

Rick said nothing.

"We should make this our last job," Bull resumed. "After this, we should skip town. Start fresh in another state or country. It's not like she gonna come looking for us. Hell, she doesn't know any of her workers. We shut the operation down, and she'll go back to being a boring ass prosecutor."

Rick was still silent.

Bull sighed. "I know you won't do it. You're too loyal. That's a gift and a curse, you know. Don't get me wrong. I like Ebony. I respect her, but I'm no fool to believe she's gonna just let us go at the conclusion of our deal. She's too much like her father."

"True," Rick finally spoke. "But she's not him."

Bull studied the side of his face before speaking. "I know you're smarter than that, Rick. There's no way in hell you believe that she's gonna just let us go. Once she finds someone to replace us, we're done."

"And who is she gonna find to replace us?" asked Rick. "Anthony bailed out on her, remember?"

"Yeah, I've been thinking about that." Bull spoke as if talking to himself. "He knows enough to bring all of us down. Hell, he's a bigger threat to her than we are."

"Of course, he is," Rick acknowledged. "But considering his absence, she's going to need us to stick around longer than she intended."

"I'm forty-five years old," Bull protested. "I can't keep at this for too long."

"Hell, I'm forty- four," Rick replied, still watching the diner. "I don't plan on doing this shit forever, but a deal is a deal. We have young guys working under us. From now on, until our time is up, we'll let them play duck-duck goose. All we have to do is point and command. A person is never too old for that."

A smile spread across Bull's face. "It sounds like you're in it for the long haul, my friend, and don't think I don't see she has a crush on you."

Rick looked over at him but remained silent.

"Don't forget who her father was," Bull warned, locking eyes with him. "His blood pumps through her veins. Maybe she has a genuine crush on you or maybe she's pretending to have a crush on you in order to throw you off the trail of her true intentions. It's called deceit. Tyrone played that game better than any hum being I've ever encountered." There was a pregnant pause before he resumed. "Despite how you feel about her, the apple doesn't fall too far from the tree."

Rick directed his gaze back out towards the diner. That's when he spotted the car entering the lot.

"There he is!"

They both watched as the gray Buick sedan eased into a spot between two pick-ups. Though it was already nighttime, they were able to identify John Pruden from Ebony's delineation, by the two streetlamps overlooking the parcel, as he dismounted, clad in a dark- colored trench coat. Raking his fingers through his hair, he made for the entrance of the diner, casting about the lot as if looking for Ebony's car. If the former investigator had a disappointing look on his face, Rick and Bull couldn't see it, being that his back was to them from the moment he began walking. He entered the establishment and chose a table closest to the rear, not bothering to take his coat off as if he didn't plan on staying long. He definitely waved off the waiter, who immediately approached to take his order. After checking his watch, he rested his forearms on the table and stared out at the parking lot.

Rick's blood seemed to boil over inside him as he studied the man who should've been murdered on the same night, he took it upon himself to fondle Ebony in that same diner while threatening her with imprisonment if she didn't agree to sleep with him. Just the thought of him sitting there in high hopes of getting her in bed had Rick ready to walk right over and shoot him dead through the large window of the diner.

"I wonder how long this clown is gonna sit there before realizing he'd been stood up," Bull asserted, encroaching Rick's thoughts.

Rick didn't care to reply as he continued to watch John Pruden, who checked his watch and ran his fingers through his hair again. Instead, he thought about what Bull said about Ebony having a crush on him. It's not like she was being subtle about how she felt, but what if Bull was right? What if she was only pretending to have a crush on him in an endeavor to conceal her true intentions, and what are her true intentions? To get him to drop his guard and believe that she would really let them go free after she's done with them? Would she really—

"Come on, Sherlock Holmes!" Bull said as John Pruden stood to leave. "You'll be using your hand tonight, buddy."

The former investigator made for the exit but stopped to say something to the waitress he dismissed upon his arrival. After a succinct exchange between them, he handed her a few bills then made his exit, moving towards his car in a menacing stride. Once inside, he immediately pulled out of the parking lot, speeding up the street as if in pursuit of a fleeing suspect.

"It's on us," Bull announced, fastening his safety belt. "He used to be an investigator, so we have to assume he's smart enough to watch his rear mirrors.

"Don't worry," Rick told him, shifting the car into gear. "I got this."

Chapter 22

Sunday

Anthony exited Shop Smart carrying a plastic shopping bag containing junk food. The sun shined brightly but the pestering wind made it hard to believe that springtime was close. Anthony had intentionally left his coat inside the rented car that was now docked at one of the gas pumps. After pulling the gas tank door release, he commenced to fuel the car while surveying his surroundings through the dark lenses of the sunglasses he purchased yesterday. Everything seemed normal, though the place wasn't crowded, but as far as he could tell, nobody seemed to be paying him any attention.

Anthony still found it hard to believe that Ebony had taken his abrupt departure lightly and had not sent anyone after him. For she was a cunning individual; someone a person couldn't turn their back on without there being any consequences. So, yes, Anthony was definitely expecting her to reveal her hand at any moment now. He just hoped that whatever it was, it didn't include his mother and son.

Now back inside the warm confines of the Audi, Anthony left the gas station and drove father up the street until he came upon another gas station that sat opposite his mother's neighborhood. This was where he decided to take up post instead of sitting in front of someone's home, which would eventually draw attention to himself. From this exact store, he could see the street that Janelle would enter and the one she would exit with Alex in tow. Therefore, he parked near the tire inflation pump that sat near the main road. Leaving the engine running, he grabbed a large bag of potato chips from the plastic bag beside him and began consuming them.

It was almost four o'clock. Church service for his mother's church started at 9:00 A.M. and ended at 12:00, so he was pretty sure that his mother was at home by now, but what he wasn't sure about was if Janelle had already collected Alex, or if Carol had taken it upon herself to drop him off on her way home from service. Even if either of these did occur, it didn't matter too much to Anthony because he ascertained where Janelle lived when he followed her home on Friday. Today, he was going to trial to make sure he'd followed her to the home where his son also resided and not the home of her current lover.

It was 5:27 P.M. when Anthony spotted the dark gray mid-size SUV. He watched as it turned and disappeared down Johnson Street. Now, he knew that it was a matter of time before Janelle reappeared via Austin Street, but it seemed like Carol and Janelle had a lot to talk about because the vehicle didn't resurface until after another twenty minutes or so. He could see the top of his son's head before Janelle made a right on the main road, going back in the direction from which she'd come. Anthony swallowed the remainder of his soda and tossed the plastic bottle onto the adjacent seat before following. The expressway wasn't overflowing with traffic, so they made it to Marietta, Georgia in no time. Anthony knew that Janelle wasn't cautious enough to think someone would be following her, so he felt comfortable tailing her at a close distance as she'd taken the same route she'd taken this past Friday; but he put a little distance between them once conceding that they were coming up on Pratt Road. He managed to make the turn ten seconds behind her, parking in front of the third house that he came to, which had no vehicles in its driveway, while

Janelle pulled into the driveway of a home several houses up, parking behind a burgundy Cadillac.

Watching, Anthony saw that there was a man seated in the driver's seat of the Cadillac. He dismounted just as Janelle was getting out. She let Alex out her side. As soon as his feet touched the ground, Alex ran and jumped into the arms of the man, who greeted him with a broad smile and a kiss on the cheek. Alex was all smiles himself, which instantly filled Anthony's heart with envy. This also caused him to reflect on Leonard, the man who assisted his mother with raising him. It's bad enough that Janelle had taken his son away from him, but were she trying to make Alex forget who his real father was by rearing him with the aegis of this stranger? Anthony still didn't have a definite plan as to how he would deal with Janelle, but he was now certain of one thing: he had to extract this man from his son's life, like Leonard was extracted from his.

***

"I'm quite sure he'll question my knowledge of his whereabouts," Ebony asserted after Rick and Bull explicated their plan to her.

They called her early that morning informing her that they'd followed John Pruden from the diner to his home and had pulled an all-nighter, casing out the house to make sure that he was the only resident. As it turned out, the former investigator was a loner which seemed to avail the older men formulating a quick plan of execution. Though Ebony was leery of the part they wanted her to play, she knew that she had to trust their judgements and go along with it. It was already Sunday and she had instructed them to handle this matter before Monday. Now, they were all assembled in Ebony's living room; Rick and Bull occupying the sofa, while Ebony paced back and forth across the coffee table from them. The men were well-dressed for the mission at hand, whereas Ebony wasn't as she was clad in a pink sweatsuit and house shoes.

"You're a government official," Bull told her. "It's nothing for you to acquire someone's address."

"True," She stopped pacing to face them. "But this guy is smart. What if he suspects that something is not right, and denies me entrance?"

"Then he'll die the moment he steps foot outside his house tomorrow," answered Rick in his normal composed tone. "If necessary, we'll sit outside his house all day. The moment he comes out, we'll ambush him."

"What about cameras?" Ebony inquired. "I'm quite sure—"

"There are no visible cameras on the outside," Bull interrupted. "We made sure to look for those."

"It's on you," Rick told her, checking his watch. "That's a plan of action with a contingency. If you're in, I advise we go ahead and move now. I don't think he'll have his guards up if you show up at a decent time."

"Then I suggest we hope to it."

"One more thing before we go," said Bull standing.

"What's that?" Ebony asked, sensing something was wrong.

"Being that Anthony is gone—" he started.

Ebony cut in, "I'll need you two to hang on a little longer. At least until I can find someone to replace you, and I'm still waiting for closure of my mother's murder, as you'd promised."

Rick and Bull left the house to allow Ebony to prepare herself for the mission. Once finished, she exited the house wearing her black leather trench coat. She gave the Solid Nation Members at the end of the street a mere glance before climbing into her car and backing out of the driveway.

Rick and Bull were parked at the top of the street in another car. As planned, she followed them until they pulled behind and abandoned building where the men got out. Rick was carrying a blonde wig and Bull a license plate and screwdriver. She rolled her window down as Rick approached.

"Put this on!" he told her, proffering the wig. "Once Bull switches your license plate, we'll roll out. Remember when we get there, circle the block. We should be in position by the time you arrive."

"Why do I need the wig?"

"For the same reason you need the license plate," he answered, looking toward the rear of the car where Bull was applying the plate. "If you're spotted, the police will get the wrong description of you and the wrong license number belonging to another Cadillac of the same make and model as yours."

"Let's move!" Bull said, approaching, handing Ebony's license plate over to her in which she placed on the seat beside her, and began adjusting her hair in order to place the wig.

"Are you having reservations about this?" Rick asked as Bull headed back to the other car.

"There's no room for reservations." Done wrestling with the wig, she looked up at him. "He made his move; now it's our turn."

Rick gave a slight nod in response, then headed back to the stolen car. As she followed them, Ebony mind reverted back to Aaron Taylor and what transpired between then in the motel room yesterday. At first Aaron protested, saying that he had to get home to his wife and grandchildren, but when Ebony started taking off her clothes and was down to her panties and bra, he could no longer stand there in the threshold of the room and watch. He closed the door and pretty much tackled her onto the bed, while drowning her in kisses and simultaneously struggling to disrobe. Ebony's deduction of Aaron being divested of sex for a long period of time could have very well been true, considering the way he edaciously performed oral sex on her before climbing on top and pounding her insides with all his might. His lack of sex, commingled with the fact that he was trying to rush home to his family was incontestably the reason why it didn't last for more than ten minutes. Surprisingly, he'd fallen asleep afterwards and she purposefully let him sleep until nine o'clock.

Now, Ebony's mind was back on business as Bull turned onto Mildred Road. She continued on as planned, sticking to the main road, moving past several small businesses that glowed in the nighttime with neon signs of various shapes, sizes and colors. She didn't know what turn to make, in order to begin circling the block, so Ebony drove at a length until she came upon a fast food restaurant in which she entered the lot and circled around. Back onto the main road, heading in the opposite direction, she drove slower, hoping to give the men sufficient time to get in position. When she entered on Mildred, Ebony drove past rows of houses on each side, purposely passing John Pruden home, where the car she'd seen him drive to the diner was parked in the driveway beside the one she'd seen outside the church at Jason's funeral. Had she been a passing resident and not cognizant of what was afoot, she would not have noticed the dark figures of Rick and Bull squatting on the side of the house.

After turning her car around in someone's driveway, Ebony cut her lights before pulling in behind the former government official's cars, lest her beams gave away the older men's positions. Cutting the engine, Ebony dismounted feeling the cold wind immediately assail her bare legs. Her heels click-clacked on the concrete walkway that was lined with marigolds and led up to the front door. Just in case Pruden was watching her from the front window, she swayed to the side a bit, to make it appear as though she was possibly inebriated. Reaching the door, she rang the doorbell, but didn't hear any indications of it beyond the door, but waited, fighting the urge to look in the direction of where the men lay in wait as she swatted at the insects that were drawn to the light that she now stood under. Just as she decided that she would try knocking, the occupant's face appeared in the transom, and yes, he was scowling at her.

Perhaps. He had company. Still intending to play her role, Ebony placed a hand to her forehead and took a half-step back as if not able to fully maintain her balance. She knew that such display would disarm the most skeptical human being. Just then, she heard the sound of security locks being disengaged. Momentarily, the door opened slowly on its hinges, revealing John Pruden, who was clad in tan slacks, a white, long sleeve shirt, and loafers.

"What are you doing here?" he hissed, darting his eyes beyond her, perhaps to make sure none of his neighbors were witnessing him get a visit from what appeared to be a prostitute in a ridiculous blonde wig with long locks.

"We had an appointment, remember?" Ebony slurred, tilting her head as if confused.

"That was yesterday." There was anger in his voice now. "And someone took it upon themselves to make me out to look like a fool."

"Something came up that needed my immediate attention," she purported. "It's not like I had a way of contacting you."

John Pruden looked as though he was considering her excuse, as he raked his fingers through his hair before crossing his arms over his chest.

"I'm here now," she pressed, unbuttoning her coat, and pulling it open to reveal the red Angela Cofer lingerie set, trimmed in black lace. "Is your offer still on the table?"

The concupiscence in his eyes stood out like a sore thumb as he gander at what he been wanting for God knows how long. Though his visage didn't show it, Ebony was sure that he was mentally celebrating what he thought was an accomplishment. After a few seconds of staring, Pruden looked around once more before stepping aside to allow her entrance. Glad to be getting out of the cold air in her scant accouterments, Ebony pulled her coat tight around her, making sure to swerve a little before crossing the threshold where she took a few steps, and purposely fell to her knees on the carpeted living room floor. She was sure this had momentarily drawn his attention, though she didn't look up to see. Just then, Ebony heard the sound of the door being crashed, which was almost in harmony with John Pruden painful cry, a millisecond before his body collapsed onto the floor a couple feet away from the spot that she was getting up from. Before the former investigator could scramble to his feet, Bull was on top of him, pounding him with his huge, gloved fists, while Rick locked the door before heading toward the kitchen.

John Pruden's plea for his life echoed in Ebony's ears as she rounded the coffee table to the sofa where she donned a pair of black gloves from her coat. Not bothering to fasten her coat for how warm the atmosphere was, she let it hang open as she sat with her legs crossed and her hands folded in her lap. Momentarily, Rick re-entered the room carrying a wooden dining chair which he placed opposite the coffee table, facing in Ebony's direction. He only gave her a mere glance before assisting Bull with planting a now battered looking John Pruden in the chair with redundant force. He was panting as he locked his swollen eyes onto Ebony, but the fight in him had abated. At this time, Bull had produced a band of duct tape, and Rick was screwing a silencer onto the barrel of a silver revolver. Though Ebony kept her eyes on Pruden who seemed oblivious to the implements of her men, she noticed how Bull kept cutting his eyes in her direction as if distracted by what she had on.

"It's on you," Rick told Ebony, handing her the gun across the table. He then regarded his comrade. "Any time tonight, big guy."

"It doesn't matter what you do to me," Pruden insisted through clenched teeth, while Bull commenced to tape his legs to the chair. "I've already sent my findings to my boss."

Ebony fixed him with a broad smile. "Really? And which boss is this? Surely, you're not talking about Chief Investigator Livingston?"

"Once he views the file," he persisted, "it'll be curtains for you and your puppets."

"Nice try, Mr. Pruden," Ebony replied, shaking her head. "I had a private chat with Livingston this past Tuesday." She paused to let her words sink in. "Yes, I know all about you being terminated in December."

Her words had hit home because apprehension was now etched on his face. "What a shame," she resumed. "You went to all this trouble to get me into your bed, and still didn't succeed, but I have to admit that you had a nice ploy going, which has me wondering how many women you've ensnared with it."

"Arm!" Bull demanded after binding Pruden's legs.

"The photos you took of me," Ebony went on. "Where are they?"

The ex-government official remained silent. Ebony looked over at Rick, who was standing off to the side with his arms folded over his chest. "Search the house!" she told him. "Find those photos. They should be in a manila folder."

"I see you have these boys trained," John Pruden sneered as Rick set out to do as directed.

Whack!

"Ah!" he cried out in pain from the close-handed blow that Bull delivered to his face, that breached the side of his top lip, which blood trickled from.

"I think you may wanna watch what comes out of that mouth of yours," Ebony warned, lying the gun on the sofa beside her and folding her hands in her lap again. "If I'm not mistaken, that was and autonomous act in which I had no influence over."

"Should I tape his mouth?" Bull asked, having completed his task of incapacitating the man.

She waved a dismissive hand. "I don't see any reason why. Besides, I think our friend has a lot to say in his last hours. Right, John?"

"You won't get away with this," he replied, locking eyes onto hers as the blood continued its stream from his lip to his chin and onto his clothes. "You may escape the authorities, but you won't escape him. He knows your every move. He knows how careless you are. He watches you like a hawk but moves like a cobra. I assume he's waiting for the right time to strike." A crooked smile slowly creased his face. "I guess your father didn't know that something he'd done would come back upon his seed."

"Don't go getting all delusional on me John," Ebony said, just as Rick approached and placed a manila folder onto the table. She looked up at him. "John was just telling me how God is waiting for the right time to strike me down, as if I didn't already know this."

"I'm not talking about God," John protested. "I was—"

"There's something you need to see," Rick intervened with a serious look on his face.

Ebony darted her eyes to John, then back at Rick.

"Right now," he prompted before turning on his heels and heading back in the direction in whence he'd come.

Ebony huffed, shot Bull a look as if telling him to keep an eye on the hostage then leaving the gun on the sofa, followed the older man to a room that had been converted into a workstation, whereas a computer and its essential components occupied a metal desk amid two cameras, video recorder, and several memory cards scattered about. Rick stood aside, quietly, for he didn't have to direct her attention to what he insisted she needed to see because what he was referring to couldn't be missed by a blind man.

Ebony stood in awe as she rivetted her eyes on the large array of 7 by 10 photos that were arbitrarily placed along the walls like exhibits at a museum. As if by some magnetic force, she moved slowly about the room, individually surveying each item that pretty much showed that John Pruden had been running surveillance on her for quite some time, considering the dates at the bottom of each photo. There were pictures of her leaving her house for work, pumping gasoline into the tank of her car, entering a restaurant, leaving the same restaurant, and several shots of her jogging through Hester Park on separate days. There were also several photographs of her leaving the courthouse, accompanied by Deputy Aaron Taylor, which were drastically disturbing, being that Taylor's face had been blotted out with a black marker in all of them. In one area of the wall, there were pictures of some Caucasian male, whom Ebony figured to be one of John Pruden's investigative projects. The older white man wasn't familiar to her, but the older-model, dark green Cadillac he was shown climbing from was. She now turned to face Rick, who was standing with his hands in his pockets, watching her. "I don't think I need to tell you what needs to be done."

Rick didn't reply.

"We've been here too long," Ebony pointed out, then made for the living room where she violently snatched the revolver off the sofa and towered over Pruden, who didn't seem threatened as he looked up into her eyes. "So, you've basically been stalking me like some psychopath from a suspense movie. It had never been about the death of my fiancé, Hell, you weren't even the initial investigator on the case, but I assume you found me attractive on our first encounter, and concocted this little scheme, hoping to get your filthy ass hands on something you probably can't handle. You let your small ass dick override that small as brain of yours, John."

"It won't be long before you join me in hell," he snarled.

"It may actually be longer than you think, John." Ebony combed the fingers of her free gloved hand through his hair, as she'd seen him do numerous of times. "I would love to stay and chat for a little while longer, but I have to get up in the morning. You know, some people still have jobs to go to. However, give my regards to Jason, will you?"

With that, Ebony fired a slug into the left side of his chest. John's eyes which had never deviated from her, enlarged with the promise of death and his breathing had become audibly laborious. His mouth opened as if to say something, but nothing came out. His strenuous breathing and whatever Rick were doing in the other room to disencumber its incriminating content, were the only noise in the house. Finally, John's head slowly dropped forward as he 'gave up the ghost.'

"Here." Ebony handed the gun over to Bull, who was regarding her impassively. "I'm going home. Rick's gonna need your help in the other room. I'll make contact tomorrow to discuss how we're gonna handle the situation with Anthony."

Chapter 23

"Is that all from the defense?"

It seemed like it had taken forever for Monday to come. Plus, last night was a drag to Ebony, being that those images of John Pruden and what she discovered at his home had deprived her of a good night's rest. She couldn't believe he'd been following her around for a long period of time, stalking her, and she had not the slightest clue about it. Just the thought of him violating her privacy rights in such a manner overwhelmed her with the sense of being naked and vulnerable. The more she thought about it, the angrier she'd become. That, commingled with the fact that she'd run out of crush was a bad combination to be explored. So, it was fathomable why she'd been in an agitated state all morning.

"Yes, Your Honor," the public defender answered the judge's question before re-taking his seat at the defense table beside his client.

Judge Jackson turned his attention to Ebony. "State, your reasons why the defendant, Mr. Hargrove, should not be granted a new trial."

"For one," Ebony replied not bothering to stand, "the defendant's claim of ineffective assistance of counsel, is null and void, as well as defendant's claim of miscarriage of justice, and prosecutorial misconduct, being that the defendant failed successfully at demonstrating that he suffered actual prejudice."

"Your Honor?" Attorney Verne Lancaster was back on his feet. "If I may, I would like to bring to the court's attention that my client's argument, corroborated with the trial's transcripts, substantially validates his claim of the ineffective assistance of counsel, prosecutorial misconduct, and also miscarriage of justice, which are blatant violations of the 6th and 14th amendments of the United States Constitution."

"Prior to defendant's trial," Ebony countered with little more force, "and according to aforementioned transcript, defendant's counsel filed appropriate motions, including discovery motions and additional motions attacking the eyewitness identification and fingerprint evidence. At trial, defendant's counsel conducted a vigorous defense on behalf of the defendant. Counsel made appropriate objections during the trial, cross-examined the State's witnesses in a thorough and effective manner, presented an alibi witness on behalf of the defendant, and made cogent and reasonable arguments to the jury. I mean what else did the defendant expect from the counsel? A proposal?"

"Let's refrain from inappropriate remarks, Ms. Davis," the judge warned, fixing her with a stern look.

"However," she continued, returning the look, "the State's review of the entire transcript reveals that the defendant received effective assistance of counsel, pursuant to the standard announced in Strickland versus Washington, and adopted by the Georgia Supreme Court in Smith versus Francis. Moreover, the record reflects no evidence of a miscarriage of justice, nor prosecutorial misconduct, as you can see for yourself, Your Honor, within the documents that have been properly placed before you."

Judge Jackson scowled at her for a brief moment before perusing the indicated papers in front of him. While he was doing this, the defense attorney re-took his seat as Ebony wondered how things were going in Judge Manning's courtroom with Samanta and Larry Hendrix, on the jury selection for the trial that they were prosecuting together. Though she didn't agree with the two working alongside each other, Ebony did want to drop in to see how her friend was handling herself, which was why she'd been anticipating a recess, so she could do just that.

"Mr. Lancaster?" Judge Jackson finally looked up. "According to the transcript of Mr. Hargrove's trial, there are no signs of prosecutorial misconduct, miscarriage of justice, nor ineffective assistance of counsel. Plus, the evidence in the case was quite overbearing, which brings me to my final decision. I, Judge Jackson, on the twenty-sixth day of February, of the year of two thousand and twenty-four, hereby deny motion for new trial, filed by Attorney Verne Lancaster, in respects to his client Mr. Randy Hargrove. Defendant will have sixty days to appeal this matter to the Court of Appeals. Prisoner may be taken into custody."

While the defense attorney gathered his things to leave and the defendant was being escorted from the room by Deputy Taylor, who'd done his best to avoid eye contact with Ebony, the judge asked, "What is your next cause?"

"Well, Your Honor," Ebony started, "being that two have been rescheduled, the next one, which is a plea and arraignment, is set up for two o'clock."

"Then, we can go ahead and get that one out the way, right?"

"Not without the defendant, Your Honor."

"And where's the defendant?"

"She's currently out on bail," Ebony answered, just as Aaron Taylor re-entered the courtroom. "And being that her case is scheduled for two o'clock, I seriously doubt she'd be anywhere near this place at a quarter past eleven."

"Well, I guess I have no choice but to call an early recess," the judge said, which was music to Ebony's ears.

"We'll reconvene at approximately one-thirty." Judge Jackson was the first to exit the courtroom, via the door to his chambers.

Ebony was half-expecting for Aaron Taylor to make his way over to her table, and offer to buy her lunch, but while getting her things together, she peered up to see him conversing with the court stenographer as if to further dodge her being that 'good morning' was all he'd said to her thus far. Ebony didn't mind. For she knew that his conscience was eating at him for giving in to his appetite, and committing the worst sin that a married individual could commit, which is something she was gratefully free of, though she had other things nagging at her psyche, more darker things.

After depositing her briefcase in her office, Ebony made it up to Judge Amber Manning's courtroom, where there were a number of people sitting and standing around in the hallway, whom Ebony assumed were there to testify as to what they knew of the case being prosecuted beyond those walls. Without a word to either of them, Ebony peered through the glass doors. Standing with her back against the inner doors was a white female deputy, whose name Ebony was not familiar with. As if sensing her standing there, the court officer turned around with a blank expression on her face. Seeing that she wasn't making any attempt to do anything other than stare, Ebony had to gesture for her to approach. The officer accessed the first set of doors with her keys, which led her into a small, insulated area.

"Do you plan on sitting in, Ms. Davis?" the deputy asked, once she got the second pair of doors open.

"Only for a few," Ebony answered. "Are they still doing jury selection?"

The woman shook her head. "No. That was completed over an hour ago. The actual trial is taking place at this very moment, and I assume that you already know that the media is present."

"Is Barbara Hutchins present?"

"Seated on the front row like a basketball coach," the officer quipped with a grin on her face. "Do you still wanna sit in?"

"Of course."

The deputy led Ebony into the courtroom that consisted of three news crews, who were stationed at the rear, 13 jury members seated in the jury box, another court officer who was standing between the jury box and witness stand where a young-looking female to be no more than nineteen years of age was seated. Judge Amber Manning, who seemed bored out her mind, a Caucasian attorney and his client seated at the defense table, Barbara Hutchins, who was sitting on the front row, directly behind the State's table where Larry Hendrix was seated, the stenographer, and Samantha Gordon, who was standing at the lectern examining the witness. Samantha, Hendrix, and Hutchins hadn't noticed her arrival, Ebony quickly took a seat on the row next to the last.

"At what time of day was this, Ms. Bell?" Samantha was asking the witness.

"It was after five in the evening," she answered. "I can't say exactly but I know for sure that it hadn't reach six o'clock."

"And what was the lighting condition?"

"It was still daytime. The sun was still out."

"You may continue," Samantha told her.

"Well," Ms. Bell started, "as I said, my boyfriend and I were standing at the bus stop waiting for the bus. I remember hearing a loud scream, but it was so distant, it sounded like someone, a child, maybe, was having fun. I mean, we were just outside of the apartment, so it was a possibility. Anyway, moments after hearing the scream, we saw a man emerge from the woods across the street from where we stood. He—"

"Let me stop you again, Ms. Bell," Samantha cut her off.

"The man you saw emerge from the woods, is he in this courtroom today?"

The witness darted her eyes to the defense table before giving Samantha a slight nod. "Yes, he is."

"Could you point him out, and tell me what he's wearing?"

She pointed towards the defense table at the bulk of a man seated beside the defense attorney. "He's right over there wearing a gray suit and red tie."

"Let the record reflect that the witness has identified the defendant, Mr. William Curtain," promulgated Samantha.

"Reflected," Judge Manning intoned.

"Now," Samantha resumed, "to clear up something for the record, when you testified to hearing a scream. It seemed as though you were implying that you were the only one to hear it. Did your boyfriend hear it?"

"No," she answered. "He had ear pods in his ears listening to music from his phone."

"Did he have anything over his eyes, sunglasses, maybe?"

"No."

"So, he was able to see the defendant, Mr. Curtain, emerge from—"

"Objection!" The defense attorney was now on his feet, clad in a dark blue suit.

"Under what grounds, Mr. Brantly?" Judge Manning inquired.

"Your Honor," he began, "it is not the witness place to testify on behalf of another witness, which would definitely be hearsay, Plus, the prosecutor is misleading the witness."

"Your Honor," Samantha stood her ground, "the witness has already testified to seeing the defendant emerge from the wooden area, so the question wasn't at all misleading."

"Yes, she did testify to that on record," Manning acknowledged. "But by law, no witness can testify on behalf of another witness, unless the latter is unable to, due to certain conditions, not if the witness is already set to testify on his own behalf. Is the witness set to testify on his own behalf?"

"Yes, Your Honor," Brantly answered.

"Does the witness suffer from any kind of condition that would encumber him doing so?"

"Not to my knowledge, Your Honor."

"State?"

"No, Your Honor," answered Samantha.

"Objection sustained."

"Thank you, Your Honor!" the attorney said before retaking his seat.

Samantha directed her attention back to the witness. "Ms. Bell, do you remember what the defendant was wearing on the date in question?"

"Blue jean shorts," she answered eyes to the ceiling as if calling up the image in her memory bank. "A yellow shirt with some kind of black logo on it and some brown, high top shoes."

"Did you notice anything peculiar about his accouterments?"

The witness looked genuinely confused. "His what?"

"His clothing," Samantha rectified. "Did anything about them stand out to you?"

"They were blood-stained."

"Are you sure it was blood?" questioned Samantha. "Could he not have wasted some kind of beverage on himself?"

"It's possible," Ms. Bell replied. "But his demeanor is what had me under the impression that it was blood."

"And what was his demeanor like at that time?"

"'It was almost scary." She shot a quick glance over at the defense table before continuing. "He emerged from the woods in a menacing stride, both of his hands were balled into fists. His face was angrily contorted, and his eyes were filled with rage.

"And what was his distance between you and the defendant at this time?"

"I really can't say," the witness answered slowly.

"Picture yourself standing at that bus stop right now, "Samantha assisted. "Try to give me a rough estimate from where you are to the rear of the courtroom."

"Probably from here to where that lady is sitting."

Well, thanks a lot! Ebony thought as Samantha, Larry Hendrix, Barbara Hutchins, and everybody else, turned their attention towards her. She was almost certain that the three cameras had panned in her direction. Though she was aware of her colleagues watching her, Ebony kept her attention on the witness to preclude making eye contact with either of them.

"So, it's safe to say that you had a clear and unobstructed view of Mr. Curtain, right?" Samantha resumed, regaining everyone's attention.

The witness nodded. "Yes."

"And what did he do after emerging from the wooded area?"

"He didn't stop," she answered. "In that same menacing stride, he headed up the street."

Samantha asked. "Did he even look in your direction?"

"It seemed like he was looking directly at us," Ms. Bell replied. "But his eyes were…Maybe he was on some kind of drugs or something."

"What did you and your boyfriend do at that time?"

"We just stared at each other in disbelief," said the witness. "I mean, it was already rare to see a white person in this particular neighborhood, but at that time, our bus had arrived. We entertained the thought of him murdering somebody in those woods but didn't know for sure until seeing it on the news the very next day."

"What did you do then?"

"Jacob and I went to the police station on that day and looked through computerized photos with a detective."

"Separately?"

"Yes."

"Were you able to pick anybody out?"

"Yes."

"And whom did you pick out?"

Ms. Bell nodded towards the defense table, "William Curtain."

"Thank you, Ms. Bell!" Samantha turned to the judge. "No further questions, Your Honor."

***

Anthony manages to leave the motel a little after 5 A.M. and drove out to Richard Street with the intent to follow Marvin's mother for today, hoping she'd lead him to her son. Considering what the old man said about Marvin possible being arrested again, Anthony had taken the initiative to call Fulton and Dekalb County jails last night only to be informed that neither facility housed anyone by the name of Marvin Harris.

Making it to Richard Street, Anthony drove past the old man's house, where it seemed as though every light inside was on, which didn't surprise him one bit. There seemed to be no sign of movement inside Marvin's mother's home. As he drove by it, he noticed a car pulling from the driveway of another house. The male occupant, who had on some company uniform, only shot Anthony a mere glance as they passed each other. The house he came from had no other vehicle in its driveway. Considering the man was on his way to work, Anthony made a U-turn at the end of the street, and parked in front of the house that was a few houses up and across the street from Marvin's mother's adobe, making sure to extinguish the lights and kill the engine.

It was close to ten o'clock when Marvin's mother finally exited her home clad in a large overcoat that seemed to swallow her small, 5'6 frame, though the weather wasn't as cold as it's been over the weekend. With her blonde locks protruding from under a brown skullcap, Louise Atkins climbed into her GMC Denali and started the engine. The rear windows were tinted, but the front windows were obfuscated by frost, so he really couldn't see what she was doing until he saw the flick of what appeared to be a lighter, and assumed she was lighting a cigarette.

Considering the frost on his own windows, Anthony started the Audi, not worrying about being spotted by Louise, whom he figured would drive off in the opposite direction, to gain access to the main road. Momentarily, with her windows as clear a wine glass, she backed out of the driveway, and rode off in the opposite direction. Anthony didn't linger. He put the car into gear and followed. Before she blew her horn, he already spotted the older man standing out on his front porch, waving at her as she passed, then like the true 'watch dog' he proven to be, he shifted his gaze to the car coming up behind her. Although Anthony had on a small ballcap, he still turned his head, feigning interest in the houses on the other side of the street. After stopping for gas, Louise drove out to Wanda Frederick's Home and Garden Warehouse. Anthony made sure to park further away from the building but close enough to not look out of place or draw suspicion from any onlookers.

The building was manufactured with extremely large windows to analogically mimic a greenhouse, so he could pretty much see what was going on within the establishment and he could definitely see Louise Atkins as she moved about the place, selecting items with one of the male customer service workers pushing a cart behind her. Needing something to occupy his mind for the time being. Anthony turned on the radio, then surveyed the area as an old song by Toni Braxton poured through the speakers at a low volume. While taking stock of his surroundings, he again wondered why Ebony hadn't sent anyone after him. This wasn't like her at all. Just the quietude of the whole situation had him on pins and needles. Perhaps, she was waiting him out, anticipating the right time to strike. Now, he was entertaining the thought of going after her, first. Of course, he would have to liquidate Rick and Bull also. With them out of the way, his mind would be more at ease.

At approximately 11:38, the older woman finally exited the store, followed by the same male employee who was pushing her loaded cart behind her. Once he loaded her purchased items into the rear compartment of her SUV, she handed him some bills, then climbed into the driver's seat as the help made his way back towards the building. Louise started the truck but made no endeavor to pull off. Anthony saw her put her cellular up to her ear. Seconds into her conversation, she appeared to become upset, considering the jerking of her head and the gesture she made with her free hand. After a minute of this, she concluded the call, then lit up another cigarette, perhaps with the false hope that the poisonous substance would emancipate her of all her worries. Momentarily, Louise was driving towards the exit of the lot and Anthony didn't bother with being cautious as he followed her for another thirty minutes or so before they entered the parking lot of some unpopular restaurant that was packed with a lunch hour crowd.

There was no drive-in service window, so he figured she would be eating in. Therefore, Anthony managed to claim a parking spot before she could decide on one, though she was able to secure one close to the entrance. Anthony was hungry himself and now inquisitive about the comestible of the unfamiliar restaurant but didn't want to risk the older woman getting a look at his face or anyone else recognizing him from his 15 minutes of fame that he received for the bank heist.

From where he was parked, Anthony could see where Louise Atkins had taken a seat, and began typing away on her mobile device. As he watched her, wondering why she hadn't ordered anything before taking a seat, a car slowly passing by drew his attention. He looked and for some strange reason was surprise to see that it was the blonde in the red sedan. The same blonde he figured to be Louise's housekeeper. He couldn't see where she parked for the array of vehicles blocking his line of vision, but she came back into view as she neared the entrance of the restaurant clad in her black, leather trench coat, dark blue dress pants, and heels with curly locks cascading down her shoulders.

As expected, she entered and took a seat across from the older woman, handing her some papers in which the older woman took a moment to peruse before regarding her tablemate. While the two women confabulated, Anthony concentrated on the younger one. Despite the distance, he was starting to see some familiarity in her. Of course, there was an affinity between the two, but the younger one looked vaguely familiar. At this time, he was ruling her out as a housekeeper. She was definitely some kin to Louise Atkins and who was more apt to lead him to Marvin than his very own sister? This revelation has most certainly changed things up a bit. Just then the two women got up from the table, with Louise leading the way towards the cashier's counter. After exchanging a few words with the male manager, they were allowed through the employee's door as if they owned the place. While Anthony was trying to make some sense of this, he saw movement from the corners of his eyes, that drew his attention. As he now looked out through the windshield at the person that seemed to have stopped in their tracks and was watching him. All he could do was stare back at them, while wondering how they'd managed to spot him, though he was in an utterly different vehicle with a ball cap pulled low over his head.

Oh, shit! he thought as they crossed the lot, moving in his direction. There was no way that he could avoid the encounter, so he had no other choice but to let the driver's side window down when they approached.

"I thought you were back in Macon," Rene said, accusingly, giving him a look of suspicion.

"I had to come back up on business," he replied, hoping she'd think he was referring to dealing drugs and not hunting down people he intended to cause harm to.

"Does your mom know you're back?"

"Not yet," Anthony answered, eyeing her, now realizing that she had on a gray jean suit and not her work uniform. "I assume this is your off day?"

"I had an appointment to see my physician," she told him, then jerked a thumb toward the restaurant. "Are you coming or going?"

"I haven't decided yet."

"They have some really great food," Rene offered. "In fact, I'm treating you to lunch. Are you allergic to fish?"

"Not that I know of."

"Great! I'll be right back."

Anthony's eyes were on her derriere as she sauntered off, while his mind was telling him that he should be as far from that place as possible by the time she returned. Rene's presence could complicate matters, which was something he didn't need at the moment. He didn't want to make her any more suspicious than she already was by intentionally pulling a disappearing act on her. For if she wasn't planning on informing his mother of this encounter, then such as stunt would definitely prompt her to do so. Therefore, he decided to stay and see how things would play out.

Rene had two people ahead of her in the ordering line, and Louise and her daughter were still somewhere in the back of the establishment. Now, he was wondering what he would do if the women exited the building before Rene. Well, he didn't have to find out because almost ten minutes later, Rene exited the restaurant carrying a plastic bag containing two Styrofoam trays. Anthony rolled his window down, expecting her to hand him one of the trays but instead she circled the car and climbed in beside him.

"Fish, fries, hushpuppies and slaw," she announced handing him one of the trays before opening the other one up on her lap. "I've been craving fish all morning."

"So, what are you seeing a physician for?" Anthony inquired, opening his tray, and eating one of the fries that seemed to have a little too much salt on it.

"A car accident that I had over a year ago." Then she looked as if she remembered something. "Damn!"

"What?"

"I forgot to order drinks."

Anthony had a plastic bag containing junk food he'd purchased earlier on the back seat. Reaching back, he retrieved two of the bottled waters, handing one to her.

"They're still cool," he said, just as the red sedan drove by, the younger woman leaving.

"All the necessities for a stake-out huh?" Rene jested with a smirk on her face as she opened the bottle to drink from it.

"What are you getting at?" Anthony asked, now watching Louise drive by with a cigarette dangling from her lips.

Rene twisted the cap back on her bottle before answering. "Nothing. It's just that when I first spotted you, you looked like you were casing out the place. I hope I'm not in the way."

Rene was no longer smiling and considering the seriousness of her inflection, Anthony couldn't help but wonder if she was making furtive reference to the bank situation he'd gotten caught up in over a year ago. That's when it finally dawned on him that she was possibly aware of that arrest, either from his mother or the World Broadcasting News. Perhaps, at this moment, she was letting him know that if he was planning to rob the restaurant, she was not going to be an albatross, and that his secret was safe with her. He didn't doubt that at all.

"That's not the kind of business I'm here to handle," he finally said, hoping to sway her mind away from that thought. "Despite how it looks—"

"Don't worry," she cut him off. "I don't judge people for the mistakes they make, nor the lives they choose to live. Hell, I'm not perfect myself."

With that she continues to consume her meal. Anthony couldn't concentrate on his food for watching her. At this moment, he was regarding her in a new light. He could definitely see himself committing to her once his vendetta with Janelle and Marvin was over and done with. She already had his mother's approval, which was a major plus on her behalf. He just hated the fact that she'd chosen this particular restaurant to satisfy her craving for fish, which caused him to miss out on following the younger woman to her adobe, and possibly to Marvin.

Oh well, he thought, figuring he may as well make the best of it. "So, what do you have planned for the rest of the day?" Anthony finally asked.

"I'll be babysitting later on."

"Babysitting who?"

"My mama and daughter," she answered, smiling, taking another sip of her water. "I have my mom's car, so she'll be carpooling with your mom, but I have to pick Rachel up from school. That's when I become Cinderella tending to their every need." She paused, locking eyes with him. "Until then, I have the house to myself. It would be nice to have a little company."

***

Due to the light caseload for the day Judge Jackson courtroom adjourned a little after four o'clock, which was a lot more convenient for Ebony, considering what she had to do. Thankful for the extra time, she didn't plan on wasting it, waiting for Samantha and she certainly didn't want to see if Aaron Taylor was going to offer to escort her to her car, as she rushed from the courtroom. Leaving him assisting the stenographer with disassembling her machine. Once gathering her pocketbook from the office, Ebony made it out the building unscathed. Knowing that she had to give her car a couple of minutes to warm up, Ebony took that moment to call Rick from her pre-paid cellular phone.

"I'm listening," Rick answered, shortly.

"Go ahead and move out!" she told him. "I'm on my way."

It took almost 30 minutes for Ebony to reach Location 3. She already told Rick not to drive that damned unmarked police cruiser, so she immediately spotted his car the moment she pulled into the lot of Clubhouse Grocers. Parking beside his car that was still running, Ebony dismounted with her keys, pre-paid phone, and prickled hairbrush.

"I haven't heard anything on that," Ebony said upon climbing in beside him, making sure to put her seatbelt on, lest the older man castigates her about it.

"Maybe he hasn't been discovered yet," Rick replied, backing his car out its parking spot.

"Were those things properly disposed of?" She was now using the mirror visor, while trying to brush her long, jet black hair back to a presentable state.

"They were burned."

"Did you see them burned?" Ebony was hoping that Rick didn't delegate this task to Bull, or any of their subordinates.

He now regarded her through his mirror-tinted sunglasses. "I burned them myself," he told her. "Everything in that room was destroyed, along with other things we found throughout the house."

"Thank you so much," she said, closing the visor, and sliding the brush into one of the pockets on her coat. "I knew that I could depend on you."

"How much do you know about this guy we're going to meet?" Rick questioned, now driving along the main road.

"We've already been through this," answered Ebony. "All I know is the name he gave me that night at the bar. I don't even remember what he looks like." She looked over at him. "Despite the convincing story I gave him about my sister cheating husband, do you think I made a bad decision by putting him on Anthony's trail?"

"I really can't say if it was a bad decision," the older man responded. "I just think that it would've been more efficient to use one of our own men."

"Anthony knows all of them."

"Suppose he knows your guy?" Rick shot back. "Suppose they're childhood buddies or something? Suppose your guy on his first day of trailing Anthony, pulled his coattail about his wife's sister hiring him to follow him and they both come up with a plan to lure us into a trap?"

"That's a very nice deduction," Ebony commented. "However, I've already toyed with that idea. We can make a million and one suppositions, but we'll never know what's what until we cross that bridge. It's all a gamble, Rick. We just have to hope for the best but be prepared for the worse."

The two of them only made small talk for the remainder of the ride to Atlanta, which took close to 2 hours. Ebony had chosen the rendezvous spot based on her knowledge from when she visited with Carol Jenkins for the first time and was able to give Rick accurate instructions on how to get to it.

True to his word, Zoe was already there, his burgundy Dodge Gladiator that was equipped with large chrome wheels, sat conspicuously amongst the other vehicles in the mall's parking lot. Rick didn't have to explain to Ebony why he'd chosen to slowly circle the entire lot before parking. She knew that he was cautiously taking stock of the area to make sure this wasn't the trap he warned her about on the drive down. She was also looking around for any signs of danger. Once seeing that everything was clear, Rick parked at a distance but in position to where he could keep an eye on the Dodge. They exchanged glances before Ebony dismounted and marched across the parcel towards the car with its heavily tinted windows, which made it hard for her to make out any occupants.

Though she didn't bring her gun along, Ebony wasn't at all worried as she pulled the front passenger side door open and climbed in beside the dark brown complexion man with a red ballcap atop his head. The interior reeked of freshly smoked marijuana and a hint of some sweet-smelling agent.

Which was probably sprayed in an attempt to disguise the smell of the drug. Despite the weather, Ebony made sure to crack her window a bit upon pulling the door shut.

"Please, tell me that you weren't following him around in this contraption," Ebony said, looking into the face that had now become familiar to her.

"I may not be a detective," Zoe replied, revealing a mouthful of gold teeth, "but I think I know better than to follow somebody around in a car with some shiny ass rims on it, shorty. Besides, I'm only back in this car because I couldn't find your friend today."

"You couldn't find him?"

"I guess he left the motel a little early, shorty," he told her. "The Lincoln was there, but the rental was gone. I drove out to the three spots that I knew he'd be at but didn't see him. Hell, we're in a big ass city, I couldn't just drive around this huge motherfucker looking for him."

"Well," she started, pulling a wad of rolled-up bills from one of her coat's pocket, "this is yours, providing that you furnish me with accurate and concrete information."

"I can't really say for sure if he has another family outside of what he has with your sister," he began. "But there's an older woman at the address you gave me. Maybe it's his mom or maybe he was stalking her. I think he was stalking somebody on Richard Street before switching to the rental. I couldn't tell which house he was watching—"

"I already know about the house on Richard," she cut him off, all too familiar with the address in Marvin Harris' file. "Did you not see any other woman than the older woman on Johnson?"

"I was getting to that," he said, apparently not liking how she interrupted him. "On Friday, while he was watching the older woman's house, another woman showed up with a child."

"Oh yeah?" This bit of information sparked Ebony's interest. "Boy or girl?"

"I really couldn't tell from where I was sitting," Zoe informed, shifting in his seat. "But he ended up following her to a house out in Marietta. He followed her to the same house on Sunday, after she picked up the child from Johnson Street."

"Here." Ebony handed him the money, then buckled her seatbelt. "Show me the house in Marietta!"

Chapter 24

March 10th, 2024

The light drizzle of rain pelted the windshield of Ebony's Cadillac that sat in the parking lot of Kroger with the engine still running. She'd only been sitting there for two minutes, which was almost twenty minutes before the time agreed upon. This had given her sufficient time to indulge in her new batch of crush, in which she now went for a second dosage of as she extracted the vial from her pink clutch she'd brought along to acknowledge the annual National Breast Cancer Awareness Month dinner.

Sprinkling a small amount of the powdered drug onto the mirror of her compact, Ebony looked around to make sure that she wasn't under the prying eyes of any passers-by before snorting the substance into her right nostril, via a rolled-up bill. As the drug slowly became active, she closed her eyes, leaned her head against the headrest, and concentrated on her breathing, while allowing her mind to wander. Though her drug-induced thoughts were sporadic and of no substantial valve, they were soon interrupted by the blaring of a vehicle's horn, which pretty much startled her. It didn't take long for her to spot the silver Mercedes-Benz that was docked at the rear of her car.

Already knowing who it was, Ebony quickly stuffed her drug paraphernalia back into her bag, cut the engine grabbed her cellular, then exited, dropping her keys and phone into the clutch bag before adjusting her white, snug-fitted dress that graced her calves. It wasn't too cold out, so the matching mini fur coat was pretty much for show.

"Nice ride!" Ebony offered, once she climbed in beside Lance Stephens, who was dapper in a cream-colored, three piece suit and matching dress shoes. "If you got this on a comedian's salary, then I'm in the wrong business."

"Well, I guess you're in the wrong business," he replied, driving on. "But I must compliment your attire. You look really nice!"

"Thanks!" She flipped down the visor before retrieving her brush from her bag. "You don't look too bad yourself, Lance. Is that suit by Drogue Apparel?"

"Posh," he answered, then glanced over at her. "I'm assuming that dress is by Kimberly Mac?"

"The shoes are," she told him. "The dress is by Angela Cofer.

"That was my next guess," Lance purported. "Those two designers are what's hot right now, but I do have a few suits from Drogue Apparel. I've even met Moerise Williams, once. He's pretty cool."

"Besides you meeting famous designers," Ebony said, brushing her hair, "how's life been treating you?"

"I can't complain," answered Lance. "The fans haven't gotten tired of my corny jokes, so I'm still able to crack on someone's one-legged grandmother and keep the bills paid. So, how's life been treating you? It seems as if someone has opened a Pandora's box in Linkton County."

"How so?" Ebony asked, closing the visor, and placing the brush back into her bag.

"The ongoing violence."

"Like everywhere else right?"

"No." He was slowly shaking his head. "According to the media, the death toll in Linkton County hasn't been this high since 2005. You all just had an ex-investigator found murdered in his home after being tied up. Then, a man who was on trial for murder was murdered before the trial ended and I think Samantha was prosecuting the case."

"She was the prosecutor on the case," Ebony confirmed, now thinking about her friend, who was still a bit distraught by the ordeal she'd cause of her anticipated victory.

"How'd she take that? Is she okay?"

"She took it pretty hard," Ebony answered, truthfully. "It was the first time something like that happened to her, but she's coming along just fine."

There was a pregnant pause before Lance asked, "Do you even feel safe there anymore?"

"It's not a matter of feeling safe lance," replied Ebony, whose attention was out the window as she spoke. "Besides, my profession won't allow me such a luxury. I am a prosecutor. I make enemies every day that I step inside that courtroom, whether it's the defendants or their loved ones, but I already knew what I was getting myself into before I signed up for it. I mean, look at what befell my father. Who's to say I won't suffer the same fate?"

"You shouldn't talk like that," Lance tried to reason.

She now regarded him. "But it's true."

Lance didn't respond, so Ebony was left to her thoughts for the remainder of the ride and quite naturally, she was thinking of her father, who was pretty much responsible for the rise in the death toll in Linkton County, in 2005, which Lance had mentioned ,19 years ago! Ebony couldn't believe that she allowed this much time to elapse without avenging her parents' death, like she'd promise herself she would do once she gets older. That realization, mixed with the effect of the drug that was still dancing through her veins had her vexed. Rick and Bull had promised, as part of their bargains, to help her gain closure for her mother's death ad has yet to hold up to that. Well, at that moment, the older men were delinquent. It was time to pay the piper.

The light drizzle of rain had surceased by the time they reached the governor's mansion, where they had to move along the line of vehicles belonging to other guests before being instructed where to park by ersatz parking attendants. As always, being that it was still daylight, the place looked too dull to Ebony, except for the drone of people moving towards, or already line up at the entrance, to celebrate the event.

"Are you ready?" Lance asked, now adjusting his necktie, which was his pink item for the evening.

Despite how she was feeling, Ebony produced a plausible smile. "Sure, babe."

Upon exiting the car, they were greeted by a number of other guests, though Lance had the biggest fan base of the two. The line was long, but it moved pretty fast, as a band of Albert Spires' guards checked off names, and adhered to their security routines at the entrance. Therefore, it didn't take long for Ebony and Lance to reach the checking point, where the only Hispanic on the Governor's security team, was holding the roster.

"Hello, Sanchez!" Ebony beamed, as cogent as possible. "How's the wife and kid?"

"They're fine, thank you!' He regarded her with a look of uncertainty before running his index finger along the names on the list. "I don't have you on here, Ms. Davis."

"That's because she's my guest," Lance stepped in, putting an arm around her waist for emphasis.

"Ah! Mr. Stephens!" Sanchez regarded his list again. "I have you accompanied by two. Your other guest?"

"My back-up comedian," replied Lance. "He cancelled at the last moment. So, I guess I'll have to serenade the crowd with my ancient jokes of why the chicken crossed the road."

"I'm sure the crowd won't mind," Sanchez spoke, looking directly at Ebony. "Enjoy yourselves!"

Clearing the security phase, Ebony exchanged her coat for an identification ticket before they entered the semi-crowded ballroom, where pink banners that expressed the purpose of the event were hung throughout the place, with pink balloons taped to them. There were also pink balloons scattered all over the floor. Pink cloth tables were placed about the room in an orderly fashion surrounded by soft-cushioned sitting chairs. On the platform as a stage a trio-member female band was doing their own version of *Savin' Me* by Nickleback. Guests were moving about, mingling with one another, while the governor's maid staff brought around appetizers and cocktails on silver trays.

"You said that you want to share a drink with Dorothy Stockholm," Lance said to Ebony as they stood just beyond the entrance. "I don't think there's a better time than this."

"Yeah, I see." Following his line of vision, Ebony spotted the gray-haired sexagenarian, sitting at one of the tables. Clad in a pink, old-fashioned skirt-set that was complemented by the pink diamonds in her watch, bracelet, necklace, and dangling earrings. Accompanying her was a much younger woman, who could very well be her granddaughter or assistant.

"I have to inform the Spires of the sudden change in entertainment," Lance now told her. "Then, I'll mingle with some of my old peers. I guess we'll find our way back to each other somehow. Just save me a dance."

"I'll remember that."

As Ebony slowly made her way towards Dorothy Stockholm's table, she scanned the crowd for the governor and his wife, who were both entertaining a small crowd over by the large windows that overlooked the vast backyard. Though she was anticipating her inevitable encounter with Albert Spires, Ebony thought it would probably be best if she prolonged it, and let it play out on its own.

"Hi, Mrs. Stockholm!" Ebony beamed, extending her hand for the frail woman to shake. "I'm Ebony Davis, an assistant district attorney of Linkton County."

"A prosecutor!" the woman exclaimed with her strong voice. She accepted Ebony's hand, then indicated her company. "My granddaughter, here, is currently taking courses in astrophysics. Maybe I've gotten too old because I have the slightest clue as to what that consists of."

The younger woman sighed with feigned exasperation. "It's the study if the physics and physical properties of celestial bodies, grandmother."

"If you want to study bodies," Mrs. Stokholm retorted, "Maybe you should consider becoming a doctor or you could take a decent profession, suck as a prosecutor, like Ms. Davis here." She now regarded Ebony. "And what is it that your husband does, Mrs. Davis? If you don't mind me being nosey?"

"I, uh…" Ebony stammered, almost forgetting about the engagement ring on her finger. "I was engaged to be married, but my fiancé was murdered before we could tie the knot."

"I'm so sorry to hear that," the older woman sympathized then gestured to one of the empty chairs. "Please have a seat!"

Ebony did so, placing her bag atop the table.

Mrs. Stockholm flagged one of the wait staff over and collected three martinis for the three of them. "And when did this tragedy occur?" she asked after taking a sip of her beverage.

"Eight months ago," Ebony answered, drinking from her own glass, while hoping that the woman wasn't going to inquire into the details of Jason's demise.

"That's just one of the many storms we have to weather in life," Mrs. Stockholm recited. "Are you a breast cancer advocate, or recipient?"

"Advocate."

"You look familiar," she told Ebony. "Have I seen you at one of my seminars?"

"Last year," Ebony answered. "Right here at the mansion."

"No." She was shaking her head, regarding Ebony with furrowed eyebrows. "I think I've encountered you more than that."

Before Ebony could think of something to say, two middle-aged women approached, apologized for the encroachment, then pretty much doted on the older woman for the local celebrity that she was, before informing her that she was set to speak in about ten minutes.

"My friend," Mrs. Stockholm now spoke, regarding Ebony. "I apologize for cutting our conversation short, but I must prepare for my opening speech. Perhaps, we could share a glass of champagne after the meal."

"That would be great!" Ebony exclaimed, though she wasn't going to count on it.

She stood with the grandmother and granddaughter, shook both their hands, then waited until all four women had moved on before looking in the direction of where she last seen the Spires. At this time, they were engaged in conversation with three people in which Lance happened to be one of the three. Ebony was almost certain that Albert Spires was staring daggers at her from across the huge room. Ostensibly, Lance had revealed her unwelcome arrival to the rotund governor, who was clad in a gray suit with pink pinstripes, but Ebony didn't stand there staring back at him. Instead, she maneuvered through the crowd, inevitably kicking balloons aside as she made for the appetizers table and began helping herself to sliced cheese on Ritz crackers, while bobbing her head to another song being performed by the feminine group.

As more people began crowding the table, Ebony helped herself to another slice of cheese and cracker, then moved closer to the stage, where Dorothy Stockholm was talking with her colleagues beside the podium as her granddaughter protectively stood by.

"You've got a lot of nerve showing your face here after our last encounter."

The inflection was menacing but the broad smile on the governor's face was award-winning. Then, to top his grammy worthy performance, he was holding two martinis, in which he held one out to her. Not one to be outdone when it came to 'stepping into character', Ebony accepted the drink with what looked to the public eye as extreme gratitude.

"Is that a way to greet a friend, Albert?" Ebony asked, bearing a smile that she was sure showed a majority of her straight, white teeth. "And speaking of friend, why wasn't Samantha invited to this event?"

"You know darn well why she wasn't invited!"

"I thought I made it clear to you that she had no parts in that," Ebony asserted taking a sip of her drink.

"The only thing you made clear to me is how low down you are," Albert retorted, nodding to a couple passing by. "And if Samantha is in association with people of your ilk, then I've done the right thing by disassociating myself from her. She's lucky to still be in existence at this moment and I'm still tempted to change that. All it takes is one call, and she'll be standing in line to meet God in less than ten minutes."

Ebony's fraudulent smile immediately dissipated, and her face took on its true form. "If anything happens to her," she spoke with malice, through clenched teeth, "I'll come for you myself! This is between you and me. Don't force me to flip this mansion upside down looking for you because I will, and trust me, I'm taking all prisoners."

The threat was enough to induce the governor to drip his front also, though his face had become crimson. "Sounds like idle talk to me," he vented. "Coming for me will definitely be a suicide mission. In fact, you need to leave before I call and notify Animal Control that I have a stray monkey running around the compound."

The racial statement stung like a slap to the face, but Ebony defied to let it show. Her first instinct was to throw her drink into his face, but that would've been condescension on her part. Instead, she gingerly handed the glass back to him, then marched toward the entrance, where she traded the ticket back in for the return of her coat. Stepping out into the late-winter air, she briefly locked eyes with Sanchez, who was still signing names off the roster. He didn't seem concerned about her early departure, so she was convinced that he was aware of the conflicting feeling between his employer and her.

Moving in the opposite direction of the remaining people making for the entrance, Ebony retrieved her pre-paid cellular from her bag and selected a number from her contacts while thinking of how disappointed Lance would be once he realizes she's no longer in attendance. It didn't matter to her because she only used him as means to gain entrance to the mansion. *Mission Complete!*

"Already?" The recipient answered the phone with acerbity.

"Did you even make it inside?"

"Just get me home!" she hissed through the device before disconnecting.

Ebony's heels click-clacked loudly on the concrete as she traveled the long driveway towards the street, with Albert Spires' insult ringing in her head. This really had her blood boiling, being that she'd never been a victim of direct racism. Just because he was the governor of Georgia, that didn't give him immunity to mistreat its citizens, right? Well, he definitely crossed paths with the wrong one. Now, she was thinking of releasing his sex video to the public, via the internet, but that would affect Samantha, which was something she was trying to prevent. Though she had to scrap that idea, Ebony knew that she had to come up with a way to get Albert back for what he said.

Making it to the street, Ebony saw the unmarked government issued sedan moving extremely slow in her direction. Then, suddenly, at about 80 yards out, it came to a halt as if the occupant didn't see her, although it was still daylight, and she was wearing a conspicuously white dress and fur coat. It took everything in her not to wave her arms in the air like a landing signal officer, as she continued towards the now idling vehicle, with the wind making a fuss out of her hair.

"Why'd you stop so far back?" Ebony inquired, upon climbing into the front passenger seat and purposefully slamming the door.

"Cameras," Rick answered, seeming unfazed by her adolescent deportment as he made a U-turn and drove in the opposite direction. "Put your seatbelt on, please!"

Had it not been for the fact that he said please, she would have pretended to not have heard him, and why not? Human beings have always had a proclivity to take their problems out on everybody but the person they should be taking them out on. Considering his affability, Ebony figured she would play nice this time. Therefore, without a word, she buckled herself in.

"So, what happened?" Rick posed. "Did you make it inside?"

"Yes, I made it inside." She retrieved the hairbrush from her bag and began brushing her hair while using the reflection from her side window. "I shared a drink with Mrs. Stockholm and her granddaughter. After a few minutes of conversating, Mrs. Stockholm had to prepare for her opening speech. While I was watching her prepare, he made his approach."

Rick fixed her with a mere glance. "And?" he urged her to continue.

"We had words," Ebony answered, replacing the brush. "Of course, he was not happy to see me. Things got heated. He told me to leave."

"I know it's not my place to ask," said Rick. "But what was your purpose for coming out here today? I find it hard to believe that it was to share a drink with a cancer survivor."

Ebony now regarded him. "That was never my purpose," she avowed. "I did it for Samantha."

"There's nothing you can do or say that would convince him that Samantha had no part in that," Rick told her. "I think you should just let the situation go before it's too late. This is the governor of Georgia we're talking about, a very powerful man. The same powerful man that you and Samantha are working under. I hope you understand what I'm saying."

"There are some things that a person just can't let go of Rick." She was gazing out the side window as she spoke. "I'll try and convince Samantha to relinquish her love jones for this guy, but it's much deeper with me right now."

"There's something you're not telling me," he acknowledged. "Were there more than words exchanged between you two?"

Ebony remained silent.

Rick drew a breath. "So, you're actually plotting against the executive head of Georgia," he stated. "I mean, if you're feeling suicidal, I could just drive this car off a bridge and be done with it. If this is true, I want all the details, so I'll know what I'm putting my life on the line for."

Ebony still didn't respond. Of course, eventually she was going to furnish Rick with the details because she would definitely need him for whatever machination she devises against Alber Spires. Right now, she just wanted to be left to her thoughts. Apparently, Rick had sensed this because he hadn't spoken another word for the duration of the ride.

"Do you need me to follow you home?" Rick asked once he brought the car to a halt at the rear of Ebony's, pulling her from her thoughts.

"Nope," she answered, curtly, disengaging her seatbelt, and pushing the door open. "If I need anything, I know how to contact you."

Rick didn't drive off until Ebony was seated securely inside her car that she allowed close to 3 minutes to warm up, before driving out the grocery store's lot, headed back to Linkton County.

Though her mind was still jumbled with thought, the most essential ones were retaliating against Albert Spires, having a heart-to-heart with Samantha, and expediting the process with Anthony before he decides to come after her first.

Entering her home, Ebony re-activated the alarm, then headed for her bedroom, where she tossed her bag onto the bed with her coat and pulled open the drawer on her nightstand. For some strange reason, she just stood there, staring down at the small silver tray that contained a little under a quarter of an ounce of crush, her employee identification card, and a drinking straw. Considering her current mind state, the drug was indeed a necessity. So, why was she just gaping at it? Unable to conjure an answer to that, Ebony took a seat on the edge of the bed and kicked off her heels before retrieving the tray and placing it atop the laminated wooden structure, where she'd intentionally left her SkyFone cellular before leaving out earlier. Not wasting another minute, she used her ID card to separate and make two lines of the powdered substance. Then, with the straw, she snorted a line into each nostril.

Lying back on the bed, she closed her eyes and welcomed the burning sensation that also made her eyes watery. As always, she went into her breathing exercise to sustain the equilibrium of her heart's pulsation and to momentarily free her mind of all existing issues. However, Ebony couldn't catch a break to save her life. It seemed like the moment she was able to lure her mind into a state of neutrality, the sound of her phone vibrating atop the nightstand instantaneously disrupted it. She found herself becoming angry all over again.

Samantha's the only person that would be calling her at this moment so, being that she intended to give her friend a ring anyway, Ebony sat up and retrieved the device, but the name on the screen did not belong to Samantha, although it was highly familiar.

"Hello?" Ebony answered, trying to conceal her aggravation.

"How are you, Ms. Davis?" the familiar, masculine voice inquired.

"I'm fine," she lied, now thinking about the death of her grandmother. "How may I help you, McAdams?"

"On yesterday," he plunged in, "the Pharmacy of America Laboratories faxed me over some documents that they received from a representative of Banner and Associated law firm, out in Dallas, Texas. Apparently, research was conducted on one of their products and supposedly had been ruled as a fatal drug that's responsible for the deaths of a great number of people. As of now, the pharmacy is facing a huge class action suit."

"Is there a specific reason why you're calling me about this?" Ebony asked, feeling a confession coming on.

McAdams was quiet for a moment. "I, um," he lingered some more. "The pharmacy also provided me with a list of alleged victims. Just out of curiosity, I perused the list, mainly focusing on the ones of Georgia."

"Okay." Ebony knew where this was going.

The doctor was still hesitant. "I saw your grandmother's name," he spoke at a length. "I wish that you would've contacted me before making a decision based upon your sentiment. I'm not saying that these people's findings are erroneous, but such findings of this magnitude have to undergo levels of research before being rendered conclusive."

"Are you telling me that these people are making an invalid claim?"

"It's possible," he answered. "And I've seen this happen more than once, Ms. Davis. Especially with tyro attorneys who are hell-bent on making a name for themselves."

"Are you under the impression that this is the case with these people," Ebony stated matter of fact.

"Perhaps."

"Look," she pressed. "I understand how people of the same profession have an implicit obligation to fend for one another. I'm amongst such union myself. However, you still haven't given me your reason for this call."

"I just don't want you to be deceived by what's been presented to you," he purported. "You've battled a great many of attorneys in the courtroom, so you know firsthand how deceptive they can be. I also want you to know, no matter how this plays out, that I'd taken every precaution with your grandmother while she was in my care. She'd never had to undergo any form of substandard treatment. As a reputable medicine practitioner, I've faithfully followed all protocol. I've also went beyond protocol to ensure that my patients were well taken care of including your grandmother."

"I understand." Ebony was still trying to discern if this was a confession or plea to make her relinquish her complaint against the Pharmacy of America Laboratories, being that he himself was susceptible of becoming a defendant in the case. "Look, Mr. McAdams," she spoke. "I just got back in and I'm in dire need of a shower."

"I apologize for the interruption," he offered, sincerely. "However, I ask a favor of you."

"I'm listening."

"If you hear anything else from this law form," he posed, "will you let me know?"

"Sure will," Ebony lied, ringing off.

Replacing the phone back onto the nightstand, she separated and helped herself to two more lines of crush. Lying back on the bed, she thought about Dr. McAdams and his unexpected call, wondering of and how much blame she should place upon him for the death of her grandmother. After all, Ebony mentally reasoned with herself, he is the one who introduced Regina to the deadly drug.

Chapter 25

It was 7:39 that night when Anthony pulled the black Chevy Impala onto the Marietta off-ramp. After encountering Rene last week at the restaurant, he thought it wise to exchange the Audi for the Chevy, lest he was unfortunate enough to be spotted by her again. As Far as he knew, she hadn't mention anything to his mother about seeing him. At least his mother hadn't said anything about it during any of their phone conversations.

Ever since that day, Anthony has had no luck with locating the blonde that he assumes is Marvin's sister. He'd been back and forth from Marvis's mother's house to the restaurant to no avail. Trailing Louise Atkinson only led him to convenient store after convenient store. Not once had she visited anyone's residence, which had Anthony under the impression that the old woman had no mutual friends to call upon, not even a clandestine boy toy. Therefore, not wanting to 'lose the bird in hand for the bird in the bush' he chose to remit his plans for Marvin and carry out the one that he concocted for Janelle. Being that he already monitored the movements of Janelle and her new beau, Anthony inferred that tonight would be the most appropriate. Plus, Alex was spending the weekend with his beloved grandmother, and well out of the way of any harm that may inadvertently befall him. Subconsciously, Anthony knew that what he was setting out to do would be considered unethical, but he was only doing it for one reason: to get back at Janell for the anguish she'd caused him when he was incarcerated.

Clearing the off-ramp, Anthony made a right turn, and alternated his eyes from the road ahead to the rearview mirror and just as he suspected, his 'company' made the same turn behind two other vehicles. For he had spied the dark green Nissan, a couple of weeks ago, while stalking Janelle's home one day.

To be sure that he wasn't being paranoid, Anthony drove around aimlessly that day. Just as he did so, the driver of the Nissan made a show of professionalism by maintaining a respectable distance behind Anthony, which to be almost invisible, had Anthony not have already spotted the car beforehand. That's when he inferred that Ebony had finally dispatched her goons, but it was quite uncanny to him because he hadn't seen the Nissan since that day, although he thought he was being followed by other vehicles at times. However, the green Nissan was back on the scene. Anthony gave Ebony the benefit of the doubt that she wouldn't just send some Tom, Dick and Harry after him, so he automatically assumed that his follower was either Rick or Bull, if not both. Though he was familiar with how coldhearted and ruthless these men were, Anthony was the least bit afraid. For he was going to liquidate the two old-timers, then go after their employer with the zeal of a runaway freight train.

Already assuming his pursuer was aware of his current destination, Anthony quickly formulated a plan of action. He knew that he had to regard and treat the situation as it was visibly presented, like a cardinal threat. Now he was coming up Pratt Street, which is where Janelle's house was located, but instead of traveling that far, Anthony made a left onto the street before it, counting houses on the right side until he came upon the seventh one, which was where he parked and immediately killed the engine and lights. It was dark but not late, so he was certain that the residents of the home were not yet asleep. Checking his rearview mirror again, he saw that the Nissan had docked in front of the first or second house upon entering the street. The black bag containing the P.98 sub-machine gun was sitting on the floorboard of the front passenger side. Extracting the p.98 from it, Anthony tucked the gun inside his coat, pulled his ballcap lower over his head, then dismounted, keeping his eyes on the house that he was parked in front of as he walked up the driveway and disappeared on the side of it, hoping that they didn't have any kind of vicious guard animal lying in wait.

At that moment, Anthony was sure that his pursuer was under the impression that he was about to make his move on Janelle's household by breaching the rear of the home, which was what he wanted them to think. He didn't bother with looking over his shoulder as he moved through the darkness because he didn't believe that his pursuer was given instructions to engage him but to monitor his movements. Thankful there was nothing deleterious waiting behind the initial home, Anthony approached Janelle's home that also had a fenceless backyard, remembering that his son's mother had a great fear of dogs. Therefore, he wasn't all too surprised when he was only met by the sound of a band of crickets.

His next mission was to exit their property without being seen, which was something he'd done with ease. As he already expected, the car belonging to Janelle's boyfriend wasn't in the driveway, being that he had not gotten in from work yet. Clearing their driveway, Anthony moved along Pratt Street in the direction of the main road, hugging the sub-machine gun against his chest and doing his best to parry some of the cold air. He didn't risk looking back just in case Janelle was looking out of one of the windows, in expectations of her man. It didn't matter how dark it was, he knew that Janelle would be able to spot him with just a mere glance. It's not like she didn't know that he was no longer incarcerated.

Seconds before Anthony reached the main road, the burgundy Cadillac belonging to Janelle's boyfriend turned onto the street with the high beams of his headlights blinding him momentarily, as it rode by. Anthony didn't divert his gaze, which probably would have made him look suspicious, though he'd only gotten a mere glance from the man. This reminded him that he would have to find another day to make his son's mother suffer, which made him madder at whomever was occupying the cabalistic Nissan that just so happened to show up at the wrong time.

The Nissan was still parked in the same spot when Anthony re-entered the street, keeping to the sidewalk, though it didn't really matter if he was spotted because the P.98 was at the ready, and accurate enough to be drawn and instantly fired upon a number of targets at once. As Anthony neared, he saw that there was only one occupant which seemed a little too strange because he was quite certain that Ebony would send more than one goon after him.

Well, it was too late to try and figure out the who, why, and what. Making it within five feet of the car that was still running, Anthony stepped off the sidewalk, brandishing the sub-marine gun, while keeping his eyes on the driver, who was wearing a dark skullcap. Coming around the rear of the Nissan, Anthony approached and stood a few feet away from the driver's door with the weapon aimed at a man that he'd never seen before. His visage didn't reveal an ounce of fear as his eyes darted from the barrel of the gun to the face of the man he'd been trailing. Just then, the whole scene went from zero to sixty in a matter of seconds. The driver jerked his upper body to the right, simultaneously raising a black handgun that was obviously sitting in his lap, but Anthony didn't flinch. Being that his gun was already aimed and ready. He squeezed on the trigger, sending a barrage of slugs crashing through the window of the driver's door and penetrating his target from the abdomen on up. The man's gun discharged in the ordeal, though Anthony couldn't tell what the bullet had impacted. Anthony eased off the trigger, once he saw that the man had expired, lying stationary across the front seats with his lifeless eyes staring up at nothing. He figured that people were now looking out of their windows to see what all the commotion was about in their neighborhood, but they were his least worry.

As he quickly stepped back toward the rented Chevy, he looked around for anyone who appeared as if they were an accomplice of the man he just murdered, but he made it to the car, unscathed. Tossing the P.98 on the front passenger seat, Anthony started the car, made a U-turn, and sped off as he wondered if he should go after Ebony and her ancient-old goons before dealing with Marvin and Janelle.

The saga continues in
Crime Boss 4: Point of No Return

Lock Down Publications and Ca$h Presents
Assisted Publishing Packages

BASIC PACKAGE	UPGRADED PACKAGE
$499	$800
Editing	Typing
Cover Design	Editing
Formatting	Cover Design
	Formatting
ADVANCE PACKAGE	**LDP SUPREME PACKAGE**
$1,200	$1,500
Typing	Typing
Editing	Editing
Cover Design	Cover Design
Formatting	Formatting
Copyright registration	Copyright registration
Proofreading	Proofreading
Upload book to Amazon	Set up Amazon account
	Upload book to Amazon
	Advertise on LDP, Amazon and Facebook Page

***Other services available upon request.
Additional charges may apply

Lock Down Publications
P.O. Box 944
Stockbridge, GA 30281-9998
Phone: 470 303-9761

Submission Guideline

Submit the first three chapters of your completed manuscript to ldpsubmissions@gmail.com. In the subject line add **Your Book's Title**. The manuscript must be in a Word Doc file and sent as an attachment. Document should be in Times New Roman, double spaced, and in size 12 font. Also, provide your synopsis and full contact information. If sending multiple submissions, they must each be in a separate email.

Have a story but no way to send it electronically? You can still submit to LDP/Ca$h Presents. Send in the first three chapters, written or typed, of your completed manuscript to:

LDP: Submissions Dept
P.O. Box 944
Stockbridge, GA 30281-9998

DO NOT send original manuscript. Must be a duplicate. Provide your synopsis and a cover letter containing your full contact information.

Thanks for considering LDP and Ca$h Presents.

NEW RELEASES

BLOODLINE OF A SAVAGE **BY PRINCE A. TAUHID**

THE MURDER QUEENS 4 **BY MICHAEL GALLON**

THE BUTTERFLY MAFIA **BY FUMIYA PAYNE**

KING KILLA 2 **BY VINCENT "VITTO" HOLLOWAY**

BABY, I'M WINTERTIME COLD 3 **BY MEESHA**

THESE VICIOUS STREETS **BY PRINCE A. TAUHID**

TIL DEATH 2 **BY ARYANNA**

CITY OF SMOKE 2 **BY MOLOTTI**

STEPPERS **BY KING RIO**

THE LANE **BY KEN-KEN SPENCE**

MONEY GAME 2 **BY SMOOVE DOLLA**

THE BLACK DIAMOND CARTEL **BY SAYNOMORE**

CRIME BOSS 2 **BY PLAYA RAY**

THUG OF SPADES **BY COREY ROBINSON**

LOVE IN THE TRENCHES 2 **BY COREY ROBINSON**

TIL DEATH 3 **BY ARYANNA**

THE BIRTH OF A GANGSTER 4 **BY DELMONT PLAYER**

PRODUCT OF THE STREETS **BY DEMOND "MONEY" ANDERSON**

Coming Soon from Lock Down Publications/Ca$h Presents

BLOOD OF A BOSS VI
SHADOWS OF THE GAME II
TRAP BASTARD II
By **Askari**

LOYAL TO THE GAME IV
By **T.J. & Jelissa**

TRUE SAVAGE VIII
MIDNIGHT CARTEL IV
DOPE BOY MAGIC IV
CITY OF KINGZ III
NIGHTMARE ON SILENT AVE II
THE PLUG OF LIL MEXICO II
CLASSIC CITY II
By **Chris Green**

BLAST FOR ME III
A SAVAGE DOPEBOY III
CUTTHROAT MAFIA III
DUFFLE BAG CARTEL VII
HEARTLESS GOON VI
By **Ghost**

A HUSTLER'S DECEIT III
KILL ZONE II
BAE BELONGS TO ME III
TIL DEATH II
By **Aryanna**

KING OF THE TRAP III
By **T.J. Edwards**

GORILLAZ IN THE BAY V
3X KRAZY III
STRAIGHT BEAST MODE III
By **De'Kari**

KINGPIN KILLAZ IV
STREET KINGS III
PAID IN BLOOD III
CARTEL KILLAZ IV
DOPE GODS III
By **Hood Rich**

SINS OF A HUSTLA II
By **ASAD**

YAYO V
BRED IN THE GAME 2
By **S. Allen**

THE STREETS WILL TALK II
By **Yolanda Moore**

SON OF A DOPE FIEND III
HEAVEN GOT A GHETTO III
SKI MASK MONEY III
By **Renta**

LOYALTY AIN'T PROMISED III
By **Keith Williams**

I'M NOTHING WITHOUT HIS LOVE II
SINS OF A THUG II
TO THE THUG I LOVED BEFORE II
IN A HUSTLER I TRUST II
By **Monet Dragun**

QUIET MONEY IV
EXTENDED CLIP III
THUG LIFE IV
By **Trai'Quan**

THE STREETS MADE ME IV
By **Larry D. Wright**

IF YOU CROSS ME ONCE III
ANGEL V
By **Anthony Fields**

THE STREETS WILL NEVER CLOSE IV
By **K'ajji**

HARD AND RUTHLESS III
KILLA KOUNTY IV
By **Khufu**

MONEY GAME III
By **Smoove Dolla**

MURDA WAS THE CASE III
Elijah R. Freeman

AN UNFORESEEN LOVE IV
BABY, I'M WINTERTIME COLD III
By **Meesha**

QUEEN OF THE ZOO III
By **Black Migo**

CONFESSIONS OF A JACKBOY III
By **Nicholas Lock**

JACK BOYS VS DOPE BOYS IV
A GANGSTA'S QUR'AN V
COKE GIRLZ II
COKE BOYS II
LIFE OF A SAVAGE V
CHI'RAQ GANGSTAS V
SOSA GANG III
BRONX SAVAGES II
BODYMORE KINGPINS II
By **Romell Tukes**

KING KILLA II
By **Vincent "Vitto" Holloway**

BETRAYAL OF A THUG III
By **Fre$h**

THE MURDER QUEENS III
By **Michael Gallon**

THE BIRTH OF A GANGSTER III
By **Delmont Player**

TREAL LOVE II
By **Le'Monica Jackson**

FOR THE LOVE OF BLOOD III
By **Jamel Mitchell**

CRIME BOSS 3 | PLAYA RAY

RAN OFF ON DA PLUG II
By **Paper Boi Rari**

HOOD CONSIGLIERE III
By **Keese**

PRETTY GIRLS DO NASTY THINGS II
By **Nicole Goosby**

PROTÉGÉ OF A LEGEND III
LOVE IN THE TRENCHES II
By **Corey Robinson**

IT'S JUST ME AND YOU II
By **Ah'Million**

FOREVER GANGSTA III
By **Adrian Dulan**

GORILLAZ IN THE TRENCHES II
By **SayNoMore**

THE COCAINE PRINCESS VIII
By **King Rio**

CRIME BOSS II
By **Playa Ray**

LOYALTY IS EVERYTHING III
By **Molotti**

HERE TODAY GONE TOMORROW II
By **Fly Rock**

CRIME BOSS 3 | PLAYA RAY

REAL G'S MOVE IN SILENCE II
By **Von Diesel**

GRIMEY WAYS IV
By **Ray Vinci**

Available Now

RESTRAINING ORDER I & II
By **CA$H & Coffee**

LOVE KNOWS NO BOUNDARIES I II & III
By **Coffee**

RAISED AS A GOON I, II, III & IV
BRED BY THE SLUMS I, II, III
BLAST FOR ME I & II
ROTTEN TO THE CORE I II III
A BRONX TALE I, II, III
DUFFLE BAG CARTEL I II III IV V VI
HEARTLESS GOON I II III IV V
A SAVAGE DOPEBOY I II
DRUG LORDS I II III
CUTTHROAT MAFIA I II
KING OF THE TRENCHES
By **Ghost**

LAY IT DOWN I & II
LAST OF A DYING BREED I II
BLOOD STAINS OF A SHOTTA I & II III
By **Jamaica**

LOYAL TO THE GAME I II III
LIFE OF SIN I, II III
By **TJ & Jelissa**

IF LOVING HIM IS WRONG…I & II
LOVE ME EVEN WHEN IT HURTS I II III
By **Jelissa**

CRIME BOSS 3 | PLAYA RAY

BLOODY COMMAS I & II
SKI MASK CARTEL I, II & III
KING OF NEW YORK I II, III IV V
RISE TO POWER I II III
COKE KINGS I II III IV V
BORN HEARTLESS I II III IV
KING OF THE TRAP I II
By **T.J. Edwards**

WHEN THE STREETS CLAP BACK I & II III
THE HEART OF A SAVAGE I II III IV
MONEY MAFIA I II
LOYAL TO THE SOIL I II III
By **Jibril Williams**

A DISTINGUISHED THUG STOLE MY HEART I II &
III
LOVE SHOULDN'T HURT I II III IV
RENEGADE BOYS I II III IV
PAID IN KARMA I II III
SAVAGE STORMS I II III
AN UNFORESEEN LOVE I II III
BABY, I'M WINTERTIME COLD I II
By **Meesha**

A GANGSTER'S CODE I &, II III
A GANGSTER'S SYN I II III
THE SAVAGE LIFE I II III
CHAINED TO THE STREETS I II III
BLOOD ON THE MONEY I II III
A GANGSTA'S PAIN I II III
By **J-Blunt**

PUSH IT TO THE LIMIT
By **Bre' Hayes**

BLOOD OF A BOSS I, II, III, IV, V
SHADOWS OF THE GAME
TRAP BASTARD
By **Askari**

THE STREETS BLEED MURDER I, II & III
THE HEART OF A GANGSTA I II& III
By **Jerry Jackson**

CUM FOR ME I II III IV V VI VII VIII
An **LDP Erotica Collaboration**

BRIDE OF A HUSTLA I II & II
THE FETTI GIRLS I, II& III
CORRUPTED BY A GANGSTA I, II III, IV
BLINDED BY HIS LOVE
THE PRICE YOU PAY FOR LOVE I, II ,III
DOPE GIRL MAGIC I II III
By **Destiny Skai**

WHEN A GOOD GIRL GOES BAD
By **Adrienne**

A GANGSTER'S REVENGE I II III & IV
THE BOSS MAN'S DAUGHTERS I II III IV V
A SAVAGE LOVE I & II
BAE BELONGS TO ME I II
A HUSTLER'S DECEIT I, II, III
WHAT BAD BITCHES DO I, II, III
SOUL OF A MONSTER I II III
KILL ZONE
A DOPE BOY'S QUEEN I II III
TIL DEATH
By **Aryanna**

THE COST OF LOYALTY I II III
By Kweli

A KINGPIN'S AMBITION
A KINGPIN'S AMBITION **II**
I MURDER FOR THE DOUGH
By **Ambitious**

TRUE SAVAGE I II III IV V VI VII
DOPE BOY MAGIC I, II, III
MIDNIGHT CARTEL I II III
CITY OF KINGZ I II
NIGHTMARE ON SILENT AVE
THE PLUG OF LIL MEXICO II
CLASSIC CITY
By **Chris Green**

A DOPEBOY'S PRAYER
By **Eddie "Wolf" Lee**

THE KING CARTEL I, II & III
By **Frank Gresham**

THESE NIGGAS AIN'T LOYAL I, II & III
By **Nikki Tee**

GANGSTA SHYT I II &III
By **CATO**

THE ULTIMATE BETRAYAL
By **Phoenix**

BOSS'N UP I, II & III
By **Royal Nicole**

CRIME BOSS 3 | PLAYA RAY

I LOVE YOU TO DEATH
By **Destiny J**

I RIDE FOR MY HITTA
I STILL RIDE FOR MY HITTA
By **Misty Holt**

LOVE & CHASIN' PAPER
By **Qay Crockett**

TO DIE IN VAIN
SINS OF A HUSTLA
By **ASAD**

BROOKLYN HUSTLAZ
By **Boogsy Morina**

BROOKLYN ON LOCK I & II
By **Sonovia**

GANGSTA CITY
By **Teddy Duke**

A DRUG KING AND HIS DIAMOND I & II III
A DOPEMAN'S RICHES
HER MAN, MINE'S TOO I, II
CASH MONEY HO'S
THE WIFEY I USED TO BE I II
PRETTY GIRLS DO NASTY THINGS
By Nicole Goosby

LIPSTICK KILLAH I, II, III
CRIME OF PASSION I II & III
FRIEND OR FOE I II III
By **Mimi**

TRAPHOUSE KING I II & III
KINGPIN KILLAZ I II III
STREET KINGS I II
PAID IN BLOOD I II
CARTEL KILLAZ I II III
DOPE GODS I II
By **Hood Rich**

STEADY MOBBN' I, II, III
THE STREETS STAINED MY SOUL I II III
By **Marcellus Allen**

WHO SHOT YA I, II, III
SON OF A DOPE FIEND I II
HEAVEN GOT A GHETTO I II
SKI MASK MONEY I II
By **Renta**

GORILLAZ IN THE BAY I II III IV
TEARS OF A GANGSTA I II
3X KRAZY I II
STRAIGHT BEAST MODE I II
By **DE'KARI**

TRIGGADALE I II III
MURDA WAS THE CASE I II
By **Elijah R. Freeman**

THE STREETS ARE CALLING
By **Duquie Wilson**

SLAUGHTER GANG I II III
RUTHLESS HEART I II III
By **Willie Slaughter**

CRIME BOSS 3 | PLAYA RAY

GOD BLESS THE TRAPPERS I, II, III
THESE SCANDALOUS STREETS I, II, III
FEAR MY GANGSTA I, II, III IV, V
THESE STREETS DON'T LOVE NOBODY I, II
BURY ME A G I, II, III, IV, V
A GANGSTA'S EMPIRE I, II, III, IV
THE DOPEMAN'S BODYGAURD I II
THE REALEST KILLAZ I II III
THE LAST OF THE OGS I II III
By **Tranay Adams**

MARRIED TO A BOSS I II III
By **Destiny Skai & Chris Green**

KINGZ OF THE GAME I II III IV V VI VII
CRIME BOSS
By **Playa Ray**

FUK SHYT
By **Blakk Diamond**

DON'T F#CK WITH MY HEART I II
By **Linnea**

ADDICTED TO THE DRAMA I II III
IN THE ARM OF HIS BOSS II
By **Jamila**

YAYO I II III IV
A SHOOTER'S AMBITION I II
BRED IN THE GAME
By **S. Allen**

LOYALTY AIN'T PROMISED I II
By **Keith Williams**

TRAP GOD I II III
RICH $AVAGE I II III
MONEY IN THE GRAVE I II III
By **Martell Troublesome Bolden**

FOREVER GANGSTA I II
GLOCKS ON SATIN SHEETS I II
By **Adrian Dulan**

TOE TAGZ I II III IV
LEVELS TO THIS SHYT I II
IT'S JUST ME AND YOU
By **Ah'Million**

KINGPIN DREAMS I II III
RAN OFF ON DA PLUG
By **Paper Boi Rari**

CONFESSIONS OF A GANGSTA I II III IV
CONFESSIONS OF A JACKBOY I II
By **Nicholas Lock**

I'M NOTHING WITHOUT HIS LOVE
SINS OF A THUG
TO THE THUG I LOVED BEFORE
A GANGSTA SAVED XMAS
IN A HUSTLER I TRUST
By **Monet Dragun**

QUIET MONEY I II III
THUG LIFE I II III
EXTENDED CLIP I II
A GANGSTA'S PARADISE
By **Trai'Quan**

CRIME BOSS 3 | PLAYA RAY

CAUGHT UP IN THE LIFE I II III
THE STREETS NEVER LET GO I II III
By **Robert Baptiste**

NEW TO THE GAME I II III
MONEY, MURDER & MEMORIES I II III
By **Malik D. Rice**

CREAM I II III
THE STREETS WILL TALK
By **Yolanda Moore**

LIFE OF A SAVAGE I II III IV
A GANGSTA'S QUR'AN I II III IV
MURDA SEASON I II III
GANGLAND CARTEL I II III
CHI'RAQ GANGSTAS I II III IV
KILLERS ON ELM STREET I II III
JACK BOYZ N DA BRONX I II III
A DOPEBOY'S DREAM I II III
JACK BOYS VS DOPE BOYS I II III
COKE GIRLZ
COKE BOYS
SOSA GANG I II
BRONX SAVAGES
BODYMORE KINGPINS
By **Romell Tukes**

THE STREETS MADE ME I II III
By **Larry D. Wright**

CONCRETE KILLA I II III
VICIOUS LOYALTY I II III
By **Kingpen**

THE ULTIMATE SACRIFICE I, II, III, IV, V, VI
KHADIFI
IF YOU CROSS ME ONCE I II
ANGEL I II III IV
IN THE BLINK OF AN EYE
By **Anthony Fields**

THE LIFE OF A HOOD STAR
By **Ca\$h & Rashia Wilson**

THE STREETS WILL NEVER CLOSE I II III
By **K'ajji**

NIGHTMARES OF A HUSTLA I II III
By **King Dream**

HARD AND RUTHLESS I II
MOB TOWN 251
THE BILLIONAIRE BENTLEYS I II III
REAL G'S MOVE IN SILENCE
By **Von Diesel**

GHOST MOB
By **Stilloan Robinson**

MOB TIES I II III IV V VI
SOUL OF A HUSTLER, HEART OF A KILLER I II
GORILLAZ IN THE TRENCHES
By **SayNoMore**

BODYMORE MURDERLAND I II III
THE BIRTH OF A GANGSTER I II
By **Delmont Player**

CRIME BOSS 3 | PLAYA RAY

FOR THE LOVE OF A BOSS
By **C. D. Blue**

KILLA KOUNTY I II III IV
By Khufu

MOBBED UP I II III IV
THE BRICK MAN I II III IV V
THE COCAINE PRINCESS I II III IV V VI VII
By **King Rio**

MONEY GAME I II
By **Smoove Dolla**

A GANGSTA'S KARMA I II III
By **FLAME**

KING OF THE TRENCHES I II III
By **GHOST & TRANAY ADAMS**

QUEEN OF THE ZOO I II
By **Black Migo**

GRIMEY WAYS I II III
By **Ray Vinci**

XMAS WITH AN ATL SHOOTER
By **Ca$h & Destiny Skai**

KING KILLA
By **Vincent "Vitto" Holloway**

BETRAYAL OF A THUG I II
By **Fre$h**

CRIME BOSS 3 | PLAYA RAY

THE MURDER QUEENS I II
By **Michael Gallon**

TREAL LOVE
By **Le'Monica Jackson**

FOR THE LOVE OF BLOOD I II
By **Jamel Mitchell**

HOOD CONSIGLIERE I II
By **Keese**

PROTÉGÉ OF A LEGEND I II
LOVE IN THE TRENCHES
By **Corey Robinson**

BORN IN THE GRAVE I II III
By **Self Made Tay**

MOAN IN MY MOUTH
By **XTASY**

TORN BETWEEN A GANGSTER AND A
GENTLEMAN
By **J-BLUNT & Miss Kim**

LOYALTY IS EVERYTHING I II
By **Molotti**

HERE TODAY GONE TOMORROW
By **Fly Rock**

PILLOW PRINCESS
By **S. Hawkins**

CRIME BOSS 3 | PLAYA RAY

SANCTIFIED AND HORNY
by **XTASY**

THE PLUG OF LIL MEXICO 2
by **CHRIS GREEN**

THE BLACK DIAMOND CARTEL
by **SAYNOMORE**

THE BIRTH OF A GANGSTER 3
by **DELMONT PLAYER**

BOOKS BY LDP'S CEO, CA$H

TRUST IN NO MAN
TRUST IN NO MAN 2
TRUST IN NO MAN 3
BONDED BY BLOOD
SHORTY GOT A THUG
THUGS CRY
THUGS CRY 2
THUGS CRY 3
TRUST NO BITCH
TRUST NO BITCH 2
TRUST NO BITCH 3
TIL MY CASKET DROPS
RESTRAINING ORDER
RESTRAINING ORDER 2
IN LOVE WITH A CONVICT
LIFE OF A HOOD STAR
XMAS WITH AN ATL SHOOTER